Wednes

By Diane E Young

Rhonda -

I hope you enjoy it!

Diane E Young

Chapter One

"Fantastic idea," Brynn was saying as she took a seat on the sofa, freshly poured glass of Pinot Gris in one hand and Anne Klein clutch in the other. "Thank you for having us, Hannah. I can't tell you how much I needed a night of relaxation!"

"My pleasure," Hannah replied with a warm smile.

"My kids are probably killing each other already," Madeline added, gulping down the rest of her wine and refilling her glass.

"Take it easy, Slugger."

"I'm not driving, Amanda. I don't have to worry about it."

"Yeah, well if your kids are killing each other, Maddy, you might not want to enter the crime scene snockered off your ass." Amanda snorted, took a seat in an oversized chair and swung her feet up on the matching ottoman. The others watched a flash of panic appear on Hannah's face at the sight of feet on her furniture, but it faded quickly with a sigh.

"I would like to make the first toast," Sydney piped in. Amanda and Maddy exchanged glances and rolled their eyes, but allowed their friend to indulge. "To the beginning of the Wednesday Wine Club. May we all relish each other's friendship with camaraderie and wine. To a safe environment of trust and compassion, where we can share our sorrows and successes in confidence, we raise our glasses to seal the bond."

The other four exchanged confused looks, but raised their glasses. Sydney stood among them with her glass raised and her eyes closed, frozen in apparent deep concentration. Five long, silent seconds passed, then she opened her eyes, exhaled loudly and smiled at her friends. She extended her glass to Brynn, who was directly in front of her, clinked them together, then raised it again toward the ceiling before taking a long swallow.

The others shrugged, clinked glasses around the room and drank. They were used to Sydney's dramatic behavior, but it never ceased to amaze them. Sydney was predictably unorthodox. They had come to expect the unexpected from her.

"You have a lovely home, Hannah," Brynn broke the silence after the awkward toast. Brynn had never seen the house before, although Hannah and her husband had moved in two years ago. Brynn was frankly surprised when Hannah offered to host their first meeting of the Wednesday Wine Club.

The club had been Amanda's idea. They were out at Tresor, one of Brynn's favorite restaurants for their weekly dinner. Although Tresor was a little pricy for the others, it was Brynn's birthday and the friends insisted they dine at her favorite spot. Brynn did not argue, but in retrospect going to Tresor was probably what precipitated Amanda's idea of hosting their weekly dinners at home. They invariably had several bottles of wine, which drove up the bill, and although the food was usually good, did they really "need" it? Wine and conversation was all that truly mattered, and maybe a snack. If they got hungry, hell they could order a pizza. They all agreed rotating the location weekly would alleviate the burden of preparing the home for guests. The host of the week could plan food if desired; the others brought the wine.

Hannah had graciously offered to host the first night. The ladies had not seen her new house yet, and she was ready to have them over. Her husband, Paolo, would be leaving soon for a meeting, and that would leave her free to visit uninhibited with her friends, and show off the new house.

Hannah was somewhat of a perfectionist and had not wanted to entertain in a half-finished house. Even after two years of decorating, painting and furnishing,

Hannah hardly considered it "done" but it was inhabitable, and it was definitely time to let her friends take a step closer into her life. In addition to striving for perfection, Hannah was also relatively reserved. She internalized much of her emotions and kept her private life out of the spotlight of the conversation. While she was a great listener and attentive to her friends' needs, she was not as forthcoming with her own and hesitated to accept any help or support. Her friends were sometimes frustrated by what appeared to be a lack of trust, but they respected that Hannah was a strong person and liked to solve her own problems independently.

Hannah's husband, Paolo – or Pauly as she called him – came down the stairs. Hannah's eyes shot from him to the ottoman where Amanda's feet had been resting but were now removed, and then back to Paolo.

"Hey, Pauly," they greeted him simultaneously.

"Good evening, ladies," he said in his smooth, patronizing voice. He flashed a smile, his teeth perfect and white. He glided across the living room floor and gave Hannah a kiss on the cheek. "Big ladies' night tonight."

Paolo was very congenial in front of Hannah's friends. He flashed his winning smile and traded a "how've you been" or "nice to see you" politely with each guest, but his olive-green eyes never actually made full contact with any of them. He had a dazzling smile and a charming, charismatic way about him. He was a good-looking man, dark and handsome but not tall. His height in no way diminished his confidence. He was probably not as attractive as he believed himself to be, but he could turn heads. His physique was lean and fit, his dark hair fell perfectly into place and he commanded attention without saying a word. He put on a gentleman-like front for Hannah's friends, but they sensed from her sudden and nearly fearful glances that their relationship had a dark side under the seeming perfection.

In spite of the niceties exchanged, the atmosphere was thick with an uncomfortable nervousness, and he left for his meeting without delay. Hannah was visibly relieved.

"Everything OK with you and Pauly?" Amanda asked.

"Fine," Hannah answered a little too quickly. "Why do you ask?"

Amanda shrugged.

"He's not much of a talker," Sydney noticed.

"No, he isn't. He is a very private person," Hannah agreed with a pang of defensiveness.

Brynn gazed thoughtfully at Hannah as she contemplated whether she should pursue this conversation or help her change the subject. Paolo was indeed intimidating, but Hannah knew what she was getting into when she married him. They had dated three years before he proposed. Brynn decided if Hannah wanted to talk about it, she would, and opted to help her out by changing the subject.

"Shall we open another bottle?" she suggested.

"Absolutely!" Maddy spoke up.

"I'll put some music on," Hannah replied, grabbing her cell phone off the fireplace mantle and connecting it to her Wi-Fi speaker. She adjusted the volume and set her phone back on the mantle. "That's better. I have some hors d'oeuvres too."

"Let me help you," Sydney offered and followed Hannah to the kitchen.

"I'm going for the red," Maddy grabbed the bottle of Pinot Noir that Sydney had brought.

"Do you think something is going on with her and Pauly, or just the normal bullshit?" asked Amanda in a low voice, once Hannah and Sydney were out of the room.

"They've always been like this," Brynn answered. "It's clear who rules the roost. I'm sure she just wants to make him happy."

"Make him happy?" Amanda spat. "She's scared shitless of him."

Brynn shot her a warning look as if to say she hadn't lowered her voice enough. Maddy started singing along to the music to cover their voices. She struggled with the corkscrew for a moment, but figured it out and poured herself a healthy glass of wine.

"Hell, *I'm* scared shitless of him," Amanda added in a lower tone. "And I'm not scared of anyone."

"He is intimidating," Brynn agreed. "He's authoritative and demanding, and is used to have things his way, but I was always under the impression he treated Hannah well."

"I wouldn't be too sure," was Amanda's response.

"Pinot noir, anyone?" Maddy asked, holding up the bottle. Amanda and Brynn held out their glasses for a fill-up.

Hannah and Sydney returned with trays of hors d'oeuvres. Hannah had painstakingly prepared a variety of finger sandwiches with freshly sliced cucumbers, zucchini and yellow squash as the bread, spread with flavored cream cheeses and topped with a colorful array of olives, peppers, prosciutto and herb sprigs. Another tray held an intricate arrangement of crackers and cheeses cut to different shapes and sizes arranged around two small bowls of cashews. The final tray was filled with skewers of fresh, colorful fruit – melons, grapes, berries, mandarin oranges, pineapple chunks and maraschino cherries. All the trays were lined with crisp, bright endive. Everything Hannah did, she did with precision and perfection.

"How lovely!" Brynn gushed.

"Hannah, you have outdone yourself, as usual," Amanda added, picking up a finger sandwich and popping it into her mouth. "Delicious!"

Hannah smiled. It was nice to have approval. Pauly never complimented her cooking – or anything else. In fact, he usually pointed out the fault in everything she did. The house was never clean enough, the meals were never quite right; God forbid she had to drive him somewhere. The only thing he didn't complain about was the sex, unless you count complaining he didn't get enough. He was absolutely insatiable, and demanded sex all the time whether Hannah wanted it or not. Hannah could never verbalize any of this to her friends. They would either say she was exaggerating, or she knew what she was getting into when she married him. Both were probably true. Whatever the case, she kept her marriage woes to herself. The girls had been around long enough to make their own judgments of Pauly.

"This is nice," Maddy commented. "I mean, I liked our tradition of going to a restaurant too, but this is much more relaxing. I can unfasten my pants if I eat too much, and no one will care."

"You've done that in a restaurant," Amanda pointed out.

"Sure, but I felt self-conscious that someone would notice. I don't care if you guys notice. You know how hard it is to hold this belly in after popping out three kids."

"I'm glad I don't know," Brynn admitted. "But feel free to indulge."

"Oh, I will," Maddy responded. "I might wear sweatpants next week."

"You wear whatever your little heart desires," Amanda told her. "I'm hosting next week."

"Are you sure?" Sydney asked. "I can do next week if you want."

"Naw, I'm fine with it."

"I'll do the following week, then," Sydney offered. "Let me pencil it into my datebook."

Sydney dug through her purse, while the others sampled from the enticing trays Hannah had set out. Amanda lost a piece of sliced pepper on the floor and quickly dabbed at the carpet with her napkin.

Hannah's expression was pure horror, but she said, "Don't worry about that. I've got club soda."

"Don't sweat it, kid," Amanda said. "I got it all."

Hannah smiled and sat down, but they all knew she would be on her hands and knees later with a wet cloth.

"We are all set for my house on the 26th," Sydney chirped. "Now, let's catch up! I want to hear what everyone has been doing all week!"

"Working," Amanda snorted.

"Wiping noses and asses," Maddy added.

"The usual," Brynn interjected, taking over the conversation. No one needed to hear about noses and asses. "I did notice something interesting the other day, though. The man in my building with the exceptionally good taste in clothing does not wear a ring."

"It's about time!" Amanda rolled her eyes. "You've been stalking him for months."

"I'm not stalking him. That's exactly why it took me so long. I don't see him very often, and when I do, he's always had a newspaper or briefcase obscuring my view of his ring finger."

"So, what's your next move?" Amanda prodded.

"I don't know …" Brynn admitted.

"Did you talk to him?" Sydney wanted to know.

"I always speak to him when I see him," Brynn insisted. "I don't know how to get past the small talk yet."

"Jump him in the elevator," Maddy suggested.

"It's not that easy. I haven't been in the dating pool in a long time. My divorce from Michael isn't even final yet."

"If you didn't have so many assets, the divorce would have been final a long time ago," Amanda pointed out. "You can't blame it on the divorce taking so long. You need to shit or get off the pot. By the time you get up the nerve to ask the guy out, he *will* have a ring on his finger."

"So be it," Brynn replied. "It wasn't meant to be, then."

"Come on, Brynn," Hannah chimed in. "You don't want to be alone forever. I think you've waited plenty long enough since your separation. It's time to get back up on the horse."

"Wish I had a horse to get back up on," Amanda snorted.

"Nate not doing it for you?" Maddy laughed.

"Eh. You know how it goes." Amanda's answer was noncommittal.

"Are you still thinking about having a baby?" Sydney asked.

"Honestly, I don't think it's the right time," Amanda replied. "I've got a shot at a promotion at work, and the position requires travel. I want to wait and see what happens with that first. I don't want to try to transition into a new job when I'm pregnant."

"I thought you were ready!" Sydney cried with disappointment.

"I thought so too, but it didn't happen, and now I've got this opportunity. I don't know, I think things happen for a reason. What about you, Hannah?" Amanda asked to redirect the focus of the conversation. "You've got the house the way you want it, ever think about a nursery?"

"Absolutely not," Hannah answered quickly, but immediately added, "not that I don't want children ever. I don't want any right now."

"I understand, Hannah," Sydney said soothingly. "I don't mean to project my desires onto the rest of you. I just know I can never have one, so I get excited when my friends are having little ones. I can't help it."

"Get a pet," Amanda suggested.

"I have a cat. It's not the same thing," Sydney pouted.

"Maybe Maddy will pop another kid out for you," Amanda poked Maddy in the ribs, nearly causing her to spill her wine.

"God, no!" Maddy blurted. "You know damn well I'm not having any more."

Amanda and Brynn laughed. Hannah was still recovering from witnessing the near spill of Maddy's red wine all over her cream-colored carpet.

"Let me know when you want me to take the kids," Sydney was saying. "I haven't taken them in a while, and I know how you and Jim enjoy a night out."

"Thanks, I'll check with Jim. I know he's out of town this weekend, but maybe next weekend."

"Sure, let me know."

"You can watch them any time, really," Maddy joked. "I will take a night out with or without Jim."

"You get a night out without Jim once a week," Amanda reminded her. Maddy flipped her off.

"I think it's time for my weekly question!" Sydney said in a sing-song voice.

Sydney's weekly question was another of her idiosyncrasies the other girls tolerated. Every week Sydney would think of a fantastic question and all five would respond with honest answers. They usually groaned at Sydney's suggestion to play each week, but humored her nonetheless. Typically, the question was controversial enough that they were all entertained by the game in spite of themselves. This week's question was no different.

"Here it is," Sydney began and paused to take a deep breath for dramatic effect. "If you could go back in time and become any femme fatale in history, who would you become and with whom would you sleep?"

"Ahhh!" Amanda reacted. "So many choices ..."

"There's the obvious, Marilyn Monroe," Maddy suggested. "Sleeping with JFK or DiMaggio. I'd have to think about that. Of course, if I were Marilyn Monroe I'd get to sleep with both, so problem solved."

"I think I'd be a Bond girl," Brynn pondered. "I would be myself, only ravishingly beautiful, and I would sleep with Sean Connery."

"Not Roger Moore?" Hannah asked.

"Oh, no. A young Sean Connery for sure."

"Good answer!" Sydney squealed.

"I'm more of a Robert Redford kind of girl," Hannah admitted. "Classic, handsome, dreamy…"

"I'm still thinking," Amanda said. "Come back to me. Who would you be, Sydney?"

"I would be Salome," Sydney announced with a flourish. "The original femme fatale. And I would seduce John the Baptist before demanding his head."

"I was thinking more like Arnold Schwarzenegger," Amanda murmured, "but OK …"

"Who needs a refill?" Maddy piped in.

Brynn raised her hand. "I have a meeting first thing tomorrow morning. I think I'll grab a glass of water, if you don't mind, Hannah."

"Sure, I'll get it. Anyone else?"

"I'm good with this," Maddy replied, holding up the bottle of Pinot Noir she'd been working on. She didn't care if she was hung over tomorrow. She would manage to deal with the kids one way or another. She didn't have to change out of her pajamas if she didn't want to – stick one kid on the bus and let the other two amuse each other. Thursdays were typically spent on the couch binge watching whatever show she needed to catch up on.

Maddy polished the bottle off by herself, before Amanda announced it was time to go. Maddy didn't argue, since Amanda was her ride, and she had consumed quite enough wine for one night. She hugged each of her friends and gushed over what a great time she had, as usual.

"My house next week," Amanda called, as she gently pushed Maddy toward the door.

"I better go, too," Brynn was saying. "I try not to schedule anything important on Thursday mornings, but this meeting was out of my control."

"I understand," Hannah replied.

"I'll stay and help clean up," Sydney offered.

Brynn graciously accepted Sydney's offer to stay, and bowed out. "Thank you again, Hannah, for having us. Your house is absolutely gorgeous. I'm so happy for you."

"Thank you! I like it. It's a work in progress, but I'm happy with what I've done so far."

"You've done a magnificent job!" Sydney confirmed, as she gathered dishes from the coffee table.

Brynn was out the door, and Sydney fluttered around collecting dishes from the living room and depositing them on the kitchen counter. Hannah had fetched the club soda and was on her hands and knees working diligently on the spot on the carpet where Amanda had dropped the pepper. She paused occasionally to check the time, praying fretfully Pauly didn't arrive home before they had the house restored to order. Thank God for Sydney, bustling back and forth between the two rooms, she had both perfectly tidy by the time Hannah was satisfied with her efforts on the spot removal.

They looked at each other and smiled at a job well done. Just in time, as a car pulled into the driveway. The blood drained from Hannah's complexion. She dodged around the house once more to ensure everything looked immaculate.

"Go out the garage," she ordered Sydney.

"Won't he come in that way?" Sydney asked, then added. "Does it matter if he sees me leaving?"

"He'll come in the back door. Trust me, he will be mad if anyone is still here. He doesn't mind me having my friends over, but he wants his house to himself when he gets home. It's the way he is. Please, just go out through the garage and I'll call you tomorrow."

"Sure," Sydney agreed, trying not to let her concern show in her expression.

"Thank you so much, Sydney! You're a life saver!"

"Of course," she said with a shake of her head and darted through the door to the garage just as the back door was opening. Sydney slipped into the dark garage and paused to allow her eyes to adjust to the blackness. She surveyed her immediate surroundings to be certain she didn't knock into anything. The garage appeared to be perfectly clean, as she would have expected. Pauly had everything neatly in place, his lawn tools hung in a neat line across one wall, rock climbing equipment on another and nothing on the floor she could possibly trip over on her departure. She could hear Pauly's footsteps passing by the door, and she could hear Hannah greeting her husband.

"How was your meeting?" she asked.

"Productive. Where is the wine?"

"There's some left. I'll pour you a glass."

Sydney heard Hannah's footsteps passing the door on her way to the kitchen. She crept back to the door and cracked it open an inch. She could see Pauly eyeing the condition living room. He removed his tie and dropped it on the coffee table. Something on the floor caught his eye and he bent to the spot where Hannah had meticulously rubbed club soda on the small stain. He ran his fingers over the still-damp carpet and frowned. Sydney watched as he turned back to inspect the rest of the room. She silently pushed the door shut. Seconds later she heard Hannah pass by again.

"Something spill?" Pauly asked.

"A tiny drop of food," Hannah confessed. "I took the club soda to it right away. I'm sure it will dry fine."

"It had better."

"It will, Pauly. Have some wine."

"I agreed your friends could come over, if they can clean up after themselves."

Sydney stayed at the door, afraid to make a sound or be discovered.

"I cleaned it up, Pauly. It'll be fine."

"I work hard to give you the house you always wanted. When I come home, I expect it to be as it was when I left. I don't know how many times I have told you, clients of mine could stop by unexpectedly any time. How would it look if my house wasn't presentable? They would never trust me to find the perfect house for them. You should take more pride in your surroundings."

"I do."

"Next time your friends come, you will host them outdoors."

"Of course. The weather should be nice by then."

"Good. Now you had your fun with your friends. It is time to take care of your husband."

Sydney heard the rustling of Pauly setting down the glass of wine and taking his wife into his arms. She could hear kissing, as she carefully backed away from the door, the sound of bodies dropping onto the couch and clothes being removed vigorously.

"Let's go upstairs," Hannah's voice pleaded between kisses.

Footsteps again, another thump on the stairwell as though they did not make it all the way up before passion overcame them.

Sydney slid silently across the cement floor of the garage and let herself out the door on the opposite wall, into the side yard. She was immediately blinded by motion sensor lighting, but there were no windows on this side of the house. No one would notice her slipping away down the side path and into the night.

Chapter Two

Hannah woke late the next morning. Pauly was long gone and wouldn't be home until Monday night. He had one of his rock climbing trips planned, which suited Hannah fine since she had to work all weekend. Today was her day off – her only day off this week – and she planned to relax and enjoy it.

As she rolled out of bed, she realized how sore she was. It took a moment to remember what had happened last night. It was the fall on the stairs. She had urged Pauly to go upstairs, since she hadn't heard any evidence of Sydney's departure. Half-way up the staircase, in their frenzy of passion, they had fallen on the steps, where Pauly took her without hesitation.

Hannah eased out of bed and surveyed the damage. Her back was sore, and some of the skin was ripped off from rubbing against the carpeting. She had a welt on the back of her head, and a few bruises on her arms, as well. She sighed. Sex on the stairs was not one of their brightest ideas.

Hannah started the day by brushing her teeth and her hair, as she did every day. She had a routine, and if she faltered from it, she felt off the rest of the day. Teeth got two minutes for the top and two minutes for the bottom. Her long, black hair got one-hundred strokes. She couldn't help but cursing Pauly after every stroke for insisting she keep her hair this long. Otherwise, she would have cut it years ago. It was thick, heavy and tangled easily. She despised it, but even if she got an extra inch trimmed off during her biannual haircut, Pauly noticed and complained. Sometimes it was easier to please Pauly than to listen to his criticism.

She knew she needed to call Sydney and thank her for her help last night, but wasn't up to the task yet. She opted to go to the gym first, in accordance with her usual routine. On Pauly's insistence, they had gym memberships at the most esteemed facility in the area. It was a thirty-five-minute drive, but it had the best equipment, trainers and amenities available. Plus, they had rock climbing walls where Pauly could keep his skills honed through the winter – not that indoor walls were much of a challenge for Pauly, but they sufficed for a few months out of the year.

Hannah had tried every available asset the gym had to offer, but had settled into a habit of a thirty-minute warm-up run on the treadmill followed by a thirty-minute nautilus circuit. She finished up with a cool-down jog around the track and a shower. On the rare occasion that she and Pauly were at the gym together, she sat in the sauna or hot tub before her shower, since her husband's workout was more intense than her own.

Days after dinner with the girls were always a challenge. Hannah's body felt sluggish after indulging in a few glasses of wine the night before. She never cut her workout short, in spite of feeling less than vigorous. Her body was tight and fit for a reason, and she wasn't about to let an ounce of fat cling to her waistline. Pauly would notice, and then all hell would break loose.

Hannah finished her workout and showered at the gym, before heading to her car to call Sydney through the Bluetooth. Hannah preferred to shower at the gym so as not to create a mess in her own bathroom. It saved one chore on her day off. She climbed into her BMW 430i (only the best for Mrs. Paolo Gianni) and started it up. It did have a pretty purr. She listened for a moment, then gave the voice command to dial Sydney. Hannah was half-hoping for voice mail, but Sydney picked up. Sydney nearly always picked up.

"Hi, sweetie! How are you today?" Sydney asked cautiously.

"I'm great!" Hannah assured her. "I just finished up at the gym. I wanted to call and thank you for your help last night. You were a life saver!"

"You're welcome, of course. It was nothing."

"No, it was very nice of you, and I appreciate it."

"I would never leave you in a bad position," Sydney replied. "Did Pauly make a fuss about anything?"

"Not really," Hannah answered, uncertain how much Sydney had heard last night. "He noticed the carpet had a wet spot, but there is no stain. I checked it this morning, and it is fine."

"Good," Sydney said, and paused. "I worry about you, you know."

"You don't need to," Hannah told her, as she wiggled in her seat to take the pressure off her back. That was some bruise she had right below the shoulder blade. Working out had been uncomfortable too, but she forced through it. She would have to take some Tylenol when she got home. Hopefully she hadn't cracked a rib.

"Someone has to, Hannah," Sydney insisted. "We all worry about you. Pauly can be very demanding, and you don't always stand up for yourself. Honestly, I'm afraid of what might happen if you did stand up for yourself."

"Pauly's a pussy cat," Hannah responded, although she did not completely believe it. She said it all the time, perhaps hoping the more she verbalized it, the better the chances of it being true. She and Sydney, and all her other friends for that matter, knew it was far from the truth.

Hannah tried to hide Pauly's questionable attributes from her friends, but she knew they noticed a lot. Hannah often had bruises which she chose not to explain, most of which were from rough sex. Was it wrong of her to like rough sex? Well, she didn't exactly *like* it, but it certainly got Pauly hot, and when Pauly was hot, he was fantastic in bed, or on the stairs, or wherever they happened to be. Hannah had never experienced multiple orgasms like she did with Pauly. She loved her husband in spite of his peculiarities about keeping the house spotless, maintaining the perfect physique, cooking all meals to his high standard of healthiness, starching his shirts stiffer than the dry cleaner, and any number of other idiosyncrasies that had become part of her typical day. Hannah had become so accustomed to Pauly's seemingly strange demands that she hardly bothered to notice them anymore. Sometimes it took the eye of an outsider to point out to her that her relationship with her husband was not the norm.

"If you say so," Sydney said uncertainly, not wanting Hannah to know how much she had heard last night. "I just want you to know you deserve the best."

"Thank you," Hannah replied with sincerity, but also with a firmness indicating the end of that topic of discussion. Sydney took the hint.

"Are you available for lunch?" she asked.

"Oh, I'm sorry, Syd. I have a bunch of errands to run. Let's do lunch next week." Hannah hurried her friend off the phone before she could object. Hannah truly adored Sydney, but sometimes she could be stifling. She could handle spending time together once or twice a week, and definitely not two days in a row. She felt guilty already for turning Sydney down, knowing Sydney didn't have a husband to spend time with like the other members of her circle of friends, but that was Sydney's choice. Sometimes Hannah envied Sydney for her independence.

Hannah's day off was her one day of freedom, and when Pauly was out of town, that made the day even sweeter. She could reconnect with herself, take her time with her routine and relax without worrying about any demanding interruptions from her husband. When Paolo Gianni wanted something done, he wanted it done ASAP with no excuses. Having Pauly away on one of his rock climbing adventures meant peace of mind for Hannah, at least for a few days.

She made a few stops on the way home, not because they were pressing, but more so to ease her conscience that she had not been lying to Sydney about having errands to run. When she got home, she fixed herself a light salad for lunch and set about her housework. Keeping up on daily chores meant no surprises when Pauly returned, and no ensuing unpleasant confrontations. Only after her housework was done, did she allow herself the indulgence of cuddling up on the couch with a book. Pauly would gape that she had her feet on the couch, but he would never know!

Hannah breathed deeply and enjoyed every second of her day of solace. She had to admit life was good when her husband was away. Even the days she worked were less stressful, knowing she would come home to an empty, quiet house. It really was no way to live, but she had chosen this path for herself, and marriage was permanent. She had been raised Catholic, and took her marriage vows seriously – until death us do part.

Hannah worked all weekend, and the time flew. She worked all day Monday, and mentally prepared herself for Paolo's return. She sighed with relief that his car was not in the driveway when she pulled in from work. She had time to change her clothes and make sure the house was tidied to his standard of satisfaction before his arrival. She hustled about, wiping counters and fluffing pillows before starting dinner. Pauly may or may not want to eat, but she should be prepared either way.

An hour passed. Dinner was growing cold. Hannah decided she'd might as well eat, fully expecting Pauly to walk in and scold her for not waiting. Her husband didn't appear, and Hannah let his dinner sit for another hour before packing up the leftovers. She didn't normally keep leftovers, as her husband preferred freshly prepared food, but she didn't want him to come home to nothing. He could eat leftovers from the same day, after all.

Another hour passed and still no Pauly. Hannah began to question whether he was returning today. Had she gotten her dates mixed up? She could have, but it wasn't likely. Pauly wouldn't want to be gone too long and miss out on any new listings. He liked to get first pick of the listings and let the rest of the sales team fight over the remains.

Hannah argued with herself over whether to call him. He hated to be bothered when he was traveling, especially if he was listening to an audio book. After much internal debate, she did dial his cell phone, and got his voice mail. She left a quick message, and retired upstairs to take a shower. She needn't wait for him to call back. If he was still on the mountain, he wouldn't have cell service, and if he was involved in an audio book, he could ignore her. She didn't anticipate he would call her back either way, so she enjoyed a hot shower and relished in her evening beauty routine. She snuggled up in bed with a book, and barely remembered to check her phone before turning out the lights for the night. No missed calls.

Hannah slept like a baby, and went to work the next day refreshed. She had a slight nagging feeling something could be wrong, but she dismissed it. She had simply made a mistake on the date of Pauly's return, or he decided to stay another day. He didn't generally stray from his routine, but he was his own boss. She certainly couldn't call him again; he would be livid after having received two voice mails from her. She went about her work day and dismissed any negative thoughts. After all, he could be home now.

When she pulled into the driveway after work, and Pauly's car still was not there, the nervousness returned. What if something had happened? What if he never came home? Hannah had to consider the possibilities. He could have had an accident. If he slipped on the mountain, would anyone even know? Or he could have had a car accident on the way home. He could be in a hospital somewhere. Would anyone know to contact her? Pauly wasn't the type of person to have emergency contact information in his phone. He wasn't the type of person to have an emergency plan at all. He was so cocky he never thought anything could go wrong that he couldn't handle.

All kinds of morbid thoughts ran through Hannah's mind. Anything could have happened. The possibilities were endless. It would be devastating to lose her husband, although she had to admit part of her would be somewhat relieved. Life without Pauly would be tolerable after the initial shock wore off. She always enjoyed her time away from him; she was able to relax and be herself for a few days. She could actually breathe easier. She realized she hadn't had a headache in three days, which was highly unusual.

Hannah didn't bother with her nightly scan of the house to make sure everything was in place. She had to stop second-guessing herself and driving herself crazy over the house. What could possibly have gotten messed up while she was at work all day? She changed out of her work clothes, and found herself whistling as she heated up last night's leftovers. She had no problem eating food that was cooked yesterday; that was Pauly's hang up. He could fend for himself when he got home – *if* he came home tonight. If he was on his way, after all, there was no reason he couldn't have returned her call. It was common courtesy.

She was nearly done eating when she heard the car in the driveway. A flush of panic waved over her. Her heart jumped and she could feel her blood pressure rising. He was home!

She let out a sigh, whether of gratitude or defeat she wasn't sure. Pauly saw the surprise on her face when he came in.

"Did you think I wasn't coming home?" he teased.

"I thought you were due back yesterday," she responded.

"I was. I decided to stay another day. The weather doesn't usually hold up this early in the season. I thought I'd take advantage of it while I could."

Hannah nodded.

"Were you worried or something?" he prodded.

"I was a little concerned, but I knew you wouldn't have cell service up there ..."

"You *were* worried," he surmised from the expression on her face. "Did you think something happened to me?"

Hannah didn't respond, but dropped her eyes to her half-finished plate.

"Or maybe you were hoping I wasn't coming back," he changed his tune. "Did you think I found another woman?"

"Don't be silly."

"Would you like that, if I ran off with a sexy little blonde, and you could have our house all to yourself?"

"Come on, Pauly. That's crazy talk."

"It's not so crazy. I meet beautiful women every day. You didn't put on any weight while I was gone, did you?"

"I don't think so."

"You better not have," he teased. "Come on, aren't you going to kiss me? Didn't you miss me?"

Hannah let Pauly lift her from the chair and softened into his arms. He kissed her passionately, and she realized she had missed him after all. She didn't miss the nit-picking or the comments about her weight, or his obsession with the house, but she had missed those soft lips. He was her husband, faults and all, and she did love him. She found herself kissing him back, matching his passion. He lifted her into his arms and strapped her legs around his waist. He pressed her backwards against the table. She barely had time to shove her plate out of the way as he slammed her body onto the table and tore at her clothes. He was on her in seconds, rock hard and insatiable. She had no doubt he had been alone the last few days. He merely liked to tease her about having an affair to judge her reactions. It was a game he played often. Sex on the kitchen table, however, was a first, and the hard, wooden surface irritated the bruises on her back. She had nearly forgotten about them, as they had been healing nicely, but his weight slamming against her brought fresh pain. She grimaced.

If Pauly noticed, he didn't let on. He took it as a queue to pound her harder against the wood. She pulled herself away from the table and held her body tightly to his chest to ease the pressure on her back. Pauly lifted her again and sat back in a chair, all the while keeping firmly implanted in Hannah. She was on top of him now, on the chair, and the only pain in her back was when he squeezed her closer to him. She forgot about the bruises, as she lost herself in the passionate sensations in her groin. The roller coaster of emotions she had felt all day dissipated into lust. Nothing mattered at that moment other than her satisfaction, and Pauly was the only man who had ever been able to give it to her. At that moment, the pain was worth it, and she welcomed more pain if it meant satiating the hunger in her loins.

This is the way she and Pauly had always been, sexually electric, insatiable for each other. She only realized the unhealthy nature of their relationship the next day, when she could barely move to get out of bed. Her back was stiff and sore, as she eased herself to a sitting position. Only now did she question whether the sex was worth it, but the memory of her lust was so fresh, she tingled just thinking about last night. Oh, it was worth it. She would do it again right now if Pauly were home.

She slid herself gently off the bed and padded to the bathroom to begin her morning ritual. It was Wednesday, thankfully her day off. She had all day to recover, and she had wine with the girls this evening. Perhaps if she drank enough, she would numb the pain by the time she got home for tonight's encore.

Chapter Three

Hannah left for Amanda's house before Pauly got home from work. There was no reason to wait for him, although she would probably be the first one there. It was simply easier for her to avoid her husband than to stick around and risk a confrontation of some sort. Amanda lived about twenty minutes away, in the general direction of the gym. Hannah was admittedly a little jealous that Amanda lived so close to the gym, but the neighborhood was less than desirable in Pauly's standards. It wasn't a bad neighborhood, by any means; it merely wasn't a neighborhood a real estate agent would show off as home to his clients. At least that was Pauly's politically-correct description at the time Amanda and her husband purchased their home several years ago.

Hannah thought the neighborhood was charming regardless if it was rather outdated. She was the first to arrive, even before Amanda herself. There were no cars in the driveway, and no cars parked on the street when Hannah pulled up. Checking her phone, she was a few minutes early, and she read her emails as she waited.

Brynn arrived shortly after and parked behind her. They both got out of their cars and greeted each other, as Sydney pulled up.

"She is not here?" Sydney asked, looking around, brown curls bobbing from side to side.

"Doesn't appear to be," Brynn answered, and the three friends walked up to the porch together. Sydney rang the bell to make sure, but no one answered. They settled in on the porch for the time being.

"Too bad we couldn't open the wine," Brynn motioned to the bottles they had brought with them.

"Ah, but we can!" Sydney announced triumphantly, digging through her purse and coming out with a Swiss army knife equipped with every tool imaginable. "But what will we drink from?"

They looked around, but the porch had nothing more than a wicker seating area with a table – no accessories, other than a wind chime and an empty flower pot.

"No, thank you," Brynn said to the flower pot. "I can wait."

"That or we share the bottle …" Hannah joked. Maddy and Amanda were the ones who would unabashedly drink from the bottle, and when Maddy arrived, that is exactly what she suggested they do. She had a look of surprise that they hadn't already come to that decision.

"Where is Amanda anyway?" Maddy pondered aloud as she waited for Sydney to manipulate a small knife out of her multipurpose tool to remove the foil seal from the wine bottle, then wiggle the corkscrew into working position and twist it into the cork. Sydney made quick work of the task and tossed the foil and the cork into the empty flower pot next to her. She handed the bottle to Maddy, who raised it slightly as thanks and then lifted it to her lips for a long swig. Sydney deftly folded the tools safely into the Swiss army knife and deposited it back into her purse for the next emergency.

"Sorry, I didn't wait for your toast, Sydney," Maddy replied as an afterthought.

"I'll forgive you under the circumstances," Sydney sighed. She accepted the bottle back from Maddy and took a drink. She offered the bottle to Brynn next, who hesitated only for a second, then shrugged and joined them. Hannah didn't hesitate in the least when it was her turn, and they passed around the bottle and chatted until Amanda finally arrived. The bottle was nearly gone, and the late April air was growing chilly.

"It's about time!" Maddy called, as Amanda climbed out of her car and gathered the supplies she had brought with her, grocery bags, bottles of wine and a couple of Enquirer magazines.

"I know, I'm sorry. I'm running late. I see you girls made yourselves at home."

"We had to open the wine to stay warm," Maddy commented.

"Well, I don't blame you for opening the wine," Amanda admitted, as she unlocked the door. "You know I would have."

The ladies settled into Amanda's living room and unpacked the bags she had brought. She had several bottles of wine, cheese and crackers and a pre-cut fruit platter. She wasted no time in fetching glasses for them, which they promptly filled.

"I already apologized to Sydney for drinking before she gave her toast," Maddy said, in an obvious attempt to prevent Sydney from giving her toast now. Sydney either didn't get the hint, or ignored it, because she forced them to indulge her once again.

"To friendship," Sydney sang, with her eyes closed and her glass raised. "Friendship is always worth the wait."

The others exchanged glances, trying to figure out if she was done with her speech. Momentarily, she opened her eyes and drank, and the others followed suit.

"Is Pauly back from his trip?" Brynn asked.

"Yes, he got home Tuesday. He was supposed to come home Monday, but the weather was so good, he stayed another day. You never know what you're going to get when you plan a rock-climbing trip in April, but he couldn't wait to get out there after the long winter."

"Does he ever ask you to go with him?" Amanda wanted to know.

"He used to, but I never took him up on it. It's not my thing. I think he gave up on me, because he doesn't ask any more."

"I don't blame you," Maddy piped in. "I could never do it either."

"It's not even so much that I couldn't do it," Hannah admitted, "I just like the fact that Pauly and I have our own interests outside of each other. I don't think we need to spend every waking moment together."

"That's for sure," Amanda snorted. "Nate is driving me absolutely crazy. I wish he would go away for a week."

"Jim could stay, if someone took the kids," Maddy sighed.

"I told you I would watch the kids," Sydney reminded her. "Let me check my calendar and get back to you. You and Jim can have a date night."

"Thanks, Syd. That would be awesome."

"No problem," Sydney insisted, then turned back to Amanda. "How is Nate driving you crazy?"

"The usual bullshit," Amanda waved her hand as though a fly was bothering her. She reached for the cheese platter and stacked a slice of Muenster between two Ritz crackers. She bit the mini sandwich in half before continuing, although her concentration was more on the food than the topic at hand. "He is always pestering me to do stuff around the house, when he is the one who's the slob. I gave up keeping the house clean. This is as good as it gets."

She gestured to the room around her as cracker crumbs toppled to the floor by her feet. Her sandwich was coming apart.

"It looks great compared to my place," Maddy offered.

"I wouldn't stress over it," Brynn added. "Clean up after yourself, and he can clean up after himself. Marriage is a partnership, after all, and you both work full time. He can't expect you to do it all."

Hannah rolled her eyes. "Doesn't every man expect the woman to do it all?"

"Michael didn't," Brynn told her. "Although he had his faults, he did clean up after himself."

"Pauly takes care of the lawn, because he doesn't trust anyone else to touch it. Otherwise, I do everything else, cooking, cleaning, laundry, errands, everything. It's bad enough cleaning up after two people, I have no idea how Maddy cleans up after five."

"Not very well," Maddy admitted, and downed the rest of her wine. "Is there any more Pinot Noir in that bottle?"

Hannah handed the bottle to Maddy. As she did, her sleeve slid up on her arm, revealing a huge black-and-blue mark.

"Hannah!" Sydney cried. "Look at your arm! What did you do?"

Hannah noticed her sleeve had creeped up and embarrassedly pulled it back down over the bruise.

"It's nothing," she said, recalling the way Pauly had slammed her against the table last night. She was relieved Sydney couldn't see her back.

"It looks pretty bad," Sydney prodded.

"It's fine. Why don't we play your game, Sydney?" Hannah changed the subject. "Go ahead, ask us your question for the week."

"All right," Sydney sighed, obviously not fooled that Hannah was attempting to distract her, but polite enough to take the bait. She closed her eyes and thought for a moment, as though she hadn't already pondered over this hypothetical question the past week. The others exchanged glances, knowing very well Sydney was simply building up for the dramatic.

"This question builds off last week's question," she began. "The difference is that last week's question was based on fantasy and this week's question is based on reality."

She paused again for effect, while the others sipped their wine and nibbled on crackers in anticipation.

"This is going to be a good one," Amanda rubbed her hands together, encouraging Sydney's folly.

"Here it is. If you could sleep with anyone you know, just one night, with no future repercussions, who would it be?"

The others squealed at the question.

"The UPS man, no doubt," Maddy answered without hesitation. Her friends laughed.

"You don't even know his name," Amanda laughed.

"Yes, I do. It's Ken."

"Oh, you read his name tag," Amanda teased.

"Who cares what his name is?" Maddy defended her response. "He's hot, and it's a one-time thing with no future repercussions, remember?"

Amanda rolled her eyes. "It's supposed to be someone you know."

"My answer is no good either, then," Brynn chimed in. "I would definitely pick the man in my building that I've had my eye on for months. I admit, I don't know his name, or anything about him for that matter, other than he is extremely good looking and dresses nice. And he has a fabulous smile."

"That's a good answer!" Sydney insisted.

"But wouldn't you want to sleep with him more than just one night?" Amanda pointed out.

"I'll let you know …" Brynn joked. She winked and took a swig of wine, finishing her glass and reaching for the unopened bottle of Chardonnay. "This is going down way too easily tonight."

"Pour me some of that, please," Hannah agreed, handing her empty glass to Brynn. Hannah was drinking at an uncharacteristically fast rate.

"What about you, Hannah?" Amanda asked. "Who is your secret crush?"

Hannah smiled, waiting for her refill before responding.

"I've given it some thought," she said, "and I have to be honest. Pauly is the best I have ever slept with. I would choose him any day of the week."

"You can't pick your husband!" Amanda groaned.

"I don't have another answer," Hannah shrugged. "I don't know anyone else I would want to sleep with, and Pauly fulfills all my needs, if you know what I mean."

The others laughed.

"You're going to have to be more specific," Maddy prodded.

"Pauly is absolutely insatiable," Hannah told them. "He wants sex all the time – anytime, *anywhere*. I thought after we'd been married for a while, he would calm down, but he hasn't. And honestly, my desires haven't waned either. I have never, ever in my life had sex so much, and so good … I'm talking multiple orgasms. It's just so unpredictable where we're going to do it next. Last night he was so horny when he got home from his trip, he did me right on the kitchen table. There was food and everything. We didn't even care."

"Oh!" Maddy squealed. "You're a freak!"

"Who would have thought innocent, little Hannah was a sex freak."

"Pauly's the one who's the sex freak," Hannah corrected Amanda. "I'm just enjoying the ride!"

"Enjoy it while it lasts," Amanda advised. "Marriage has a way of putting out the fire in your sex life, if you know what I mean."

"So do kids," Maddy added.

"At least you have an option," Brynn reminded them. "Being divorced hasn't done anything for my sex life."

"You need to put yourself out there," Amanda told her. "No one knows you're back on the market."

"I know," Brynn admitted. "I'm not going to meet anyone cooped up in my apartment. What about you, Amanda? Who would you sleep with?"

"I'm picking Pauly," Amanda declared matter-of-factly.

"Can I change my answer?" Maddy piped in, which drew a good round of laughter from the others.

"Sorry, ladies, he's all mine," Hannah told them. "Besides, I wouldn't wish Pauly on any of you. The sex is good, don't get me wrong, but it can get rough. And he's not always pleasant to live with."

"That explains the bruise," Amanda grunted.

"Is that where you got this?" Sydney exclaimed, pulling up Hannah's sleeve for the others to see.

"Sort of," Hannah blushed.

"He didn't beat you, did he?" Sydney asked with a wave of apprehension.

"No, he didn't beat me," Hannah answered quickly, suddenly aware she had to explain now that she'd said so much already. "My arm bumped into the table last night when he was lifting me up there. It's no big deal. I didn't feel anything at the time. I didn't even realize it was bruised until today."

"I'm sure this isn't the first battle scar you've come away with," Sydney commented, remembering what she heard from her hiding place in Hannah's garage last week. "You have to be careful, or he is really going to hurt you."

"He's never hurt me," Hannah lied, wishing she had kept her mouth shut about the table incident.

"He'd better not," Sydney warned.

"Seriously, Hannah," Brynn added, "Pauly's a lot bigger than you. He could really hurt you."

"I'm a big girl. You don't need to worry about me. Sometimes the sex gets a little rough, but it's worth it. I can handle it."

"You know that's not normal, right?" Brynn kept on her.

"What is normal?" Hannah challenged her. The wine was making her unusually outspoken. "The fact that my husband is still hot for me after two years of marriage is probably not normal. The fact that he gives me multiple orgasms is definitely not normal. Coming away with a few bruises may not be normal either, according to your definition, but I will take abnormal every day of the week. I am undeniably sexually satisfied, which is more than the rest of you can say. No offense," she added.

"I can't argue with that logic," Amanda replied, then redirected the discussion. "Sydney, you haven't answered your own question. Who would you sleep with?"

The others turned their attention to Sydney expectantly. They were all relieved to take the focus off Hannah and her unprecedented confession.

Sydney looked taken aback for a second, as though she had forgotten all about herself. She collected her composure and smiled, picturing her answer in her head with obvious relish.

"I have a thing for the reverend at my church," she admitted sheepishly.

"You bad girl!" Maddy scolded.

"Isn't he married?" Brynn recalled.

"Oh, yes, he's happily married. I would never want to mess that up in real life, but that's what makes him so attractive to me. In the fantastic nature of this game, where I can have anyone I want for one night with no future repercussions, it would be him. And it would be marvelous."

"This is what you think about in church," Amanda stated flatly.

Sydney shot her a look.

"At least she goes to church," Maddy pointed out. "I wouldn't dare drag those three rug rats to church. Can you imagine?"

No one commented on Maddy's rug rats.

"I admit, I dreamed up this question in church on Sunday," Sydney told them. "He is just *so handsome*. Sometimes I think I go to church just to see him."

"Blasphemer," Amanda kidded. "You go to church for the sole purpose of committing adultery."

Hannah laughed loudly and hiccupped.

"I never claimed to be a saint," Sydney offered. "Are you all right, Hannah? Do you need some water?"

"I'm fine. I got the hiccups." Hic.

"I'll get you a glass of water," Amanda stood. "Anyone else?"

"Sure. Why not," Maddy agreed.

"I'll help you," Sydney stood as well and joined Amanda in the kitchen. Once they were out of earshot, she pounced on Amanda with questions. "Do you think Hannah's OK? She's had a lot to drink tonight. Do you think Pauly hits her? Rough sex is one thing, but I've seen bruises on her before, and I don't think she's being completely truthful with us."

"I don't know." Amanda was noncommittal.

"Do you think she can drive home? I don't think we should let her drive like this. She never drinks this much."

"You're probably right about that. Carry these."

Sydney accepted two of the glasses of water from Amanda and followed her back into the living room.

"I have an idea," Sydney said, as she handed one of the glasses to Hannah. "Next week at my house, I am going to cook us dinner. We really need to eat something more substantial than cheese if we're going to be drinking this much."

"You don't have to go out of your way," Brynn replied.

"It's my pleasure," Sydney insisted. "I'll make something delightful. We will have full bellies and full hearts."

There was no arguing with Sydney. They sipped their water and helped Hannah remedy her hiccups. No one drank much more of the wine, since they didn't want to encourage Hannah to get any drunker than she already was. When the fiesta started to break up, Amanda told Hannah she would drive her home.

"What about my car?"

"Your car will be fine here overnight. I'll pick you up in the morning to come get it, if you want."

"Pauly's not going to be happy about this…"

"Would he be happier if you drove drunk?" Amanda pointed out. "Come on, kid. You're making a big deal out of nothing. Grab your purse."

Hannah did as she was told and hugged each of her friends in turn.

"Thank you for a wonderful evening," Sydney was saying to Amanda. "And thank you for taking care of Hannah."

"That's what friends are for," Amanda answered and gave Hannah a gentle shove towards the door.

Chapter Four

Amanda loaded Hannah into the car and took it easy on the drive home. Hannah babbled the entire way about what a fuss Pauly was going to make, and Amanda continuously reminded her she made the right decision not to drive.

"He can't very well be angry with you for choosing *not* to drive drunk," Amanda told her.

"He will be angry I drank so much that I couldn't drive," Hannah argued.

"He'll get over it."

"You don't know Pauly ..."

"Do you seriously think he's going to be mad? Nate wouldn't notice if I didn't come home at all."

"He will be mad all right."

"Listen, Hannah. Do you want me to stay with you? He's more likely to behave himself if I'm there."

"Oh, no, I'll be fine. I just hate going home sometimes."

Amanda stole a glance at Hannah, but she was staring out the window. She shrugged to herself and put her eyes back on the road. She was honestly relieved that Hannah didn't want her to stay, but she pondered if she should at least walk her inside. By the time she pulled into the driveway, Hannah seemed more like herself.

"Thank you so much, Amanda! You're the best!"

"You got it, kid."

Hannah jumped out of the car without delay and waved as she hurried into the house. Amanda watched her go inside.

"That answers that question," Amanda said aloud to herself. She took out her cell phone and called Nate. He had graciously gone out to a bar to watch the baseball game with some friends, to allow Amanda to have the girls over for wine night. One thing about Nate, he was easy-going and agreeable. Amanda got his voice mail.

"Hey, Babe. I'm taking Hannah home, because she had a little too much to drink. I think I'm going to crash on her couch, make sure she's OK. I'll talk to you tomorrow. Love ya."

Next, she texted the single word "myah" to a number not stored under her contact list.

She took one last look at Hannah's house for any evidence of activity between her and her overbearing husband. All was calm. Amanda backed out of the driveway and headed south, not the way she had come, and not the direction of her home. Twenty minutes later, she pulled into an alley behind a row of duplexes. It was an old neighborhood, and garages lined the alleyway behind the buildings. She parked in front of one of the garages, about midway down the block and turned off the car.

She pulled her phone out and checked it. No missed calls, but she had a return text, "excellent."

She slipped through the darkness of the small backyard and went in through the back door. It was unlocked. The entryway led into the kitchen, and the light was off, but she could see the glow of the television from the next room. She headed toward the light and the faint sound of gunshots.

"Whatcha watching?" she asked.

"I don't know, some movie, but I'm lost. I must have dozed off," he said and sat up on the couch. He looked as though he had been sleeping, but he was still sexy as hell. He had on the same jeans he had worn earlier, but had taken off his shirt. His dark hair was mussed, his blue eyes clear and piercing in the dim flickering of the TV screen. "I can't believe you're here."

"I can't either. If I knew I was going to get back over here tonight, I wouldn't have let you make me late for girls' night."

"How did you manage it?"

"It was almost too easy," Amanda admitted. "Our Wednesday Wine Club was going along as usual, but Hannah was drinking like a fish. It's not like her. She is usually more reserved. It's not like her at all! She was telling us things about her sex life, talking about her husband. She *never* does that. I never knew the first thing about Paulo except he's scary as fuck. Honestly, I don't know why she stays with him."

Amanda tossed her purse on the coffee table and joined Dalton on the couch.

"I was blown away. I don't think I've ever seen her drunk before. She had this huge bruise on her arm – which isn't the first time I've seen bruises on this woman – but she actually told us it happened during rough sex."

"Is that what you're getting at?" Dalton teased. "You want to spice things up?"

"No, I'm just saying … well, maybe. I don't know. I never thought about it," Amanda laughed. "I just couldn't believe she was telling us this. Her private life has always been kind of a secret with her. She's very introverted, you know, quiet, keeps things to herself."

"Now you know why," Dalton laughed, running his hand through his hair. He was beginning to come back to life after his nap.

"At any rate, none of us thought Hannah should drive herself home. I've never seen her drink like that," Amanda shook her head. "I felt like it was kind of my responsibility to get her home safely, since she was at my house, so I offered to drive her. On the way to her house, she was starting to freak me out, saying how mad Pauly was going to be. I just wasn't getting a good vibe, with that big bruise on her arm. Who knows what goes on behind closed doors, you know what I mean? So, I offered to stay, thinking he can't very well beat her or rape her or whatever he does if I'm there. She said no, of course, but Nate doesn't know that. I told him I was staying over there, and here I am!"

"Myah," Dalton smiled.

"Myah," Amanda repeated, their code word for "Meet you at home." She threw her arms around her lover and kissed him.

'Do you think we should change our code word, now that we've used it?"

"I think it's fine," Dalton assured her. "No one knows, right?"

"Hell, no!" Amanda confirmed adamantly. "It seemed weird at first, not telling my friends, but it's better no one knows. Funny thing happened today, though. I told you every week at our Wednesday gathering, Sydney comes up with a hypothetical question for the group, and we all have to answer honestly. This week she asked if we could sleep with anyone we wanted, but it had to be someone we knew, for just one night with no repercussions, who would it be?"

Dalton smiled and waited for Amanda to finish her story. He was humoring her, letting her get all the talking out before whisking her off to the bedroom. He was becoming aroused watching her present her animated recollection of her night.

"I could have told them about us, right then and there. But I kept my mouth shut. I mean, I am dying to tell someone about you. I hate keeping all this inside! I've never been so happy in all my life. But I know, for this to keep working, I've got to keep it to myself. It's so hard!"

"It's getting hard ..." Dalton said, and leaned in to kiss her. One quick kiss and he pulled back and asked, "who did you choose, then?"

Amanda blushed slightly, which was an oddity.

"You can tell me ..." Dalton urged, taking her around the waist and pulling her onto his lap. As she straddled him on the couch, she could feel he was, in fact, getting hard.

"It's funny, actually," she started, her cheeks still flushed, but more from the excitement of rubbing against him than the embarrassment of the recollection of her answer. "That was when Hannah was opening up about Pauly being into rough sex, and wanting sex all the time, and she was bragging how he is so good he gives her multiple orgasms. I was like, I'll sleep with Pauly," she laughed.

"You think this Pauly guy is better than me?" Dalton teased, as he rubbed his thumbs over her hip bones.

"I don't think I'll ever get the chance to find out. Let's see what you can do, big boy."

Dalton easily lifted her up as he stood, and carried her to the bedroom with her legs still wrapped around his middle. Neither gave Pauly another thought. They had the entire night together, and all their focus was on each other.

Amanda was thrilled to spend the whole night with Dalton. They had only been able to arrange it once before, and it felt wonderful to wake up in his arms after a full night of lovemaking. She hadn't been looking to have an affair, six months ago when Dalton had walked into the restaurant. Her marriage was not struggling at the time, and she and Nate had been discussing starting a family. She had never believed in love at first sight, but she had no other words to describe it. There was something about Dalton that she was madly attracted to, something she had never experienced before.

Dalton knew Amanda was married. It didn't deter him from asking her out, and she couldn't say no to him. It was an unexplainable attraction which neither could resist. Amanda had no idea where the relationship was going, but it didn't matter. It was all about fulfilling each other's needs, at this point. She would sneak off to see Dalton at every possible opportunity.

It was getting more and more difficult to leave Dalton and go back to her regular life. She lingered longer after every encounter, kissed him goodbye a hundred times, before pulling herself away reluctantly. Eventually she knew she was going to have to make a decision about their future, but for now she was riding the wave, enjoying every stolen second with her lover, and keeping every delicious detail of their affair a secret. It was hard not to confide in her friends, but she kept her mouth shut for her own good.

After her lengthy goodbye the next morning, she would barely have time to drive back to Hannah's before heading home to change for work. She texted Hannah from the car to let her know she was on her way. Hannah texted back promptly that Pauly was going to drive her over later to get her car, no need to go out of her way.

Amanda breathed a sigh of relief and changed her plan of action. She wouldn't go home at all. She would drive straight to work. She had a change of clothes in the break room, and she had already showered at Dalton's. It would be easier not to have to face Nate until later.

She found herself whistling as she arrived at work and went inside the restaurant to change. The breakfast crowd was filling in, and it appeared she would have a busy start to her day. It was just as well; if she kept busy, the time went faster. Amanda wasn't overly enamored with her waitressing job at The Diamond Diner, but there was something special about being in the place where she'd met Dalton. She went about her day with a smile on her face, which perpetuated her good mood and helped earn her tips at the same time.

Her shift was nearing its end when a familiar figure at the counter caught her attention. It was a man, not overly tall, but of strong stature. He exuded confidence and authority as he ordered his coffee to go, tossed a bill on the counter and stepped back to wait. It took Amanda a closer look to realize it was Paolo Gianni.

He wore a trench coat over an ostentatiously expensive suit. He flicked his wrist to force his cuff up far enough to check his watch. Amanda caught the glitter of a diamond inset where the twelve would be. She remembered that was how Hannah had met him – she had sold him his watch. Whether that was the same watch, Amanda had no clue. It had been several years, after all. Better to think about Hannah's story about the watch than her rendition of their sex life, Amanda reminded herself.

Paolo looked up and caught her gazing at him.

"Amanda," he said with a half-smile. His voice made a shiver run up her spine. That and the fact that he was looking her dead in the eye. The last time she'd seen him, he had barely made eye contact, as though he had merely greeted her for the benefit of his wife. Today his gaze was purposeful.

"How are ya?" she managed meekly. She was positive she had never seen him in the restaurant before today. He was here for a reason. He was here to see her.

"I'm well," he answered politely but briefly, and he did not return the courtesy of asking how she was.

She stared, her heart beating out of her chest as she waited for his next move.

"Thank you for taking care of my wife last night," he said in his odd way of speaking, annunciating each word, with a hint of sarcasm in *taking care of*.

"He knows," Amanda thought in a wave of panic. She mentally reminded herself to breathe. How could he possibly know? Unless he had spoken to Nate, but Nate was undoubtedly at work when he and Hannah had picked up her car. She sucked in her breath slowly, her mind racing, debating how to respond.

"My pleasure," Amanda said aloud, trying to sound casual. She forced a smile.

Paolo was staring at her intently. It felt like he was looking straight through her, reading her thoughts.

"Your coffee, sir." Debbie was behind the counter, leaning over to hand a large to-go cup to Paolo.

"Thank you," Paolo said to Debbie as he accepted the cup. He nodded toward Amanda, then spun on his heel and headed for the door. His phone was ringing, and he popped it to his head on the way out the door.

"Paolo Gianni," Amanda heard him answer before the door swung shut behind him. He strode to his car without a backward glance.

Amanda forcibly exhaled, not realizing she'd been holding her breath. She was frozen for a second, chilled to the bone by the sound of his voice and the piercing stare of his olive-colored eyes. He was one scary mother fucker, she thought as she regained her senses and turned back to work.

The smile she'd worn all day was gone, and she was barely conscious of what she was doing the rest of her shift. Her body was on auto-pilot, while her mind raced.

What the hell was that all about? She knew Pauly's visit was intended as a warning, rather than a thank you. He wasn't in the neighborhood coincidentally. She knew Paolo Gianni wouldn't be caught dead selling real estate in this neighborhood. He didn't get his fancy clothes and diamond-studded watch by doing business on the South Side. No, he had made a special trip just to see her, to "thank" her for "taking care of" his wife last night.

But how much could he really know… He couldn't possibly know Amanda hadn't gone home last night. And if he did know, why would he care? It had nothing to do with him. Besides, he couldn't possibly know. She didn't know what time they were at her house picking up the car, but Nate certainly couldn't have been home. Even if he was home, Amanda reasoned, they wouldn't have spoken to Nate. There would have been no reason to knock on the door. Hannah knew she wasn't home.

Honestly, she was acting paranoid, she told herself. Her perfectly orchestrated plan to spend the night with her lover was her secret. No one could possibly know.

Then why did Pauly stop in here? Amanda couldn't answer that question. She didn't know Pauly very well, but she knew him well enough to know he didn't do things out of the goodness of his heart. He did things for a reason – as a means to an end. He was a purposeful man. Everything he did was done with foresight and the expectancy of a specific outcome. He wasn't the type of person to drive out of his way to get a crappy cup of coffee at the restaurant where his wife's friend worked, for the sole purpose of thanking her for getting his drunk wife home the night before.

She wished she had someone she could talk to about it – someone neutral to bounce her ideas off, someone to smack her across the face and tell her to stop being so paranoid. But she knew deep down it wasn't paranoia. Paolo Gianni somehow knew that she'd told her husband she was spending the night at the Gianni residence, when she was actually shacking up with her lover.

Amanda shook her head fiercely. The thought was so ridiculous that Paolo could possibly know, yet it had just enough plausibility to make her nervous. He was a very, scary man. If he did know, he would use that information to his advantage any way he could. But that was silly! He had literally no interest in his wife's friends – what use could it possibly be to learn that his wife's friend was having an affair?

Amanda made herself put the thought from her mind, but it continued creeping back the entire week. It ate away at her every night, when she pulled into the driveway after work and wondered if a confrontation was waiting for her. She didn't dare call Hannah and ask her about it. She didn't want to raise any suspicion on Hannah's part if she didn't know anything. And she couldn't risk Pauly hearing her talking to Hannah and knowing she knew that he knew. It was all so awful, not knowing who knew what!

Amanda struggled through the week, worrying constantly and playing every possible scenario out in her head. She barely spoke to Dalton all week, which was the worst part of it. She didn't want to take any unnecessary chances going to see Dalton or talking to him; she didn't even tell him about the incident. She tried like hell to keep a low profile and prayed nothing was amiss. She would wait it out. Next week, at their Wednesday gathering, she would casually ask Hannah about getting her car back, under the pretense she was simply making sure everything went smoothly. She would make it about Hannah, suggesting she was concerned after all Hannah's fretting over how mad Pauly was going to be. Wednesday couldn't come quick enough!

Chapter Five

Sydney lived in the house that had belonged to her grandmother. It was north of the city, just over the county line. Sydney had moved in with her grandmother when she became ill, eight years ago. She passed away two years later, leaving the house and all its contents to her beloved granddaughter. Sydney had not changed a thing since her grandmother's passing, which made for an atmosphere that was both comforting and eerie.

Amanda said as much when she arrived.

"I feel like Lawrence Welk should be on TV," she said.

Sydney smiled and took Amanda's jacket.

"I like the warmth Grandmother created. I'm afraid if I redecorate, I will lose everything she worked so hard to create. We have such good memories in this home!" Sydney sighed and looked around, mentally reminiscing. Her trance was broken by a rap on the door, and she flitted off to greet her next guest.

Hannah had arrived. Amanda could hear Sydney fawning over Hannah, spewing compliments about her hair, her outfit, her knack for timeliness. As Sydney crooned on, Amanda started opening drawers looking for a corkscrew. She needed to get alcohol in her system ASAP.

Sydney and Hannah entered the huge, eat-in kitchen where Amanda was rummaging guiltlessly through a drawer. Sydney nonchalantly passed by her, pushing the drawer shut and opening the one next to it in one swift movement. She continued on her way through the kitchen, to take care of the jackets without a word. Amanda pulled the corkscrew triumphantly out of the drawer Sydney had opened. She spun around and attacked the bottle of wine she'd brought, slitting the foil and tossing it aside.

"How are ya, kid?" she asked Hannah, as she struggled to remove the cork from the bottle. Sydney was back from the coat closet in perfect time to relieve Amanda from her struggle and pull the cork free. Amanda stared in awe, as Sydney handed her back the cork screw with the cork still attached, retrieved wine glasses from a cupboard and set them on the table on her way through the kitchen, back to the door to greet her next guest. Amanda shrugged, set down the cork screw without bothering to dislodge the cork and poured herself a glass. After downing half of it and deeming it drinkable, she topped it off and then poured some wine into a second glass for Hannah.

"I'm great, and you?"

"Living the dream," Amanda answered, raising her glass in affirmation. "You aren't planning on getting tanked up again tonight, are you? It's a pretty long drive home from here."

"No," Hannah was saying with a flush of embarrassment. Sydney had reentered the room, with Brynn on her heels.

"Hannah can drink all she likes," Sydney answered for her. "I am the hostess for the evening, and I will ensure all guests are delivered home safely. Of course, you can always crash here. There's plenty of room at Grandmother's."

Amanda rolled her eyes at Sydney's insistence on calling the house Grandmother's six years after her death. "Hey, Brynn."

Brynn waved hello, then excused herself to the ladies' room, as she had come straight from work.

"I do not intend to drink that much tonight," Hannah assured them, "but I do want to thank you, Amanda, for taking me home last week. You were absolutely right that I should not drive in that condition."

"Don't mention it, kid. That's what friends are for. I'm just glad you made it home safely. No problems getting your car?"

"No."

"Was Pauly mad he had to drive you over to get it?"

"No, he was fine. I needn't have worried."

"You had *me* worried," Amanda told her. "What time did you get the car?"

"I don't remember, exactly. It was shortly after you texted me."

"Was Nate home?" Amanda wanted to know.

"I didn't even notice. Pauly pulled up and I jumped out."

"What did Pauly say? You sure he wasn't mad?"

"He didn't say anything. He got a phone call from a client right when we pulled up. He was still sitting in his car when I drove away. By the time he got home from work, he had forgotten all about it."

"Good," Amanda said absent-mindedly. She hadn't gotten the answers she had hoped for. Pauly theoretically could have spoken to Nate and learned the truth about her whereabouts.

Sydney was bustling around the kitchen, checking the food in the oven and slicing a fresh loaf of bread. She appeared distracted, but was actively listening to the conversation and giving Hannah concerned glances.

"I feel better!" Brynn announced as she returned from the ladies' room. "Sydney, it smells fabulous in here!"

"Thank you! I hope it tastes as good as it smells."

"I'm sure it will. You're an excellent cook," Hannah told her.

Maddy was at the door. Sydney looked frazzled, her hands covered with pot holders.

"I'll get it," Brynn offered.

"Thank you!" Sydney chirped as she continued bustling from the oven to the table, setting hot pans on trivets and collecting serving utensils for each pan. The table looked lovely, set for five. Sydney had set out place mats and linen napkins, and had prefilled water glasses. She was using her grandmother's good china and freshly polished silver.

"What is that smell?" Maddy asked as she came around the corner into the kitchen.

"We have home-made macaroni and cheese, southern fried chicken and fresh sweet potato fries," Sydney announced. "Comfort food!"

"You didn't have to go through all the trouble, Sydney, but I'm so glad you did!" Maddy laughed. "I haven't had a home-cooked meal that I didn't cook in ages!"

"I don't remember the last time I had a home-cooked meal," Brynn admitted. "I mean, I cook most nights, but it's nothing special. Cooking for one is never anything fancy."

"Well, I cook for five daily," Maddy said, "but it's nothing fancy. The kids like hot dogs, hamburgers, chicken nuggets and pancakes. That's about the extent of it."

Sydney wrinkled her nose. "That's exactly why I felt we needed an old-fashioned family dinner. We are, after all, family."

The ladies took their seats at the table, as Sydney brought the sliced bread from the counter. Amanda filled their wine glasses, or refilled as the case may be. Sydney took her place at the head of the table, and raised her wine glass to make her traditional weekly toast. A large orange cat slinked in from another room and settled itself under Sydney's chair.

"To friends," Sydney began, then stopped and looked around for her phone. Finding it on the counter, she shut it off, then resumed her position at the head of the table. "Grandmother's rule. No phones when we have company. Now, where was I? Oh, yes. Friends, for we are friends that have become family, and our family of five has a stronger bond than many blood relatives. I am grateful for each of you and honored to call you my family."

"To friends," Brynn repeated. They clinked their glasses and drank, then wasted no time digging into the delectable spread Sydney had prepared.

"So good," Maddy said between bites.

"Delicious," Brynn agreed.

Amanda and Hannah ate silently, both either lost in thought or mesmerized by the food. Sydney smiled modestly and nodded, scooping a second helping of macaroni and cheese onto her plate.

"Just what the doctor ordered!" Sydney sang delightedly, watching with satisfaction as her friends satiated their appetites.

None wanted to move by the time they were done eating, they were so full. Brynn mustered the will to move first and started clearing the plates from the table. Sydney and Hannah joined in, while Maddy excused herself to the ladies' room and Amanda stepped outside to make a phone call.

"What's with Amanda?" Sydney asked when she was safely out of earshot. "She's been awfully quiet tonight after hounding you with twenty questions about last week."

"She has been quiet," Hannah agreed distractedly, ignoring the reference to the question and answer session. Sydney tried again.

"Why was she so worried about you, Hannah? Did Pauly act badly when she dropped you off, or something?"

"No," Hannah turned her attention to Sydney. "I don't know. I guess I made her worried that Pauly was going to be mad."

"And was he?" Sydney prodded.

Brynn turned her head to watch Hannah's reaction.

"He wasn't happy, but he didn't say much. He was acting more like a father than a husband, said he was disappointed I chose to drink so much."

"You don't have any more bruises this week, do you?" Sydney asked, acting matronly herself.

"No, no. No new bruises," she answered and walked away. She headed towards the ladies' room, and passed Maddy on her way back through to the kitchen.

"You don't think he beats her, do you?" Sydney whispered to Brynn.

"I hope not," Brynn shook her head. She honestly didn't know what happened between Hannah and her husband behind closed doors. Hannah obviously wasn't going to give them any further details.

Brynn and Sydney locked eyes for a moment, both wondering the same thing.

"She wouldn't tell us if he did," Brynn surmised. She went back to the dishes, while Sydney readied dessert.

"I don't think I can eat another bite," Maddy told her.

"It's homemade apple pie!" Sydney teased.

"Maybe a sliver," Maddy conceded.

Sydney prepared five plates whether her friends wanted dessert or not. She set the plates around the table and presented a dessert wine to accompany it. No one refused the pie or the wine, including Amanda who had returned from outside.

"Did you make this crust, Sydney?" Hannah asked.

"Yes, I did. I made it just like Grandmother taught me!" She said proudly.

"It's delicious," Hannah told her.

"So good," Maddy said, shaking her head. "I wish I had time to bake."

"You will, when the kids are older," Sydney assured her. "Which reminds me, I can definitely watch them Saturday, if you and Jim want to get out of the house alone together."

"Really? That would be awesome!" Maddy gasped. "It's been *so long* since Jim and I had a night out. I feel like we don't even talk any more. Sometimes I wonder if he has a girlfriend."

"No…" Brynn interjected.

"He certainly isn't interested in me! And I'm not interested in him half the time either, but that's not because I have a boyfriend. It's because I'm dead tired!"

"That's understandable when you have three kids," Hannah pointed out.

"I don't think he'd have a girlfriend," Brynn added. "He's probably exhausted too."

"He'd better not! I'd kill him."

"I *wish* Nate had a girlfriend," Amanda snorted. "Get him off my back for a while."

"Amanda!" Brynn scolded. "That's terrible."

"You're a fine one to talk," Amanda retorted. "You know exactly what it's like to want out of a relationship – even if only for a night. Or two."

"Yeah, or forever," Brynn admitted. "I guess I do know where you're coming from."

"Pauly's going rock climbing this weekend," Hannah offered. "Maybe he would take Nate with him."

"I wouldn't be so lucky," Amanda told her.

"Oh!" Sydney squealed excitedly. "I have the perfect question!"

"Let's have it," Amanda said, resigned to playing along with Sydney's weekly folly.

"You all complain about your husbands a lot. What if you could arrange for your husband to be gone forever? How would you do it?"

"You mean murder?" Hannah asked.

"Could be murder," Sydney nodded, then raised her eyebrows suggestively. "Could be an *accident.*"

"What would be the motive?" Amanda wanted to know.

"Your husband is cheating on you," Sydney told Amanda matter-of-factly. "Hypothetically, of course. Hannah, your husband beats you. Brynn, your husband is trying to swindle you out of your inheritance. Maddy, your husband robbed you of your youth."

"Not bad," Amanda mumbled.

"And you, Sydney?" Brynn asked. "If you had a husband?"

"My husband is but a shadow of a man. He is not there for me. He's a disappointment in every aspect of his life."

"Considering my husband is cheating on me," Amanda jumped right in. "First, I'd have to snip off his balls. Then I would stuff them in his mouth and tape it shut until he suffocated."

"That's sick," Maddy frowned. "What the hell is wrong with you?"

"It's just a game," Amanda rebutted.

"Exactly," agreed Brynn. "And since it's a game, I would be rich enough to hire an assassin. The divorce hasn't finalized yet, which would give me control of all Michael's assets. He would never see it coming, and it would never be traced back to me."

"Good!" Sydney encouraged.

Maddy was still unsure and gave her an appalled look.

"Pauly would die in a mysterious rock climbing accident," Hannah chimed in. Her eyes were glossed over as though she were picturing it happen in her head. "I'm not sure how I would manage it, but no one would suspect foul play."

"Of course!" Sydney exclaimed. She clapped her hands together in approval.

"I think you guys have all been watching a little too much 20/20," Maddy told them.

"I love that show!" Brynn and Sydney both blurted out.

"Come on, Maddy. Play along. He robbed you of your youth!" Amanda reminded her.

"Literally," Maddy rolled her eyes.

"Choose your revenge!" Sydney declared.

"I guess I wouldn't want anything too gory to happen to him. Maybe he has a car accident or something."

"Because he was texting his girlfriend while he was driving," Amanda added.

"Sure," Maddy said hesitantly, then turned to Sydney. "Do you mind if I open this bottle?"

Sydney fetched Maddy the cork screw.

"How about you, Syd?" Amanda asked. Her foul mood had dissipated and she was beginning to be more like herself, as she indulged in Sydney's fantasy game.

"I actually like Maddy's idea of the car accident. I would have, of course, toyed with the breaks or something to make it look like an accident. That might be too obvious. Perhaps poison. Is it antifreeze that is undetectable? I could add a bit to his morning coffee, and he would be none the wiser. Actually, in the spirit of the game, I'm going to go back in time and have him beheaded by the guillotine for the unspeakable crimes he committed against the royal family."

The others laughed.

"That would be more your style," Hannah agreed.

"Indeed," Sydney answered distractedly, smirking as though relishing the thought.

"You're never going to find a husband with that attitude," Maddy told her. "Brynn, any progress with your mystery man?"

"None," Brynn sighed. "I only saw him once this whole week, and he had his head buried in the newspaper. Maybe I'm just not ready to get back into dating yet."

"There's no rush," Hannah assured her. "It will happen when the time is right."

"Or not. I'm going to enjoy being single for the time being," Brynn shrugged and stretched. "Hey, I'm not rushing anyone, but I need to get home. It's a bit of a drive, and I have an early meeting."

"I understand," Sydney replied, although her face showed disappointment.

"I can't thank you enough for the lovely dinner," Brynn stood. "Everything was fabulous!"

Brynn hugged each of her friends in turn, while Sydney went to retrieve her jacket.

"My house next week!" Maddy reminded her.

"I'll be there!" Brynn smiled. She accepted her jacket from Sydney and gave her a hug. "Thank you again!"

"You're welcome! I'll walk you to the door."

Amanda and Hannah left shortly after Brynn. Maddy lingered to finish her glass of wine. It was her one night-a-week out of the house, and she wasn't ready for it to end yet.

"Are you sure you don't mind watching the kids Saturday?" she asked.

"Don't give it another thought," Sydney waved her hand. "I've been promising you for weeks. What do you think you and Jim will do?"

"Probably go out to dinner, maybe a movie."

"Stay out as long as you'd like."

"Pack an overnight bag, so you can pass out if you don't feel like waiting up," Maddy told her. "We only get out about twice a year without the kids, I plan to make it worth it!"

Chapter Six

Maddy helped Sydney finish tidying up the kitchen before she went home. Somehow cleaning at someone else's house didn't seem so daunting. Plus, cleaning up after adults was not nearly as bad as cleaning up after messy kids.

She was wishing she was back at Sydney's the next day, when she was cleaning up after breakfast. Jim was off to work, and Little Jay was off to school, which left her home picking up after three-year-old Trinity and eighteen-month-old Ryan, who could mess up the house quicker than she could tidy it. Her slight hangover only added to the chaos. She reminded herself that getting a job was a moot point with the cost of daycare these days. She didn't have the skills required for a job that paid enough to enable her to afford day care.

This was the life she'd chosen, or at least the hand she had been dealt. Things could be worse, but she couldn't help feeling jealous of her friends' lives. Brynn had more money that she knew what to do with, even if she ended up losing some of it in the divorce. Amanda and Hannah had jobs, husbands, and no kids. Sydney had no one to worry about except Sydney. How nice that would be, to have responsibility for no one except yourself! Maddy didn't know. She had gone from high school to newlywed to motherhood all in the same year.

Other than high school dates, she and Jim had never had the opportunity to be a couple and enjoy romantic evenings alone together. She was so grateful to Sydney for watching the kids once in a while so she and Jim could get out! If only she could find someone to take them for a week so she and Jim could fly away some place warm for the honeymoon they never had – even a weekend or an overnight trip. At this point, she would have to settle for a date night. She had only to get through today, and tomorrow would bring her one night of freedom.

The day passed quickly enough, and as uneventfully as a day can be with two toddlers. She went to bed exhausted, but woke up Saturday refreshed and excited for her night out.

Sydney arrived around four to give her time to get ready in peace. What a doll! Maddy didn't know what she would do without her. It was highly unusual for Maddy to be able to take a leisurely shower without having young company, or at the very least the threat of being interrupted. She savored the occasion and emerged refreshed and ready for adventure. She came downstairs to find Sydney fixing dinner for the kids. Trinity was "helping" her and Little Jay was sitting on the floor with Ryan, playing quietly.

"You are an angel," Maddy told her.

Sydney smiled. "I enjoy it as much as you do."

Maddy knew it was true. Sydney had known she couldn't have children for several years, and it was devastating for her. She felt inadequate as a woman, and had trouble forming companionships with men because she was afraid the subject of children would come up eventually.

Maddy offered to help with dinner, but Sydney ordered her to sit at the table, where a glass of wine was waiting.

"It's your time to relax," Sydney insisted.

"You don't have to tell me twice," Maddy joked as she took a seat at the table and sipped her wine.

"I ran into Hannah on the way here," Sydney was saying, as she busied herself at the stove.

"Really? Where?"

"At the grocery store down the street. I stopped to pick up a few things for dinner, and some popcorn for later. She was on her way home from work, doing the same thing."

"Yeah, I guess it's on her way," Maddy thought aloud.

"The thing is," Sydney said, turning the burner down on the stove and lowering her voice as she stepped towards the table. "She had a huge bruise on her face. It looked awful."

"How did she get that?"

"Well, she said she fell down the stairs, but I have trouble believing that. I pressed her a little bit, but she teared up and shook her head."

Maddy met Sydney's gaze, but said nothing for a moment. The back door opened next to her and Jim came in from work. He set his things down on the table, kissed his wife's cheek and greeted Sydney, before being smothered by shouts of "Daddy!" and hugs from the kids.

"You don't think Pauly would hit her, do you?" Maddy asked.

"I can't think of any other explanation," Sydney shrugged. "She admitted they get rough, and sometimes she gets hurt. To me, it doesn't matter if the injuries are accidental or intentional. He knows what's happening, and he's causing it. No one should have to walk around with bruises after a normal day."

"But she didn't say he had anything to do with it this time," Maddy pointed out.

"She won't, either."

"So, what can we do?" Maddy asked rhetorically. "We don't know exactly what happened."

"I don't know," Sydney shook her head. "but I feel like I should do *something*."

Jim finished his nightly rough-housing with the kids and sent them off to get washed up for dinner.

"Do you want me to rough him up?" he asked, half-jokingly.

"You'd squish him," Maddy laughed, appreciating her husband's over six-foot height and muscular physique.

Jim was twice Paolo's size, and twice as intimidating with his shaved head, grizzly beard and tattooed neck.

"I wish somebody would do something," Sydney said wistfully.

"I'm going to shower," Jim announced.

"That's not exactly what I meant," Sydney pouted.

"Be quick!" was Maddy's response. "I'm going on my second glass of wine."

Sydney took note of Maddy's nearly empty glass and refilled it. Maddy could tell by Sydney's face she was still riddled with concern for Hannah.

"Face it, Sydney. There is nothing we can do for Hannah if she doesn't want our help. We have given her chances to talk to us about it, and she doesn't."

"Maybe she's scared of what he'll do to her if he finds out," Sydney pointed out. "I, for one, don't want to get a phone call one day that Hannah is in the hospital, because he beat her to a pulp."

"I don't either, but I don't know what we can do to stop it. We don't even know for sure if he hit her, or if she really fell down the stairs."

Sydney put her hands on her hips and gave Maddy a look. "We know. I don't know what we can do about it, but we know the truth."

"I'll call her tomorrow," Maddy suggested. "Maybe she'll confide in me one-on-one."

Sydney wasn't listening. She crossed her arms in front of her and gazed out the window behind Maddy. The kids bounded back into the kitchen and proudly showed their mother their clean hands.

"He'll get what he deserves," Sydney muttered, then snapped back to the present and helped the kids get settled at the table for dinner. She said to Maddy, "You get out of here. Enjoy your night!"

Maddy sighed and stood.

"Thanks again, for doing this!" She gave Sydney a quick hug, polished off her wine and gave the kids each a kiss good-bye.

"Be good!" she warned them. "Do what Sydney tells you, and no fooling around!"

Thirty minutes later, she was sitting across from her husband at Lombardo's Restaurant, enjoying another glass of wine and soaking in the tranquil atmosphere. It felt amazing to be free of the children for one night. She almost felt guilty for thinking that, but the guilt passed as quickly as it had come. Everyone needed a break at times. It was natural and healthy to get away. She said so much to Jim, as they waited for their salads to be served.

"I really, really needed a night out," she said. "I feel bad saying it, because I actually do miss the kids, but I am so excited to sit down to a delicious meal, that I didn't have to cook, that I don't have to clean up, and we can actually have a conversation while we eat it."

"And you look beautiful," Jim added.

"You're sweet. I am a lucky lady," she smiled.

Jim smiled back at her. "I'm the lucky one."

He raised his beer mug, and Maddy tapped her wine glass against it. She felt silly for feeling jealous of her friends earlier that evening. Sure, Brynn had plenty of money, but she had no one to spend it with. Amanda's job at the restaurant was nothing to covet, and she didn't have three beautiful children to go home to. Hannah apparently had a wife-beater for a husband, and Sydney had nothing but the ghost of her grandmother to talk to at night. Maddy's life might be mundane and hectic all at once, but it was all she ever wanted. She wanted to be a wife and have a family, and that's exactly what she had. She was grateful.

They enjoyed a relaxing dinner, then walked a few doors down to a sports bar. Baseball season was well underway, and they had their choice of several games on the TV monitors. They found a high-top table and pulled over two stools.

"Isn't that your friend's husband?" Jim asked, pointing to guy a few tables away. It took Maddy a few minutes to recognize him, since he had on a baseball cap and had seemingly put on a few pounds.

"Yeah, that's Nate," she answered. "I wonder if Amanda is here? I'm going to go say hi."

She hopped off the stool and stopped to talk to Nate for a few minutes, before rounding her trip off with a visit to the ladies' room. She was back with her husband ten minutes later.

"Amanda's working," she announced. "Too bad."

"That's not the guy you were talking about earlier, is it?"

"No, that's Nate. We were talking about Pauly, Hannah's husband."

"That's what I thought. Good thing, I don't feel like getting in a fight tonight."

"You're good," Maddy laughed. "Nate's a good guy. Pauly's the one we're worried about. I'm not sure what's going on with them, but Hannah always has bruises, and Sydney is convinced Pauly is beating her."

"Do you think he is?"

"I don't know if he's *beating* her," Maddy said tentatively. "She told us last week he gets rough during sex, and she comes away with bruises, but she seemed to like it."

"Kinky."

"Kinda sick if you ask me," Maddy shrugged and sipped her wine.

"Aw, I was just kidding. You know how I like it." Jim's blue eyes twinkled.

"If we could ever have a night alone!" Maddy cried. "I wonder how we had Ryan sometimes. Having sex with kids in the house is next to near impossible."

"They are growing up fast," Jim reminded her. "Enjoy them while they're little."

"Oh, I do. I'm just saying there needs to be a balance. We need to do this more often."

"We definitely need to get out more," Jim agreed.

"You know what I really want to do?" Maddy asked, but didn't wait for Jim to guess the answer. "This might sound weird, but I want to go see a movie. A *real movie*, rated R. None of this Disney shit."

"Let's go," he said.

"All right!" Maddy gulped down the rest of her wine, Jim chugged his beer, and they headed for the door. They decided to stop for a coffee on the way to the movies, since Maddy had consumed enough wine to doubt her ability to stay awake through an entire movie. She suggested they stop at The Diamond Diner, since it was on the way, and Amanda was working. Maybe they would get the coffee for nothing.

Maddy ran in, while Jim waited in the car, but Amanda wasn't working. Maddy paid for the coffees and took them to go.

"Amanda was gone," Maddy explained. "I had to pay for the coffees."

"That's OK," Jim said, accepting his cup and taking a taste before placing it in the cup holder between them. Maddy didn't mention to Jim that the girl had told her Amanda wasn't working today at all. It seemed odd that Amanda's husband would tell them she was working when she wasn't, but Maddy brushed it off. Maybe Nate didn't want them to think he was rude for going out without his wife. Who knew. Maddy sipped her coffee and checked the movie listings on her cell phone.

It was close to 2AM when they got home after the movie. All was quiet in the house. Sydney was asleep on the couch, and the kids were each tucked neatly into their own beds. That was a feat in itself most nights, but Sydney had handled it.

"Looks like they wore her out," Jim laughed, as they crawled into bed. Maddy was already half-asleep, smiled wanly and drifted off. Her vague hope of having sex tonight had succumb to fatigue. Her body wasn't used to being up this late, and it knew the kids were going to wake her early. Maybe Sydney would stay and fix breakfast for them all ...

However, Sydney was gone when they got up the next morning. It was after seven, which was later than usual for Jay and Ryan both. Trinity could sleep until eight or nine most mornings, but the boys were usually up by five. Maddy would take 7AM, but she was still disappointed to miss out on one of Sydney's home-cooked meals. She sighed, pulled the cereal out of the cabinet, then stopped.

"Who wants pancakes?" she called.

"We do! We do!" the response was unanimous.

Maddy put the cereal back and selected the box of Bisquick from the cabinet. If Sydney could do it, so could she. She stirred together the pancake mix, threw some frozen sausage links in a pan, and even cut up some fresh strawberries. There was no point in sitting around waiting for her life to start. She had to start living the life she had.

After the family devoured breakfast and helped her clean up, she figured it was late enough to call Sydney and thank her. The call went straight to voice mail, so she left a message. It wasn't very heartfelt to leave a thank you message on someone's voice mail, so Maddy made a mental note to try her call again later.

Next, she dialed Hannah, who answered. Hannah sounded fine, and Maddy told her all about date night before approaching the subject of her fall.

"How on earth did you fall down the stairs?" Maddy asked, not wanting to seem accusatory of any foul play.

"I was vacuuming," Hannah said. "The vacuum is kind of heavy and awkward, and I guess I got caught up in the cord. I only fell about six steps, but the vacuum went down with me, and gave me quite a black eye."

"That's what you get for cleaning," Maddy joked, and Hannah laughed along with her. "Seriously, Hannah, if that's what you say happened, I believe you. Sydney seems convinced that your bruises had something to do with Pauly. You guys weren't getting rough again, were you?"

"No," Hannah said quickly. "Pauly's not even home. I mean, he was home later that night, but he wasn't here when it happened."

"What did he say?"

"He told me not to be so clumsy!"

"He didn't tell you to stop cleaning?" Maddy laughed.

"Unfortunately, no. But that's fine. You know I'm a clean-aholic."

"As long as you're OK," Maddy replied carefully, holding back the urge to point out that Pauly was the one obsessed with a clean house; Hannah was merely the one who had to do it all.

"I'm fine," Hannah insisted.

"If you ever feel like, you want to, uh, get out of the house, I'm pretty much always home."

"Thank you, Maddy. I appreciate the offer. I'm good for now. Pauly left yesterday for his rock climbing trip. I'm going to relax by myself – when I'm not at work, that is."

"Did he go to Pennsylvania again?"

"No, he's up in the Adirondacks this time."

"Isn't there still snow up there?"

"There could be ... I don't think that bothers him."

"He's crazy," Maddy told her. "You wouldn't catch me rock climbing for a million dollars."

"It's not my thing, either ..." Hannah agreed.

"When is he due back?"

"Monday night."

"All right, well, remember my offer. I'm home all next week if you need to get out of the house after he gets back from his trip."

"I appreciate it, Maddy. I'm sure everything will be fine."

"I hope so," Maddy told her. "I'll see you on Wednesday, then."

"Wednesday at your house," Hannah agreed, and they said their goodbyes for the time being.

Maddy called Amanda next.

"Hey, kid," Amanda answered.

"Hey, there. Did Nate tell you we saw him last night?"

"No, I haven't talked to him. I worked late last night and I'm on my way back there now."

"Oh, that sucks," Maddy said, confused.

"Where'd you see Nate?"

"We stopped at the Double Play for a drink after dinner last night. I guess he was there with some friends."

"Yeah, he said he was going to watch the Mets game. Did he talk to you?"

"We said 'hi,'" Maddy answered. "Too bad you weren't there. That would have been fun."

"Yeah, too bad. We'll have to do that sometime," Amanda answered non-committedly, then added, "when I'm not working."

"Yeah," Maddy responded vaguely, not knowing what else to say. Should she tell Amanda they also stopped into the Diamond last night and she was well aware that Amanda was *not* working?

"Well, see ya Wednesday," Amanda said.

"Yeah. Have fun at work," Maddy said hesitantly.

"You got it, kid," Amanda said.

Maddy didn't need to end the call, because Amanda had already hung up. Maddy's cell phone went back to the home screen, leaving her dazed and open-mouthed. She needed to talk this out with someone to figure out what was going on with Amanda. She tried Sydney again, but no answer. She didn't bother to leave another voice mail, but sent her a text to call when she got up. She contemplated dialing Brynn. She had Brynn's contact information pulled up on her phone, but she stopped before touching the Call button.

There was no point in dragging Brynn into this. Besides, Brynn had a way of making her feel inadequate. She was certain Brynn didn't do it intentionally, but she couldn't help feeling that way nevertheless. Brynn just had everything in her life together – divorced or not. Brynn was confident, she had a career and she had enough money to do whatever the hell she wanted without a man to depend on. Hanging around with Brynn always made Maddy feel like the dowdy housewife. She had made so much progress today, she wasn't about to take a step backwards. She had actually cooked a real breakfast, and somehow enticed all the kids and Jim to help with the cleanup.

She had to keep the momentum going. If she was going to be Super Mom, she had to get off her ass and stop feeling imprisoned in her own house. She had to take charge and turn her home into a well-oiled machine. As Jim settled into the Lazy Boy with the Sunday paper, she sat at the kitchen table with a pen and pad. She made a list of age-appropriate chores for all the kids. She planned dinners for the week and wrote out a corresponding grocery list.

She fizzled out a bit by lunch time and fixed a couple boxes of macaroni and cheese. The kids were perfectly happy with that, so she didn't beat herself up too badly for feeding them a not-exactly-nutritious meal. After all, macaroni and cheese was one of the few meals all three of them would eat. It wasn't worth the fight sometimes to try something new.

Maddy had a new outlook on life, and it was all thanks to Sydney taking the kids for the night. Somehow having a night out with her husband had refreshed her, given her a sudden zest for life, a desire to be a better wife and a better mother. She needed to stop wishing for a life she didn't have and start living the life she had. She was lucky, after all. She didn't have to deal with Brynn's loneliness, Hannah's abusive husband, Sydney's infertility, or Amanda's ... well, whatever it was Amanda was dealing with. Maddy wasn't sure what that was all about, but she intended to find out on Wednesday.

Chapter Seven

Maddy went about her week with her newly-discovered positivity. Monday was grocery day, and she loaded the two little ones into the car and headed to the market with the list she had put together. She had added a few things for Wednesday night's gathering, which she was hosting this week. Their Wednesday Wine Club, as they had come to call it, was the highlight of her week. Jim was taking the kids to his mother's house for dinner. It was an hour drive for him, but it was a better option than trying to take them to a restaurant. Plus, they would undoubtedly fall asleep on the car ride home, which would enable her to put them straight to bed when they returned.

She had wished so many times that Jim's mother lived closer, but that presented an entirely new set of issues. She conceded things were "what they were" and left it at that.

Tuesday was cleaning day. She banished the kids to the family room and put up a baby gate, while she cleaned the downstairs bathroom. They seemed perfectly content, since they had plenty of toys in there. She tackled the living room next, throwing all the toys she found into the family room as she went. She cursed herself for not thinking of this method earlier. The kids squealed with excitement every time a new round of toys came flying over the baby gate. The kitchen was a lost cause, but she did what she could, at least to give herself room to cook and set up some snacks.

She took a break from cleaning to call Hannah. She wanted to re-extend her offer, if Pauly was home from his trip and wreaking havoc. Hannah actually sounded cheerful, and indicated she was fine. Pauly had not, in fact, returned home yet.

"He didn't?" Maddy prodded. "Is that typical?"

"I wouldn't say typical," Hannah replied, "but he did stay an extra day last time. He said the weather was so nice, he had to take advantage of the opportunity while he was there. I'll call his cell phone later, but sometimes when he's up in the mountains, he doesn't have any cell reception."

"So, he just shows up when he shows up?" Maddy asked, incredulously.

"Pretty much. I mean, he's only done this once before, but I understand. He can't call me if he doesn't have any cell reception."

"Well, if you change your mind and you want to come over, I'm here."

"Thank you, Maddy, but I'm fine. I'll see you tomorrow night."

Maddy hung up and shook her head. No way would she put up with Jim taking off for three days with no check-ins. She said as much to Hannah the next night, when she arrived for their weekly Wednesday Wine Club. Brynn and Sydney were already there, and they were gathered in the freshly-cleaned living room.

"It's normally not a big deal," Hannah told her friends. "It's only a long weekend. Amanda's husband goes to hunting camp for weeks at a time, and she doesn't freak out."

"She looks forward to it," Brynn laughed. "Where is Amanda, anyway?"

"Haven't heard from her today," Maddy said. "She was late last week too."

"Late and grouchy," Sydney added. "I hope she's in a better mood this week."

"I hope so…" Maddy agreed. She couldn't help thinking about Amanda's lie about working Saturday night. Amanda was lying to her husband and her friends, which wasn't like her. Amanda's life was usually an open book. Maddy struggled whether she should tell the others about it. She decided to keep it to herself for now. Maybe Amanda would explain for herself when she arrived.

Maddy went about setting out the snacks – chips and dip, and tray of precut veggies. She had a large pan of ziti baking, which was the easiest thing she knew how to cook. She had boiled the pasta, thrown it in a baking dish with jarred sauce, sprinkled some cheese on top and popped it in the oven. It was simple, but filling enough she wouldn't need to worry about anyone drinking too much wine on an empty stomach. She certainly didn't intend to chauffer anyone home. Her night of hosting meant her night of drinking all she wanted. Jim could account for the kids and her friends could account for themselves.

"So, what was Pauly's excuse for coming home a day late?" Maddy asked Hannah.

"Two days late," Hannah confessed sheepishly.

"What? He didn't come home until today?"

"He wasn't home yet when I left," Hannah said, her eyes fixated on her wine glass, as she fingered the stem and avoided her friends' gazes.

"He's two days late now, and he hasn't bothered to call you?" Maddy demanded.

"Aren't you worried?" Brynn added.

"I am a little concerned, but he did the same thing last trip. He came home a day late because the climbing conditions were so good, he couldn't pass up the opportunity."

"Did you call him?" Maddy asked.

"I left him a voice mail yesterday," Hannah said. "There's no point blowing up his phone if he's out where there's no cell service."

"I'd be blowing up Jim's phone," Maddy said adamantly. "I'd be packing three kids in the car and driving my ass up there to drag him home."

"That's because you have kids," Hannah defended herself. "I would do the same thing if I were you, but my situation is different. It's kind of peaceful being home by myself."

"You should enjoy it, then," Sydney offered. "Pauly is a grown man. He can take care of himself."

Maddy was about to interject, but her phone was buzzing on the table. The caller ID showed it was Amanda.

"Hey, where are you?" Maddy answered. The others waited silently, while Maddy listened. The conversation was short and ended with Maddy saying, "we'll miss you. Feel better."

"She's not coming?" Sydney surmised with obvious disappointment.

"She said she's sick," Maddy told them.

"That's too bad," Brynn said. "I can't remember the last time one of us missed a Wednesday gathering."

"We might as well eat," Maddy shrugged, and retrieved the ziti from the oven.

"I'm sorry, Maddy," Sydney said. "I know you worked hard on dinner."

"It's not even that," Maddy replied and shook her head. She didn't bother to elaborate that she had a suspicious feeling Amanda was lying about being sick. Instead, she changed the subject. "I know the ziti won't come close to Sydney's dinner, but it will fill our bellies."

"It smells great," Brynn assured her.

They piled their plates with ziti from the pan on the stove and filled in around the table, where Sydney was waiting with glass raised to perform her toast.

"My dearest friends, we gather tonight one short, gone from our presence but not gone from our hearts. Time heals all wounds." She paused, eyes shut lightly as though honoring Amanda with a moment of silence.

She's not dead, Maddy thought. *She didn't even sound sick.*

"Until we are joined together again, we will miss our companion, but we shall carry on. To friendship, to us that put friendship before all else, let us flourish in spite of absence and tighten our bonds."

Sydney paused again, and the others looked at each other blankly. Was she finished? Sydney raised her glass, opened her eyes and drank deeply. The others followed suit.

"Amanda would have appreciated that," Hannah said kindly.

Brynn and Maddy couldn't help but laugh.

"No, she wouldn't," Maddy shook her head, and Brynn agreed.

"Who, Amanda?" Sydney said absent-mindedly. "No, I suppose she wouldn't have liked my toast, but then again, she doesn't usually enjoy my toasts."

Sydney shrugged and drank some more wine. The others gaped at Sydney's admission, but said nothing about it.

"Let's eat!" Maddy directed to break the silence, thinking, *Sydney is so weird. How did we ever become friends with her in the first place?*

Maddy reminisced in her mind, as she ate her dinner. They had met at Body Art Gym years ago, where they were all taking a cycling class. The gym wasn't even open anymore, as Maddy recalled last seeing a furniture store where Body Art used to stand. They used to gather around the water cooler and chat. Little Jay had been a baby, and Maddy was trying to lose the pregnancy weight. Brynn was the only other one married at the time, but even back then things with Michael were less than blissful. Amanda, Hannah and Sydney all worked at the Diamond Diner – Hannah and Sydney both studying for associates degrees at the community college.

Sometimes after their workout, they would meet across the street at the donut shop for a cup of coffee or an energy drink, avoiding the donuts at all costs, of course. Eventually, their gym visits fizzled out. Brynn became absorbed in her career, Sydney's grandmother became deathly ill, and Maddy got pregnant for Trinity. They kept in touch, meeting at the donut shop sporadically, until Hannah suggested they frequent someplace healthier. Thus, the weekly gathering began, the five friends choosing a different restaurant each week.

"Dinner is delicious," Brynn complimented. "I am going to have to do some serious thinking about what I'm going to serve next week!"

"Don't fuss," Sydney told her.

"I made the easiest thing I knew how," Maddy admitted.

"My turn will come around again in two weeks," Hannah was thinking aloud. "I was hoping the weather would be nice enough to host outdoors." She left out the fact it was at Pauly's insistence that she host outdoors.

"It should be," Brynn agreed. "That would be nice."

"Wouldn't it be?" Sydney gushed. "I am sick of being inside. I don't care if I never see snow again."

"Well, we haven't seen snow in a while," Maddy pointed out. "That's a good thing."

"That reminds me of my question!" Sydney exclaimed, ignoring Maddy's comment completely. Maddy rolled her eyes, but Sydney continued unsolicited. "If you could live anywhere in the world, where would it be?"

"Germany," Brynn answered without hesitation. "I've been there six times, and if I could figure out how to stay, I would."

"I would go someplace tropical," Maddy said with a sigh. "I've never been anywhere, so I can't be more specific than that – maybe the Bahamas or Costa Rica – someplace where I could braid hair on the side of the street for a living."

"Didn't Amanda go to the Bahamas on her honeymoon?" Hannah asked.

"Was it the Bahamas?" Brynn posed, "or was it Trinidad and Tobago?"

"I thought she went to Jamaica," Sydney added.

"I don't remember …" Maddy admitted, annoyed. "If she were here, we could ask her."

"I'm sure you could braid hair on the side of the street for a living in any of those places," Brynn offered. "And I can just imagine the tan you'd have!"

"I know! I can feel the sun on my body right now, if I think about it hard enough!" Maddy laughed. "I really want to get a pool this summer. The kids would love it almost as much as I would!"

"You should go for it," Sydney encouraged her. "That would provide hours of entertainment and exercise at the same time!"

"Maybe I will …" Maddy was deep in thought.

"What about you, Hannah?" Sydney asked. "Where would you live? Anywhere in the world."

"I would like to live in Amsterdam," Hannah said after considering for a moment.

"Amsterdam?" Maddy repeated in disbelief.

"Not Amsterdam, New York, silly. The Netherlands. That's where my grandparents came from, and I've always wanted to explore my heritage."

"We'd practically be neighbors!" Brynn pointed out.

"Even better!" Hannah agreed.

"I wouldn't be far from you either, in Ireland!" Sydney revealed.

"Ireland is beautiful," Brynn admitted.

"Great, and I'm halfway around the world," Maddy replied sarcastically.

"I'm sure we can find you a tropical location in Europe," Sydney assured her. "The Mediterranean perhaps."

"Do they braid their hair?" Maddy pouted.

"You could start a trend," Brynn suggested. "You'd have a monopoly on the market."

"I guess," Maddy agreed. "As long as I could be closer to my friends."

Maddy rose to clear the table, and the others jumped in to help.

"Take a break, Maddy," Sydney told her. "We'll take care of the clean-up."

"Are you sure?"

"Of course!" Sydney insisted. "You have to clean up after people every day. You deserve a break."

"You don't have to ask me twice," Maddy laughed and poured herself another glass of wine. She sat back down at the table, while her friends washed the dishes and put away the leftovers. The topic of moving to Europe continued throughout the clean-up, and the ladies found themselves seated back around the kitchen table fantasizing about all the places they could visit. Living in Europe brought an entire realm of possibilities for Wednesday Wine Club, and the friends agreed they would have to sample wines from their prospective regions on their night to host.

"Next week's theme is Germany!" Brynn announced. "Everyone bring a German wine, and I'll coordinate my menu."

"I don't know the difference," Maddy confessed.

"That Gewurztraminer I brought last week was German," Brynn told her, "but Riesling is big in Germany."

"Just go to the Germany section in the liquor store," Sydney said as an aside, and Maddy agreed she could handle that.

They were interrupted by the back door bursting open, and Jim and the kids pushing their way in. Little Jay was first, followed by Jim carrying a sleeping Ryan and tripping over Trinity. Trinity looked half-asleep herself, and went straight to her room. Jim greeted the ladies on his way through to put Ryan to bed. Little Jay wanted to join the party, and Maddy set him up with a very small glass of chocolate milk to drink before bed. It was a school night, after all.

Little Jay drank his milk and gave everyone a hug goodnight. He ran off to get ready for bed with very little coaxing, much to Maddy's surprise.

"Such a good kid," Sydney was saying.

"Most of the time," Maddy agreed. "He has his moments. Trinity is the one who causes most of the drama around here, but I have a stinking feeling Ryan is going to be even worse."

"Too soon to tell?" Brynn laughed.

"He's trending in that direction, unfortunately," Maddy admitted.

Jim came back downstairs after getting all three children settled into bed for the night.

"Mind if I join you?"

"It would be our pleasure," Sydney announced for all of them.

"Have a glass of wine, honey. You deserve it!"

"I think I'll have a beer," Jim grabbed a can from the refrigerator. "I am exhausted!"

"How's your mom?" Maddy asked.

"Exhausted too!" Jim laughed, cracking the can open and downing half of its contents.

"How would you like to move to the Bahamas?" Maddy asked.

"The Bahamas?" Jim repeated with a chuckle. "Where did that come from?"

"Just a little game we were playing," Maddy told him. "I was thinking about becoming a hair braider."

"You can practice on Trinity, if she'll let you touch her head," Jim responded.

"Her hair's long enough," Maddy agreed, "but I don't think she'd sit still for me. She might sit still for Sydney, but not me."

"She is such a doll," Sydney agreed. "I had a great time with them Saturday night."

"Why did you take off so early?" Maddy asked. "We got up and you were gone!"

"I meant to leave when you got home, but I fell asleep on your couch. Like you said, those three are exhausting. Still, I would trade anything in the world to be able to have children. Since that is not to be, I have to satisfy my mothering instincts with other people's children."

"Have you considered adoption?" Brynn asked.

"I would absolutely adopt, if I were in a stable relationship. I don't think I would want to raise a child alone. I feel a child needs two parents, to reinforce each other's morals and support each other. Being a single parent would put too much stress on the parent and the child, in my opinion."

"Where is my purse?" Hannah asked randomly, nearly in a panic when she reached for it on the back of her chair and it wasn't there.

"It's on the counter," Maddy pointed.

"I can't believe I almost forgot to take my pill," Hannah zoomed across the kitchen to retrieve her purse and the plastic dispenser of birth control pills inside. "That's the last thing I need is to get pregnant."

The others laughed, but Hannah was on a serious mission. She popped a small pill out of the case and swallowed it with some wine. She finished off her glass and set it back on the table.

"Refill?" Maddy asked.

"I guess I could have one more," Hannah agreed, checking the time. "If Pauly does show up tonight, he can take a turn waiting for me. Give this pill a chance to get into my system."

"You sure you'll be able to drive?" Brynn asked, picking up the wine bottle but waiting for an answer before refilling Hannah's glass.

"I can always drive her home," Sydney offered.

"I'm fine to drive," Hannah assured them.

Either way, Brynn was satisfied that Hannah had a safe ride home and poured her another glass.

"I still can't believe he hasn't even called you," Maddy was saying. "First of all, I wouldn't let Jim go off on a mountain climbing trip without me, let alone an indefinite one – not that you'd want to," she added for Jim.

Jim shrugged and finished his beer. He knew it was best to keep his mouth shut when Maddy was on one of her rants, especially when she'd been drinking. He tossed the empty can into the sink and grabbed a fresh beer from the refrigerator.

'I'm sorry, but I don't get it," Maddy went on. "Even if you two don't mind being apart for days at a time, it's common courtesy to let your spouse know where you are."

"I know where he is …" Hannah replied meekly.

"But he was due home *two days ago!*" Maddy argued her point. "That is unacceptable, whether the two of you are enjoying yourselves or not! It's just wrong for him to tell you when he's going to be home and not show up. And not call. For two days! I would be furious."

"I don't know if I'd be furious," Brynn interjected diplomatically, "but I would be a little worried."

"I am a little concerned," Hannah admitted. "Anything could happen up on the mountain. It's petrifying to think that some accident could have happened, but I know Pauly. He's the best rock climber I've ever seen. It isn't likely that anything bad happened. I'm sure he's having the time of his life and simply can't drag himself back to solid ground. It's a rush for him, and it's early in the season, only his second time out. He's been cooped up all winter; I'm sure he's staying as long as he possibly can."

"It seems kind of odd. If *you* can't get in touch with him, neither can *his clients*," Maddy pointed out. "I don't see him missing a sale for a few extra days on top of a mountain."

"He plans his trips strategically," Hannah said with a wave of her hand. "He doesn't go if he has a big sale pending."

"He's not the number one sales agent in his office for nothing, I guess," Brynn laughed.

"Indeed," Sydney agreed. It was the first she'd said throughout the conversation, and she said it as though she hadn't been listening at all.

"I should get home and see if Pauly is there," Hannah said, and she said it again every hour on the hour until it was well after midnight. Jim had long since excused himself to go to bed, and the four ladies had moved from the kitchen table to the living room.

"Let him wait," Maddy was saying. "He can whack himself off until you get there."

Hannah actually laughed along with her friends.

"Looks like we're all going home to lonely houses," Sydney sighed.

"Is that your phone?" Brynn asked Maddy, who was completely oblivious that her cell phone was vibrating frantically on the coffee table.

"Who could that be?" Maddy wondered aloud as she reached for the phone.

The others couldn't help but listen to Maddy's responses, which were short and didn't provide any clues as to who was calling.

"What the hell?" she said as she set the phone back on the coffee table. "That was Nate."

"Is Amanda OK?" Sydney said breathlessly.

"I don't know, but she's not home sick like she told us she was. Lie number two."

"What did Nate say?" Brynn asked.

"He wanted to know if Amanda was still here!" Maddy filled them in. "I said, *Nooo*. He wanted to know what time she left, and I told him I wasn't sure. What else could I say? If she's not home, where is she?"

"Call her cell phone," Brynn urged.

"Nate said he called and she didn't answer. That's why he called me."

"Try it anyway," Brynn directed.

"She obviously doesn't want us to know where she is," Maddy retorted, but she tried the call regardless. It went straight to voice mail. Maddy had it on speaker phone, made a face as if to say, "I told you so," and hung up without leaving a message. She filled in the others about Amanda's lie Saturday night.

"She obviously doesn't want Nate to know where she is either," Brynn surmised.

"I didn't have the heart to tell him that she hadn't been here all night. Do you think I should have?"

"What if something is really wrong?" Sydney asked. "Should we call him back?"

"She's lying to him," Maddy started another rant. "She's lying to us. If she wanted us to cover for her, the least she could do is tell us where she is! I have a good mind to call him back and tell him everything."

"You think she's cheating on him?" Brynn wondered, mulling over the possibilities in her head.

"It sure looks that way," Maddy spat.

"Maybe she's with Pauly," Hannah offered lamely, trying to make light of the situation, while pondering if there could be some truth to it.

"Don't be silly," Sydney rubbed Hannah's shoulder. "Of course, she's not with Pauly."

"How can you be sure?" Hannah demanded. "You heard her say she wanted to sleep with him. We all heard it."

"I don't think she was serious," Brynn shook her head.

"She was joking," Maddy agreed. "I said the same thing, for hell's sake. It was just a joke. Besides, she wasn't at work Saturday when she said she was, and Pauly was out of town."

"He left on Saturday," Hannah pointed out. "Plenty of time to hit her on the way out of town and again on the way back."

"You don't seriously believe that," Maddy had a look of disbelief mixed with disgust.

"Come on, Hannah," Sydney prodded. "I'll drive you home. Maybe Pauly is there wondering where you are."

"I hope he isn't," Hannah muttered, as she stood to take up Sydney on her offer.

Chapter Eight

Sydney helped Hannah from the car and walked her to the door. The house was dark inside, giving no indication that Paolo was home. She took Hannah's house key from her and unlocked the door, pushing it open and helping her over the threshold.

"I can't believe I drank so much ... again," Hannah murmured.

"It was a special occasion," Sydney cooed.

Hannah gave her a questioning look, but didn't respond. She dropped her purse on the floor by the door and stumbled to the couch.

"He's not even home. Thank God. He would have been pissed that I'm drunk again."

"Hannah, you can't live your life worrying about what Pauly will think. You have always been a strong, independent woman, and it saddens me to see you so meek and jumpy all the time. You need to pick up the pieces of you that are left and start being 'you' again."

"I know, I know ..." Hannah agreed without contestation. "He's sucking the life out of me."

"Exactly. I'm glad you recognize that."

Hannah kicked off her shoes, swung her feet up onto on end of the couch and rested her head on a throw pillow at the other end.

"I'll be fine," she said.

"You won't be fine if you keep going the way you are. Tell me, how often does he hit you?"

"He's only hit me a couple times," Hannah answered. She was intoxicated just enough to speak without guarding her words. "I'm *so* glad he didn't get home yet. I need sleep."

"Let me help you upstairs," Sydney offered. "You probably don't want him to come in and find you sleeping on the couch."

Hannah complied. She straightened herself up and even picked up her shoes and purse on the way upstairs. Drunk or not, it was imbedded into her brain to clean up after herself or face the consequences. She went straight to the bathroom to brush her teeth, while Sydney rifled through her drawers for sleepwear.

"I really appreciate everything, Sydney," Hannah called from the bathroom.

"That's what friends are for," Sydney responded automatically. She located a night shirt and laid it across the end of the bed. She pulled the sheets open so Hannah could easily slip underneath them.

"Can I ask you one more favor?" Hannah was finished in the bathroom and stood in the doorway of the master bedroom. She looked exhausted, and older somehow. Sydney realized how much Hannah had aged over the last two years, and she knew very well it was all at the hands of that monster of a man she had married.

"Of course," Sydney replied.

"Would you mind staying the night?" she asked sweetly, almost childlike. "I don't want to be alone when he gets home."

Sydney sighed. She hated seeing her friend so defeated, scared of her own husband. It wasn't right. It wasn't the Hannah she'd known for years, and she vowed to do everything in her power to get her friend back.

"Of course, I'll stay," she said.

"I'll get you some bed clothes." Hannah scurried to the dresser. "Anything else you need is in the guest bathroom."

"I'll find what I need," Sydney told her. "You go on to bed and get some rest."

"Oh, no. Wait a minute. Can you actually sleep on the couch? That way Pauly will see you if he comes home. I'm sorry."

"No worries. Good night."

Hannah climbed into bed and pulled the covers up around her neck. Sydney sighed, turned out the light and shut the door behind her. She didn't mind sleeping on the couch, as long as it gave her friend peace of mind. She changed her clothes and used the guest bathroom, then grabbed a blanket off the guest bed and headed downstairs. She didn't think she would get much sleep, but once she fell asleep she slept soundly.

She was abruptly awoken by a knock on the front door. She had no idea what time it was, but it was still dark out. She peeked outside from behind the curtain, and there were two police officers standing on the porch. She wrapped the blanket tightly around her like a robe, and opened the door a few inches.

"Mrs. Gianni?" the office closer to the door asked.

"No, I'm not. I can give her a message."

"I'm Detective Harris, and this is Detective Rowley." The office flashed his badge as he spoke. "We have important business with Mrs. Gianni. Do you know when she'll be home?"

Sydney's heart was pounding in her chest. She closed her eyes and tried to slow her heart beat. Should she get Hannah or let the officers continue to believe she was not home. She hated to interrupt Hannah's sleep, when she so desperately needed it, especially for something as unpleasant as a visit from the police department. She couldn't keep them away forever, though. There was no point prolonging the inevitable. She opened her eyes and met Detective Harris's gaze.

"I'll get her. Please, come in."

The officers entered, as Sydney swooshed upstairs to fetch Hannah. They were still standing by the front door when she came downstairs, Hannah following closely behind her.

"I'm Mrs. Gianni," Hannah said, as she took the last step and make her way across the living room floor.

The detectives showed their credentials again before alluding to the purpose of their visit.

"May we have a word alone?" Detective Harris asked.

"I'd prefer my friend stay, if that's all right," Hannah answered curtly.

Detective Harris exchanged glances with his cohort, who gave a slight shrug.

"Mrs., Gianni," he began, "I have some news that may come as a shock to you. Would you care to sit?"

Hannah crossed her arms defiantly in front of her chest, but sat on the edge of the ottoman. She stared, blinking at the officer who loomed over her. His face bore no expression, and he glanced over his notes before he spoke again.

"We received notification from the State Police in Lewis, NY of a hiker's body recovered outside of Keene. The identification gathered at the scene indicates the hiker's identity as a Paolo F. Gianni of 4425 Carnation Lane. Ma'am, I'm deeply sorry to inform you that the hiker discovered is deceased, and is believed to be your husband. We would, of course, ask for visual confirmation, if you would be so kind as to accompany us downtown to identify the body."

Detective dropped his eyes for a second while speaking, but now stared at Hannah intently, in anticipation of a reaction. Sydney also searched Hannah's face for a sign of understanding, but Hannah didn't move. Her expression did not change, her eyes staring straight ahead blankly. Sydney held her breath, as she waited for Hannah to do something. Seconds ticked by in absolute silence.

"Mrs. Gianni?" Detective Harris prodded.

Hannah lifted her eyes to meet his, but did not speak.

"I am very sorry for your loss. Of course, there is a chance the body recovered is not, in fact, your husband, but in this case, the ID was procured directly from the body. I must prepare you for the worst, I'm afraid."

Hannah nodded slightly and dropped her eyes again. She looked dazed for a moment, then attempted to stand, wavered and sat back down heavily on the ottoman. Sydney jumped to her feet and was immediately at Hannah's side.

"Take a breath," Sydney said. She rubbed Hannah's back as she recovered her stature and her dignity. She did as Sydney instructed, inhaled deeply and attempted to stand again.

"Let me get dressed," she mumbled vaguely and headed for the stairs. Sydney was by her side the entire time, holding her arm and whispering comforts in her ear.

"Will you come with me?" she asked, when they were safely in her bedroom.

"Of course!" Sydney guided Hannah to the master bathroom and shut the door gently behind her. She could hear her retching, as she entered the adjoining walk-in closet and picked out clean clothes for Hannah to change into. She found a conservative button-up oxford and gray pants and laid them out on the bed. It seemed so long ago that she had lain out Hannah's bed clothes for her, when it had been less than six hours. Sydney grabbed a clean pair of khakis and a turtle neck for herself out of Hannah's closet, stopping at the bathroom door to listen for a second. She rapped lightly.

"You OK, hon?"

"I will be," Hannah answered weakly.

Sydney sucked in her breath and took the clothes to the guest bedroom to change. She washed her face and brushed her hair and teeth, and found some deodorant in the drawer under the sink. Her heart was beating out of chest in spite of her efforts to remain calm for Hannah.

Oh my God. Oh my God. Oh my God. They found Pauly's body…

Sydney told herself to focus, Hannah needed her right now more than ever, and she had to keep her emotions in check. She quickly dressed, inspected herself in the full-length mirror and hurried back to Hannah's room.

She rapped lightly on the door before entering. Hannah was sitting on the bed next to the clothes Sydney had picked out. She was staring at the floor, unmoved when Sydney came in. Sydney didn't know what to say. She wanted to give Hannah hope, tell her maybe it wasn't Pauly they had found, but she knew it would be false hope. The sooner Hannah dealt with the truth the better.

Sydney was atypically tongue-tied, so she grabbed a brush off the dresser and started brushing out Hannah's long, dark hair. It went half-way down her back, and was knotted from sleeping on it. Sydney's own brown curls were mousy and uncontrollable. She was frankly jealous of Hannah's beautiful, silky mane. Hannah sat a moment, then jerked her head away.

"I hate this stupid hair," she cried. "Let's just go."

"Don't you want to change your clothes?" Sydney cooed soothingly.

"I guess I should at least do that," Hannah sighed and started stripping down on the spot. Sydney politely ducked into the hall to wait. Hannah was but a few minutes, and she had changed and brushed her hair when she emerged from the master suite.

Sydney took a quick inspection of Hannah head-to-toe and turned to head downstairs. Hannah grabbed her arm, pulling her back.

"Sydney," she whispered desperately.

Sydney turned.

"Don't leave me alone. I don't care what they say or do, don't leave me alone."

"Of course," Sydney nodded and patted Hannah's hand, which was still clutching her forearm. Hannah's grip loosened gradually, and her hand fell back to her side. She took a deep breath, crossed her arms in front of her chest and folded her hands around her ribs, hugging herself as she trudged downstairs to comply with the detectives' request.

They rode in the back of the police car, locked in like convicts. Sydney watched the houses pass by out the window, but Hannah stared down at her lap, her arms limp at her sides. Sydney stole a glance at Hannah once in a while, and reached over to pat her hand. The poor darling was in shock. The silence was broken by the occasional static-ridden voice projecting from the police radio. Sydney listened intently to the messages, but only understood half of what the choppy voice was saying.

When the officers parked and came to open their doors to escort them into the station, Sydney whispered to Hannah, "Don't say a thing."

Hannah said nothing, but her eyes demonstrated understanding. Her door opened and she climbed out of the car, accepting Detective Harris's hand for support. He kept her arm tucked under his own as he ushered her towards the stony, cold building. Sydney wasn't sure if the detective was holding Hannah to prevent her from collapsing, or to prevent her from running, but she followed as closely as possible. She was not leaving Hannah's side. Hannah had asked her to stay, and she would do exactly that. They weren't going to bully her friend into doing or saying anything she didn't want to. Hannah was a victim here, and from the harsh, empathy-lacking tone Detective Harris used when he spoke, Sydney had a sour suspicion that Hannah was not only here to identify the body, but also here to face an investigation.

She could hear Hannah's own words from last night, "Anything could happen up on the mountain. It's petrifying to think that some accident could have happened, but I know Pauly. He's the best rock climber I've ever seen." *If Pauly is such a good rock climber, he wouldn't have fallen.*

Sydney crossed her fingers and hoped that Hannah took her advice and kept her mouth shut. She pushed a curly lock of hair out of her eyes and took a stealthy glance over her shoulder at Detective Rowley. He was walking so close to her, she could practically feel his breath on the back of her neck. She quickened her step.

They were brought to a holding area, where they waited for over an hour, before Detective Harris came back to retrieve them.

"I apologize for the delay," he sounded more business-like than sincere, repeating the words he was trained to use in this situation. "They are ready for us in the morgue."

The morgue had a separate entrance from the opposite side of the block, but Detective Harris led them through a maze of halls within the building that ended at a back entrance to the morgue, which was evidently attached to the police station. Detective Rowley caught up with them, as they filed through a door into a short corridor. They stopped before another door.

"Please be prepared that the body may be bloated and distressed from the fall. We have been informed the hiker was dead upon discovery, and possibly had been for several days."

Sydney did the math in her head, as Detective Harris opened the door and stepped through, holding the door with one hand for the others. Detective Rowley entered last and approached a steel gurney with a gray body bag atop. He worked to unzip it, as Sydney held her breath and watched Hannah. Hannah was standing so still, she could have been a statue. Her arms were at her side, but her hands closed tightly into fists. Her lips were parted, and she was breathing through her mouth. Her eyes were not blinking.

Sydney blinked her own eyes several times to make up for Hannah's dry-eyed stare. She watched closely, as Detective Rowley unzipped the bag and slowly peeled the cover down away from the head of the body. Sydney gasped. She looked at the dead face only for a second, and although it was bloated and discolored, it was most definitely Pauly. She turned her head quickly to witness Hannah's reaction.

Hannah looked as though the air was punched out of her lungs. She bent and clutched her stomach. The anguish on her face made Sydney's heart ache. Hannah covered her mouth and turned away, the tears flowing freely now.

"It's Pauly," she sobbed. Her whole body was shaking as she gasped for breath. "It's Pauly."

Sydney was at her side in a second, Detective Harris took her other arm and together they guided her to a chair. Hannah collapsed into the chair, as Detective Rowley quickly pulled the body bag back up over the face and zipped it closed. Sydney put her arm around Hannah's shoulder. Hannah still had one hand over her mouth, the other clutching her stomach, and rocked back and forth in the chair with uncontrollable adrenaline.

"Ms. Mitchell," Detective Harris stated flatly, "do you concur as to the identity of the body?"

"I concur," Sydney said, and pulled Hannah's head to her chest. She smoothed Hannah's hair as the tears soaked through the front of the turtle neck she had borrowed. The detectives stood by in silent respect and allowed the newly-widowed woman to mourn.

Sydney wasn't sure how much time elapsed before Detective Harris spoke again.

"Mrs. Gianni, we can go back to the station and talk if you prefer."

Hannah nodded and stood, letting Sydney guide her back through the chain of corridors to the police station. They took a seat in Detective Harris's office, and waited while he retrieved water and a box of tissues.

"Mrs. Gianni, I need to ask you a few questions, when you're ready, and I will assist you with the process of releasing your husband's body."

"Can you just give her a few minutes?" Sydney snapped.

"No," Hannah raised her hand in protest. "I need to know what happened."

"The circumstances surrounding Mr. Gianni's fall are being investigated, I assure you. We will do our best to determine the cause of the fall. The injuries sustained are consistent with a fall, but the coroner's office will perform an autopsy to verify the time of death and rule out the possibility of any foul play."

"Foul play?" Hannah repeated.

"Shhhh," Sydney soothed her friend. "We don't know that, do we Detective Harris?"

"As I said, the cause of the fall is under investigation. We will pass along any pertinent information as it becomes available." He turned his focus to Hannah. "Mrs. Gianni, was your husband an avid hiker?"

"He was a rock climber," Hannah replied.

"Does Mrs. Gianni require a lawyer?" Sydney blurted.

"Not at this time," Detective Harris answered in his level tone. "We merely need to ask a few questions to understand Mr. Gianni's background."

"But she has a right to an attorney," Sydney insisted.

"Ms. Mitchell," Detective Harris began, emphasizing the *Ms.* "No one is under arrest. We are asking that Mrs. Gianni provide us with some background information on her husband in order to assist in our investigation. Your participation is strictly voluntary, Mrs. Gianni, although I don't know why you wouldn't want to assist in the matter."

"Of course, I want to assist," Hannah said quietly. "Ask me anything you want."

"If Ms. Mitchell would be so kind as to wait outside my office."

Sydney looked at Hannah for affirmation. Hannah nodded. Sydney huffed, stood and strode out of Detective Harris' office, purposely leaving the door open behind her. She took a seat in the hallway.

Detective Harris paid no mind, shuffled some papers around on his desk and pulled out a note pad before continuing. Detective Rowley appeared, rapped on the open door, then entered, closing the door behind him. He took a seat in the chair Sydney had vacated. He had a steno pad as well, and was poised to take notes.

"How long have you been married?"

"Two years."

"Practically newlyweds. I'm sorry. How long has your husband been gone?"

"Since Saturday."

"Did he make any contact with you after he left your home?"

"No."

"How many times a year would you say your husband rock climbs?"

"At least once a month, spring through fall. In the winter, he climbs indoors."

"Was it his first time out this year?"

"No, it was his second."

"Had he ever climbed in Keene before?"

"I believe so," Hannah said.

"Did your husband have any prior training?"

"Of course. He's been climbing for years."

"Then, in your opinion, he was a rather skilled climber?"

"Yes, of course," Hannah answered. "He was an excellent climber."

"Have you ever gone mountain climbing with him?"

"No."

Detective Harris glanced at Detective Rowley, who was scribbling frantically. He waited for his partner to catch up before proceeding.

"Mrs. Gianni, even skilled climbers can make mistakes."

"I can't imagine Pauly ever making a mistake," Hannah blurted. "He is very particular in everything he does, a perfectionist."

"In that case, do you have any reason to believe your husband's fall was not, in fact, an accident?"

"What do you mean, not an accident? What else could have happened?"

"We are going to find out what happened, Mrs. Gianni. I merely want to cover all the possibilities. That you are aware, did Mr. Gianni have any enemies?"

"No enemies," Hannah shook her head. "His coworkers envy him for his success in real estate. He is top salesman in the office every month, but that doesn't qualify them as enemies."

"Was there any indication that Mr. Gianni was suffering from depression or unhappy with his life, to the point where he may have committed suicide?"

"No, not that I know of."

"And when was Mr. Gianni due to return?"

"He was due back Monday night."

"He takes a week off once a month to go rock climbing, and still manages to achieve employee of the month in real estate? That's quite a salesman – and to be able to take a week off every month of the year, I have to admit I'm jealous myself."

"He doesn't go for a week every month."

"Just this month?"

"No, he was due back Monday. That's barely a long weekend."

"I see. I thought you meant next Monday. So, he was due back this past Monday?"

"Yes."

"Today is Thursday. Had you reported him missing?"

"No."

Detective Harris stared at Hannah with cool blue eyes and waited for her to continue.

"I didn't know he was missing... "Hannah started crying again. "I just thought he was late getting back."

"Is he typically late coming back?"

"Not usually, but he was late coming back last month. The weather was so nice, he stayed on the mountain. I just thought he decided to stay an extra day or two. He can't call me while he's in the mountains. There's not always cell service, and he doesn't like to bother me at odd hours."

"I see," Detective Harris said curtly.

"What happens now?" Hannah asked between sobs.

"Mrs. Gianni, the coroner is going to perform an autopsy on your husband's body. Was he an organ donor, do you know?"

"I don't know."

"The coroner's office will take care of that. It should be on his license. When the autopsy is completed, the remains will be turned over to the funeral home of your choosing. Any personal belongings that are not deemed evidence in the investigation surrounding his death will be returned to you at that time. Will the funeral be local?"

"I ... I believe so," Hannah murmured. "His only family is in Italy."

"I am truly sorry for your loss," Detective Harris said and stood. Detective Rowley was nearer to the door, and opened it to allow Hannah to depart. The detectives followed her into the hallway, where Sydney rose to greet her.

"I would ask that you not leave town until the investigation is completed," Detective Harris added.

"I don't understand what there is to investigate," Sydney broke in. "The man fell to his death, whether it was human error or equipment failure makes no difference to my friend. She's lost her husband! Your attitude is completely insensitive!"

"I'm sure Mrs. Gianni will find some comfort in learning the cause of her husband's death. I wouldn't be doing my job otherwise."

Sydney's jaw dropped for a second, then her agape mouth snapped shut.

Chapter Nine

Sydney kept her thoughts to herself for the rest of the time they were in the presence of the officers. When they were safely back at Hannah's house, and the patrol car out of site, Sydney let her true feelings be known.

"I am so sorry they treated you like that," Sydney burst. "You must be simply devastated, and there they are interrogating you like a criminal."

"I didn't feel like they were interrogating me. I honestly don't know what to feel. I can't believe he's gone."

"Sit down, Hannah. What can I get you? Would you like some water or some hot tea?"

"Nothing right now, Sydney. Thank you, though. Thank you for everything. I never could have done that by myself." Hannah sat in the chair by the ottoman. She took her shoes off before putting her feel up and leaning into the back of the cushiony chair. "I guess I don't need to worry about getting the ottoman dirty."

"You don't need to worry about anything. He can never hurt you again."

Hannah looked up sharply.

"I'm sorry, that was very insensitive of me. I know you loved him. I'm just searching for the silver lining, and it's there whether you see it right away or later. You will never, ever be abused at the hands of that man again."

Hannah's face softened again.

"I think I'd like to lay down for a while. Would you mind staying? I don't want to be in the house alone."

"I don't mind at all! Whatever you need, Hannah, just say the word."

"Help yourself to whatever you need," Hannah said and lifted herself slowly from the chair. She looked as though her body weighed a ton and it was a great effort merely to stand. She paused for a moment before turning towards the staircase and heading up to her room – the room she used to share with that monster.

Sydney felt terrible for what Hannah was going through, but she saw silver lining everywhere she looked. Pauly was an evil person, and she was glad he was gone. She promised herself she would try to be more empathetic with her words when Hannah came back down, but she had a feeling Hannah was feeling as much relief as she was grief. Her nightmare was finally over.

Sydney went to the kitchen and made herself a cup of tea and a sandwich. She felt like she should do something to help Hannah, but the house was spotless already. She took a shower and put her borrowed clothes back on. Hannah room was still quiet when she listened through the door, so she decided to make a list of things Hannah might need to do, such as calling relatives, choosing a funeral home. Did Hannah even have life insurance on Pauly? She must have. Pauly wasn't the type of person to leave any loose ends. She hoped they had life insurance on their mortgage. Hannah might not be able to afford to live in this house on her own income, although Hannah may not want to live in this house by herself. Sydney wrote "house?" on her list.

When Hannah emerged two hours later, Sydney tucked the list swiftly into her pocket. She didn't want to upset Hannah with discussions she wasn't ready to have. Calling relatives and choosing a funeral home were things that needed to be cared for as soon as possible, but the other things could be tackled later, after the shock wore off.

"How are you doing?" Sydney asked.

"Honestly, I don't know. I feel like I should cry more, but I'm not."

"You're still in shock," Sydney told her.

"I guess," Hannah nodded. "I feel overwhelmed. I know I have to call people and tell them, but I just can't. Every time I think about it, I panic."

"I can make some phone calls for you," Sydney offered, "but I think you should call his family personally."

"I know. I will. Let me get my head together. I'm going to take a shower, and then I'll find my address book. I have a sheet in there I used to plan our wedding. I know I have phone numbers on there."

"Would you like something to eat?"

"Not yet, but thank you, Sydney. You're a lifesaver. Have you told the girls yet?"

"No, I haven't told anyone."

"That's OK. Let me call his family first, and then you can let the girls know, if you would."

"Of course."

Hannah went back upstairs, and a few minutes later Sydney heard the shower running. She was surprised how well Hannah was handling everything. Maybe the reality that Pauly was gone hadn't fully hit her yet. Maybe she was still in shock. Or maybe she was relieved he was gone. After all, he was arrogant, abusive and controlling. More than likely Hannah was feeling a mix of emotions. Once the initial shock wore off, Sydney had a feeling she was going to start seeing her friend's old personality re-emerge.

Hannah was upstairs long after the water stopped running. When she came down, she announced she had called Pauly's brother in Italy, and he was going to notify the rest of the family.

"Leo is coming," she said.

Sydney raised her eyebrows.

"Leonardo Gianni, Pauly's big brother," Hannah explained. "He came to our wedding, and I've never seen him since."

"I remember him," Sydney said, more to herself than to Hannah.

"He's coming to the United States," Hannah repeated, and Sydney couldn't tell if she heard disdain or fear in her friend's voice. "He said he will leave his ill father's side out of respect for his brother, and he has no doubt he will find his father worse if not dead when he returns to Italy."

"That's what he said?" Sydney was aghast.

"Quote-unquote."

"I'm sorry, Hannah."

"I am too. It's bad enough I have to deal with all this, and then his brother on top of it all. He is not an easy man to get along with."

Neither was Pauly, Sydney wanted to say, but she kept her mouth shut. She did remember Leonardo from the wedding, and he was harsh, blunt and intimidating. He did not smile. He was all business, always serious and always staring at people with a look of disgust on his face. It was obvious he didn't want to be at the wedding, and Sydney could only imagine what his demeanor would be at the funeral.

"Are there any other relatives nearby?" she asked instead, to take her mind off Pauly's monstrous brother.

"There are aunts and uncles on Long Island. Leo is going to contact them. Everyone else is in Italy and probably won't make the trip. His father is very ill – has been for some time."

"I'm sorry," Sydney said again. "Please let me know what I can do."

"You can call the girls now, at least Brynn and Maddy. I don't know if I want to bother with Amanda."

"Why not?"

"I know this will probably sound silly, but it really bothered me that she lied to us last night. You don't really think there's any chance she was having an affair with Pauly, do you?"

"I don't know where she was last night, but she certainly wasn't with Pauly," Sydney answered, perhaps too bluntly.

"Maybe she was supposed to meet up with him, and he didn't show," Hannah pointed out.

Sydney wasn't sure how to respond. She had no reason to believe Amanda was having an affair with Pauly, but she also had no reason to defend her. "We will have to confront Amanda to learn the truth, I'm afraid, but we don't have to call her today. I will call Brynn and Maddy, and any other phone calls you want me to make."

"Thank you, Sydney. I'm going to go upstairs to call my brother. There was no love lost between him and Pauly, I can tell you that."

"He will want to be here for you," Sydney assured her. Hannah's brother, Jeff, was the only family she had since her parents passed away nearly fifteen years ago. He had been very protective of her, but he couldn't stop her from marrying Pauly. He would probably be relieved Pauly was gone. It was only a matter of time before Pauly did serious damage to Hannah physically, and Sydney often feared what might happen. Jeff would undoubtedly rush to Hannah's side to comfort her and help her through her loss. Sydney was thoroughly relieved it wasn't her calling Jeff to give him bad news about Hannah, as would have been her inevitable fate living with that abusive jerk.

Sydney called Brynn and Maddy and broke the news. They were both shocked, to say the least. Brynn wanted to come over, but Sydney advised she would stay, and quite honestly although Hannah insisted she didn't want to be alone, most of the day she was in her room, alone. Sydney fixed them dinner, which Hannah barely touched, and cleaned up the kitchen. Hannah insisted Sydney go home that night.

"The cat needs you," Hannah said.

"The cat probably hasn't even noticed I'm gone," Sydney retorted, but she went home overnight and returned the next morning to help Hannah research funeral homes and buy a cemetery plot. She had not settled on which funeral home she would use, but she was decisive at the cemetery. She picked out a single plot and wrote a check for the full amount. The manager gave her the name of a local monument mason where she could order a headstone.

"You don't want a double plot?" Sydney asked, when they were settled back in the car.

"I have my whole life ahead of me," Hannah responded flatly. "My children can make that decision when the time comes."

Sydney was relieved to hear Hannah speaking positively about her future, but it seemed oddly sudden. She took Hannah home and made sure she ate, before heading on her own way. Hannah insisted she would be fine by herself tonight, and Sydney respected her friend's wishes.

Saturday afternoon, Sydney got a call from Hannah, who was an absolute mess.

"Calm down, Hannah. I can't understand what you're saying."

"Please come get me," Hannah cried. "I can't stay here with him."

"Slow down! I'm only catching every other word."

"Leo showed up today, and insists on staying at the house. He is asking me all kinds of questions and making accusations and blaming me that Pauly fell, as if I could have prevented it! I can't stay here with him. He can have this place; I don't care. I can't take it!"

"All right, Hannah. Pack a bag. You can stay with me. I'll be there as quick as I can."

Sydney grabbed her keys and ran to her car without even grabbing a jacket. It was pouring rain. She couldn't remember if she locked the house, but she didn't go back to check.

Hannah must have been watching for her, because she flew out the door the second Sydney pulled into the driveway. Sydney admittedly was relieved she didn't have to go inside and face Leonardo Gianni. Hannah popped her suitcase in the back seat and jumped into the passenger side of Sydney's car.

"Thank you so much," she panted, as she shook rain water from her arm and reached for her seatbelt.

"Of course," Sydney told her. "You can stay with me as long as you'd like." Sydney was sincere, but she couldn't help but wonder by the size of Hannah's suitcase how long she had been planning on staying.

"He is an evil person!" Hannah spat. "If you think Pauly was unpleasant, you should meet his brother!"

Sydney didn't bother to point out she had met Leo at the wedding, and she already knew he was ten times more irritable than his brother. Pauly at least was congenial to your face. Sydney always wondered if under that hard exterior, Pauly had a soft side that had appealed to Hannah, but over time, the steady decline of her friend's character blared truths of her husband's demeanor. He had a certain charisma which he used to his advantage with his clients, and which he obviously had used to enamor Hannah into marrying him. Sydney resolved that Pauly had no underlying tenderness in his personality, and Leo lacked even a speck of decency, let alone tenderness.

"How can he think he can barge in and take over your house uninvited? I can't believe he would even want to stay there with you. You hardly know each other. Wouldn't he be more comfortable in a hotel?"

"I'd have thought so, but he feels he has a right to what was his brother's. He is so overbearing!" Hannah's face was red.

"Does he think he's going to come in out of the blue and take over everything?"

"He was already questioning every decision I've made. He is insisting there be a traditional Catholic funeral in a church. Pauly and I didn't get married in a church, we never went to church, and he definitely wasn't a practicing Catholic. I don't see anything wrong with having the services at the funeral home. Then, he had the nerve to insinuate that I had something to do with Pauly's death!"

"Why would he think that? What did he say?"

"He said, 'I will avenge the death of my brother.' And he shook his finger in my face. It was obviously directed at me!"

"I think you might be overreacting. I mean, his brother died unexpectedly. He is obviously grief-stricken. He's undoubtedly exhausted from travelling all day. Maybe you should give him time to settle down."

"There is no settling down Leo Gianni. He is a bull!"

Sydney couldn't argue on that one. She turned north on the interstate to head home.

"Oh, darn it! I should have had you drop me at Maddy's to pick up my car!"

"I didn't even think about it. I'm sorry."

"I really need to go to the gym and sweat out some of this pent-up frustration."

"You can work out at my house," Sydney offered. "I have a whole gym set up in the basement, everything you need."

"You do?"

"State of the art," Sydney told her. "When my grandmother got sick and I had to quit Body Art, I started furnishing my own home gym one piece at a time. I have a nice variety of equipment. I think it will do very well for you."

"I'm sure it will," Hannah agreed, "but I'm still going to need my car."

"Why don't you get your workout in and shower first, then I'll take you to get your car. The most important thing right now is your health."

"That'll work," Hannah conceded. "I have some errands to run."

Sydney got Hannah set up in one of the extra bedrooms and got her some clean towels. Hannah evidently approved of Sydney's personal fitness center, because she worked out for well over an hour, and then hit the shower. Sydney offered to accompany Hannah to run her errands, but Hannah insisted on going alone. So, Sydney dropped her off at Maddy's to get her car and swung over to the market to pick up something for dinner.

Hannah had not been specific regarding what errands she needed to run, but she was gone quite a while. Sydney had completed her shopping, put away all the groceries and started dinner before she heard Hannah's car pull in. Hannah showed herself in, which was good because Sydney was busy stirring her sauce on the stove.

"In the kitchen!" She called.

"It smells wonderful!" Hannah breathed deeply as she came into the kitchen and dropped her purse on the table.

"Bolognese sauce!" Sydney announced. "Would you like a taste?"

"Sure!" Hannah said, and joined Sydney at the stove. Sydney took one glance at Hannah and nearly dropped her wooden spoon. Sauce spattered across the stove, as she fumbled not to lose grip on the spoon.

"You didn't!" Sydney gasped.

Hannah had chopped her hair off! It was above the shoulder and tapered around her face. It was beautiful, but shocking. Hannah's long, black hair had been her look for years.

"Do you like it?" Hannah gushed.

"I do, but it's so drastic!"

"You know what's drastic? That I kept it long for so many years when I hated it! I feel free. I am no longer a slave to Pauly. I feel reborn!"

"You look incredible!"

"I feel incredible! Do you know Pauly wouldn't so much as let me put my hair up in a ponytail, unless I was at the gym? One day I made the mistake of pulling my hair up before I left the house, and he made me take it down. He said I could put it back up when I got there. When I asked him what difference it made, he nearly slapped me! I think he just raised his arm to make a point – I don't really think he would have hit me over something so trivial – but his point was made. Pauly was my boss, and what Pauly said, I did."

"I can't believe you lived like that," Sydney empathized.

"No more!" Hannah answered adamantly.

Sydney wiped her hands on a towel, then reached out and touched Hannah's hair. It was like she was looking at the old Hannah she had known in high school. She had been so vibrant and full of life back then! It was devastating to witness how Pauly had changed her. Over the last few years, Hannah had built a wall around her life and retreated into her own little hell. She had become introverted and timid, compliant to every demand Pauly made. She had lost a part of herself, and Sydney had feared the old Hannah was gone forever. Yet, here she was, standing in her kitchen, renewed, beautiful, and confident.

Sydney grinned and threw her arms around her dear friend.

"I am so glad to have you back!" she cried.

Chapter Ten

The calling hours were Wednesday. Hannah defied Leonardo's demand for a Catholic funeral and arranged for calling hours and funeral to be held in one session at the funeral home. The police had generously released the body to the funeral home after gathering all the forensic evidence they required, although the autopsy results were not yet complete. Although Leo was anxiously awaiting the results, Hannah's priority was getting the body in the ground and moving on with her life.

Hannah met the funeral director an hour before the start of calling hours to go over the itinerary for the day. Leonardo arrived very shortly after to put his two cents in regarding every detail. He had not recognized Hannah when he walked in, with her short hair. She wore a fitted black suit with a black lace camisole under the jacket, and trendy black leather boots with a thick, spiked heel that added several inches to her stature. The result was a formidable span between the top of Leonardo's head and the point of Hannah's chin, which gave her a reinforced sense of authority over her deceased husband's interfering brother.

"The priest is coming over from St. Mary's," she told Leo.

Leo was startled by her voice, then realized it was his sister-in-law speaking to him.

"Grazie," he said automatically with a nod. He removed his overcoat and handed it to the funeral director, who was hovering nearby.

Hannah turned away and went to sit in front of the open casket. She stared at her husband in disbelief. They had done well enough making him look as close to how he had looked in life, but his skin had a pallid glow from the makeup they'd applied. His hair was actually a wig, which had been necessary due to the injuries sustained on his head. Looking closely, Hannah could hardly tell it was a wig, and those that didn't know him as intimately as she had would probably not notice. She had provided his best Dolce and Gabbana suit for the occasion.

People started to arrive shortly thereafter to pay their respects. Hannah's brother Jeff sat by her side and held and patted her hand dutifully, as the rush of sympathizers knelt to embrace her and murmur condolences. Leo sat on Hannah's other side, although their chairs were separated by a large space as though to indicate they were not together. Many of Pauly's colleagues and clients made an appearance, as well as family that made the trip upstate from the city.

The Wednesday Wine Club crew was there, Sydney and Brynn came up to her together, followed by Maddy and Jim. Amanda entered alone. Brynn and Maddy had both called Amanda over the course of the weekend, unaware of Hannah's festering suspicions that she and Pauly were having an affair. Hannah hugged Amanda in turn, as she did all the other guests, and thanked her for her kind words.

The priest from St. Mary's, approached and spoke a few words to Hannah as well as Leo, before beginning the funeral service. His tone was soothing, but the words rang hollow to Hannah. After all, this pious man had never met Pauly, let alone known him as she had. He knew nothing of Pauly's life, other than a few tidbits he had undoubtedly gathered from the obituary in yesterday's paper.

The obituary was penned blandly by Hannah and proofread by Sydney. The coroner had provided the date and time of the death as 9AM Sunday, which saddened Hannah to think he had been lying in the cold for over three days before anyone discovered him. She had struggled with wording the obituary, so she provided as little detail as possible.

Paolo L. Gianni, 38, died unexpectedly on Sunday, April 29, 2018. Born on January 28, 1980 to the late Maria and Lorenzo Gianni, of Italy, he worked at Charles Brockway Real Estate for the past twelve years. He is survived by his wife, Hannah (Doherty), father Lorenzo, and brother Leonardo, (Italy) aunts, uncles and cousins (Brooklyn). Services will be held on Wednesday, May 9, 2018 at 11AM at Oliver & Rush Funeral Home followed by graveside services at City Memorial Cemetery.

Hannah stared at the wedding band on her finger, as the priest's voice droned on methodically, repeating the Hail Mary over and over again. Not particularly paying attention, Hannah had not realized he was actually saying the rosary, and she was supposed to be praying along with the group. Her mind was riddled with questions and guilt. No matter how many times she told herself there was nothing she could have done to prevent Pauly's death, the guilt would not subside. Her guilt of feeling partial responsibility was compounded by her guilt of feeling relieved he was gone. She scolded herself for being an evil, ungrateful wife. She couldn't wait for this day to be over so she could move forward with her life!

The services ended soon enough, and the funeral director asked the pall bearers to wait in the hallway and all others except immediate family to step outside. Amanda caught up with Brynn and Sydney in the parking lot. Maddy and Jim were saying goodbye to each other, as Jim was heading back to work, and Maddy was to ride to the cemetery with Sydney.

"What the hell?" she said. "I feel like I haven't seen you guys in ages. When did Hannah cut her hair?"

"I hadn't seen it until today," Brynn advised.

"She did it over the weekend," Sydney told them. "She said she only kept it long because Pauly liked it that way, and from now on she is going to do what she wants for herself."

"It looks fantastic," Amanda remarked, "but kind of abrupt. I wasn't expecting it."

"I know what you mean," Brynn agreed.

"Hey, stranger," Maddy said as she approached. "What happened to you last week?"

"I had some kind of bug," Amanda replied. "I couldn't stay out of the bathroom all day."

"That's awful," Sydney cooed.

"It sounds awful," Maddy began, "but is it true? You know, Nate called looking for you when you were late getting home."

"Oh, that. Nate's a gem. I was asleep on the back couch. He didn't even realize I was there," Amanda brushed it off. She reached into her purse and pulled out a box of cigarettes, then fished around and pulled out a lighter.

"When did you start smoking again?" Maddy demanded.

"Couple weeks ago. Hey, it's the stress. I'll quit again when things calm down."

"What's been bothering you?" Sydney asked kindly, intercepting Maddy from tearing into Amanda. Maddy looked ready to blow. She crossed her arms in front of her and waited for Amanda to respond.

"Well, one of my best friends' husband just died," she answered dramatically, as if it were obvious. "Thirty-eight years old. How does a thirty-eight-year-old man in perfect physical condition suddenly drop dead?"

"Lower your voice," Brynn said, glancing around as other attendees were making their way to their vehicles to drive to the cemetery. "He had some sort of accident when he was rock climbing."

"And that doesn't freak any of you out?" Amanda looked from one to the other. When no one responded, she felt compelled to remind them of their conversation a few weeks ago. "Hannah says her husband is going to die in a mysterious rock climbing accident, and next thing you know, bam! Pauly falls to his death. That's quite a coincidence."

"What are you insinuating?" Sydney pressed.

"I'm not insinuating anything, I'm just saying what we're all thinking …" Amanda answered. She went back to puffing on her cigarette, as another small group of people passed by.

"I didn't realize Pauly was that much older than Hannah," Maddy changed the subject.

"Eight years," Sydney nodded.

"I'm sorry to bail on you guys, but I have to get back to work," Brynn interjected, before Amanda could turn the conversation again. "Let's plan on getting together next week at my place, as long as Hannah is feeling up to it."

"You're not going to the cemetery?" Sydney was disappointed.

"No. I'm lucky I was able to sneak out of the office for this long," Brynn explained. "I told Hannah I would call her later."

Brynn was off in a flash, heading across the parking lot and down the street to where she'd parked her car. The others looked after her wistfully.

"I wish I had to work," Amanda snorted. "Going to the cemetery is the last thing I want to do."

"Suck it up," Maddy told her.

"Do you want to ride with us?" Sydney asked.

"Thanks, but I'll drive myself." Amanda wasn't planning on staying a second longer than necessary, and she didn't. As soon as she placed the rose she was given on top of the casket, she gave Hannah a hug and rushed off to her car without so much as a glance towards the others. Maddy stared after her in disbelief.

"Hannah thinks Amanda and Pauly were having an affair," Sydney said with a sigh.

Maddy turned her attention to Sydney.

"She's not serious," was Maddy's response.

"She seemed intent on asking her," Sydney shrugged. "Maybe that's why Amanda took off so quickly."

"If she was having an affair with Pauly, do you really think she'd have the nerve to show her face at his funeral?" Maddy pointed out.

"Maybe she had to see for herself that her lover is dead."

"I don't think so," Maddy said, but she had to admit there was some logic to Sydney's theory. She glanced over at Hannah, who was standing dutifully in front of the casket and accepting words of sympathy from the other mourners. She had obviously been crying, but she still looked magnificent. Her new hairdo looked especially chic with her tailored black suit. It had to be hard for her, losing her husband at such a young age, when they had only been married for two years. She had loved Pauly in spite of his faults, but she hadn't been overly worried that he was late getting home from his trip. Was there any truth to her suspicion that he was cheating on her – with Amanda? Amanda was admittedly acting strange, but would she stoop so low to have an affair with her friend's husband? It could explain why Amanda was the only one to bring up their conversation about killing their husbands … Maddy shivered at the thought.

"Are you cold?" Sydney asked, noticing.

"Just a chill," Maddy shook the negative thoughts from her head.

Hannah joined them shortly and asked them to come to lunch with her, and Pauly's family.

"Leo insists," she said, and neither could say no. At least, neither could think of an excuse to get out of it.

"How long do you have a sitter?" Sydney asked.

"Jim's mother is staying all afternoon and having dinner with us," Maddy told her. She was suddenly jealous

Amanda was able to slip out early. Having lunch with strangers mourning the loss of a loved one was not Maddy's first choice of activities when she was fortunate enough to have a babysitter for the entire afternoon. However, friends like Hannah didn't come along every day, and Hannah so seldom asked for anything. Maddy couldn't deny her this one simple request. Besides, Leo was buying. There was no point turning down a free lunch.

Maddy climbed into Sydney's car, and they followed the funeral service's limousine to a nearby Italian restaurant neither had frequented. Hannah rode with Leo in the limo, accompanied by her brother, Jeff, and Leo's aunt and uncle from Brooklyn.

"I think this place is authentic," Sydney whispered, as they followed the group of Paolo's family inside.

"As long as the menu is in English," Maddy said back. Even if it wasn't, she was sure she could pick something out – spaghetti or linguine had to be the same as English, she figured.

They were seated at a long table layered with lush, scarlet-colored linen, with Leo at the head of the table, Hannah to his left, followed by Jeff, Sydney and Maddy. To Leo's right sat his Uncle Vito, Aunt Sofia, cousins Vincent, Marc and Uncle Luciano and Aunt Ilaria. Maddy had straightened it out in her head that Vito was the brother of Lorenzo, Leo and Paolo's father, while Luciano was the brother of Maria, Lorenzo's deceased wife. Vincent and Marc belonged to Vito and Sofia. Luciano was the only one who was at all friendly. His wife Ilaria apparently didn't speak English. Vito and Leo spoke to each other in Italian, while Sofia rolled her eyes and crossed herself repeatedly. Vincent and Marc said next to nothing, which left Maddy and Sydney making small talk with each other and staring at the opposite wall, which was ornately decorated with antique sconces and a huge painting of the Last Supper.

Leo ordered wine, which Maddy and Sydney graciously accepted. Maddy wanted to suck it down, but refrained. She was grateful of her decision when Leo lifted his glass to make a toast.

"I speak on behalf of my father, Lorenzo Gianni. He is very ill. He cannot travel. He is very troubled over the loss of his son. It is not natural that the son passes before the father. His heart is broken. He will no doubt join his son soon. I swear on the head of my father, I will find the cause of Paolo's death."

Sofia crossed herself again.

"Abbastanza per mio fratello," Vito ordered.

Leo held up a hand as a gesture of apology, but continued speaking regardless.

"My voice will be heard. Mark my words. I will leave no stone unturned. I will have answers for my father when I return to Italy, may he still be breathing when I return. The life of my brother ended too soon. Some would say it was his time. I do not believe it. God rest his soul. We will share this meal in his honor."

Leo drank, and the others followed suit.

"This is really good wine," Maddy whispered to Sydney.

"Chianti. The real deal, I saw the label," Sydney whispered back.

"We're having wine and it's Wednesday," Maddy noted. She couldn't care less what the quality of the wine was.

Leo ordered food for the table, family style. Maddy and Sydney stole glances at Hannah, but couldn't hear much of the conversation at the other end of the table. Hannah seemed to be holding up well enough, although she didn't eat more than a few bites.

"How do you think she's doing?" Sydney asked Jeff in a hushed voice.

"She's holding it in," Jeff nodded knowingly.

"She's going to have to let it out eventually. How long are you staying?"

"Just overnight. I'm going to the police station with her tomorrow to follow up on their investigation. I'm sure Leo will be joining us, from the sound of his speech.

"I'm sure. You're welcome to stay at my place."

"We're going back to the house," Jeff informed her. "She needs to get back to her normal routine, as much as possible."

"It would be good for her," Sydney agreed, "but you are both welcome any time, if you change your mind."

"Thank you. You've done so much for Hannah. I can't thank you enough."

"No thanks necessary," Sydney insisted. "I'm happy to do whatever I can. All of us are," she gestured to Maddy.

"Of course," Maddy nodded between bites.

"What do you think the police will have to say tomorrow?" Sydney asked. "It was faulty equipment or something?"

"They should have the autopsy results. Maybe there were drugs or alcohol in his system, I don't know. As good a rock climber as he was, it seems there has to be some explanation other than he lost his footing."

"I never knew Pauly to do drugs," Sydney responded quietly, so the others at the table would not overhear. "I guess you never know. Sometimes you think you know someone, and then you find out you didn't know the first thing about them."

"I have a bad feeling about the whole thing. From what Hannah told me, the police treated her more like a criminal than a widow. I'm not letting that happen to her again."

Sydney tried not to take offense at Jeff's statement. He may have known that she was at the police station with Hannah, but he didn't know how she had stood up for her, asked about her rights and scolded the detective for his insensitivity. Sydney didn't bother to defend herself to Jeff. She had done her best to support Hannah, and she would continue to support her friend in any way she could. Sydney excused herself to go to the ladies' room to ensure she didn't say anything to Jeff she might regret. She thought Hannah might rise and join her, but she barely glanced up from the food she was mindlessly shifting around on her plate with her fork. Sydney couldn't help but notice she was wearing Paolo's wedding band around her thumb.

Sydney returned with a renewed attitude to let Jeff's verbal dig slide. She was here for Hannah, as he was. They had a common cause and should not concern themselves with whom was doing a better job. She did wish Hannah had asked her to accompany them to the police station tomorrow, but she had to rest assured Jeff would do what was in Hannah's best interest.

Sydney suffered through the rest of the awkward meal. Maddy didn't seem bothered by the tense atmosphere, as she was simply appreciative to have food, wine, and an afternoon off from the kids. Hannah hugged them both goodbye and thanked them profusely for coming with her. She looked exhausted, and Jeff put his arm around her and led her away.

"Do you think she's going to be OK?" Maddy asked, when they were belted into Sydney's car.

"Hannah is one of the strongest people I know," Sydney told her. "I think she will be OK in time, with the support of her friends."

"I'm glad her brother is with her, anyway," Maddy replied. "It would creep me out having Leonardo staying at my house. He talks like Pauly was murdered or something. His little speech was not what I was expecting."

Sydney put the car in drive and said nothing. Leonardo Gianni was scarier than his brother, but he would be returning to Italy soon enough. Then, Hannah would be able to start the healing process and get her life back.

Chapter Eleven

Brynn checked in on Hannah later that evening, as promised. Hannah was exhausted physically and mentally, and only spoke for a few minutes, but promised to call Brynn in the morning.

Brynn fixed herself a Lean Cuisine and settled down for the night. Her apartment was modest in size, decorated with modern furnishings, but it was comforting to her, nonetheless. She hadn't wanted to keep the house when she and Michael separated, but she hadn't wanted him to keep it either. It seemed a slap in the face that he could go on living there without her and start a new life. She needed to relocate and start fresh, with entirely new surroundings, new furnishings. He wanted to refinance the mortgage into his name alone. She wanted to sell the house and split the proceeds. They had accrued equity, after all, and the market was a seller's feast right now. Why should she walk away with nothing?

She had spent many an evening alone, fussing over Michael and the divorce. It didn't feel like an end was in sight. They simply couldn't agree on anything. She couldn't help thinking about Sydney's silly little game and how much easier her life would be if Michael were to disappear. She had thought about it often since that Wednesday Wine Club at Sydney's house. She didn't wish Michael dead; she merely wished him out of the picture. He was such a selfish bull, this divorce was never going to be finalized!

She couldn't help wondering at the coincidence that Paolo Gianni had fallen while rock climbing after Hannah had wished him dead in that very fashion. Hannah had never come out and said how, exactly, her husband happened to fall. It certainly seemed odd that such a seasoned rock climber could make a fatal mistake. Of course, anyone could make a mistake. Perhaps the oddity was more so the fact that it happened after Hannah fantasized about it. Hannah must feel horrible!

Brynn resigned to speak with Hannah tomorrow. In the meantime, she ate her Lean Cuisine and thought about the funeral. Amanda had been right when she said they were all thinking the same thing. Brynn didn't think she would ever have verbalized it to the others, but since Amanda had, she couldn't stop thinking about it. It was a terrible coincidence, indeed.

When she finished her dinner, she called Maddy. Normally, she would have kept suspicious thoughts to herself, but since Amanda had drawn attention to it, she needed to hear what the others thought. She needed assurance there was no validity to the theory.

Maddy was happy to rehash the day's events with Brynn. She told her about the conversation in the parking lot after she left the funeral home, how Sydney had said Hannah suspected Amanda and Pauly were having an affair. She told her about the awkward luncheon at the authentic Italian restaurant, every detail from the painting of the Last Supper on the wall behind their table to the bizarre toast Leonardo gave in Pauly's honor on behalf of his dying father. She also repeated what she had heard of Sydney's conversation with Jeff, regarding the visit they were making to the police station tomorrow to try to get some answers surrounding Pauly's fall.

"I wish I had been able to go with you, but I'm also glad I wasn't there," Brynn admitted.

"I don't blame you. If I had an excuse I wouldn't have been there. I was mad Amanda took off so quickly with no excuse whatsoever. But I also didn't want to spend any more time with her than necessary. I still can't believe she lied to me."

"I think she lied to all of us about being sick," Brynn pointed out. "She said she was home the whole time, but I don't believe it. There's no way Nate wouldn't have known she was home all those hours."

"I agree. She's probably lying about that, too. But I blatantly caught her lying about being at work that night. I went into the diner for coffee, and she wasn't there. I even asked for her, so I know she wasn't on break, or out back smoking, or whatever."

"I can't believe she started smoking again," Brynn commented.

"She said it's stress."

"The stress of having an affair?" Brynn suggested.

"She's definitely up to something," Maddy agreed. "I think Hannah might be letting her imagination run wild believing Amanda and Pauly were an item."

"I thought Hannah was joking when she said that."

"I thought so too, at first, but Sydney confided in me yesterday that Hannah was serious."

"I think Hannah's emotions are wreaking havoc on her sensibility," Brynn said. "I absolutely believe Amanda is having an affair, but not with Pauly."

"I agree," Maddy said again. "I can't see Amanda and Pauly together, but Amanda is definitely up to something."

"I just had a thought," Brynn began. "Do you think Amanda brought up that stuff about Hannah's prediction of Pauly's death coming true just to deflect the conversation from herself? I mean, we know she's lying, but she doesn't know you stopped into the diner that day. She doesn't know she got caught in a lie. If she is having an affair, she's making a huge effort to hide it from her friends. Maybe that was her way of taking the attention off herself, and getting us to wonder about Hannah instead."

"It had the opposite effect on me," Maddy debated. "It made me wonder if there was any truth to Hannah's suspicions. Maybe Amanda and Pauly *were* having an affair. Amanda could be trying to blame Hannah for Pauly's death *because she was sleeping with him*. Call me crazy, but I can't help thinking Amanda knows something she isn't telling us. Why would she lie to me about being at work that day, and stand us up for Wednesday night Wine Club, and then take off so early from the funeral with no explanation?"

"I don't know," Brynn admitted. "I honestly don't think Amanda believes Hannah had anything to do with Pauly's death. I think she just said that to redirect the conversation from herself."

"She wouldn't be the only one with suspicions. You should have heard Pauly's brother's speech at the restaurant. Leonardo doesn't believe Pauly's fall was an accident. He said so in front of the whole table, with the painting of the Last Supper hanging on the wall over us. And Sydney told me Hannah's been staying with her since Saturday, because she had to get away from Leo. She told me he pointed his finger in her face and swore on the life of his dying father he would avenge the death of his brother."

"Those Italians are so dramatic!" Brynn cried. "They always want to blame someone else. Pauly's death was an accident. Either he misjudged something, or slipped, or didn't have his equipment on properly. Leonardo doesn't want to admit that his brother was negligent and fell to his death. There is no other explanation!"

"You know that, and I know that," Maddy pointed out, "but Leonardo Gianni has a mind of his own. No matter. It will all be resolved tomorrow, when Hannah and Jeff go down to the police station and get the autopsy results. I'm sure Leo will go with them to hear the truth for himself."

"I'm sure he will," Brynn agreed. "He will have his answers from the horse's mouth. Then he can get on a plane and go back to Italy where he belongs. I swear, that man is more disruptive than consoling."

"He definitely didn't come to console Hannah. He came to make her life more difficult. He tried to take over the funeral plans. He *did* take over her house. She finally went back home tonight, but only because Jeff was with her. Otherwise she would have gone back to Sydney's."

"It was good of Sydney to have her."

"Yes, it was. Any one of us would have taken her in. Sydney just happened to be there at the time. She has a kind soul."

"That she does," Brynn said. "I'm not sure I'd want to live with her for more than a couple days, but she does mean well."

Maddy laughed.

"I told Hannah I'd call her tomorrow," said Brynn. "She was absolutely exhausted when I called tonight. I'll call her later in the day, after she's made her trip to the police station. I can give you a call and let you know how she made out."

"Sounds great," Maddy agreed.

Brynn hung up the phone and shook her head. She felt better after speaking with her friend. Maddy was generally down-to-earth. She could let her imagination run wild occasionally, but for the most part she looked at things practically. She gave people the benefit of the doubt until she was proved wrong. She hadn't wanted to believe Amanda was lying to her until she actually caught her lying.

Maddy had certainly made Brynn feel better about the entire ordeal. She had confirmed Brynn's doubts were justifiable. She had also presented some alternative theories as to what may have happened, but overall Brynn felt certain Amanda was not having an affair with Pauly, nor did she have anything to do with Pauly's death. Furthermore, she was certain Hannah had nothing to do with Pauly's death, in spite of the horrid coincidence of what had happened.

Brynn felt better at the moment, but she didn't sleep well that night. For once, she didn't dream about the divorce, but rather was haunted by a menagerie of dreams about her friends. Amanda was having an affair with

Michael, not Pauly, and she was flaunting it in all their faces. She and Hannah and Maddy were outraged with Amanda. Sydney was there, too, but she wasn't mad at all; she kept saying, *We are all friends. We need to forgive and forget,* in her sing-song voice, as she danced, her arms spread wide as she spun around in circles. Then Amanda turned on Michael and pulled out a gun. She blamed him for breaking up their friendship, and pulled the trigger.

Brynn sat up with a start. She was breathing hard and fought to catch her breath. She regained control of her breathing and reached for her cell phone. It was 4:17AM. She was never going to get back to sleep after that weird vision! She got up, showered, and went into work early. There was nothing better than delving into her work to take her mind off her personal problems.

She worked straight through until 6:00PM that evening. She didn't feel like another Lean Cuisine for dinner, so she called Tresor and ordered an entrée to go. As it wasn't quite ready when she arrived, she sat at the bar and had a glass of chardonnay while she waited. She adored Tresor. It was her favorite restaurant in the whole world, and she was so lucky it was on her way home! How odd, in her travels all over the world, her favorite cuisine could be found right here at home.

Brynn enjoyed her glass of chardonnay as she soaked in the atmosphere. She tipped the bartender, collected her meal and made her way home to eat it. It was a typical day for Brynn, work, go home alone, work, go home alone. She seldom varied from her routine, other than her Wednesday night outing with her girlfriends. She had missed their gathering this week.

She parked in the garage under her building, got into the elevator and pressed 8 for her floor. She was busy thinking about her turn to host Wednesday Wine Club next week. The elevator stopped at the lobby, and the gorgeous guy she so often prayed to see, stepped into the elevator with a smile.

"Something smells good," he told her, as he pressed 6. Brynn couldn't help looking at his finger to confirm her previous observation that he wasn't wearing a ring.

"I stopped at Tresor on my way home," she told him. "I treat myself once in a while."

"It's a great place," he agreed.

"I'm Brynn, by the way," she heard herself saying, and she freed up one of her hands to shake his. "I feel like we see each other often enough, we should know each other's names."

"Tanner Evans," he said, accepting her hand and shaking it warmly. "Nice to meet you officially."

"Yes, it is," Brynn agreed.

The elevator made no stops between the lobby and the sixth floor, which gave Brynn little opportunity to have a conversation with her mystery man, but at least she had finally spoken to him.

"See you soon," she smiled, as the elevator doors swooshed open.

"It was nice meeting you, Brynn," he said and exited.

"You too," she replied, as the elevator doors slid shut once again. The elevator pushed up two floors, and she exited with a smile on her face. Now she could put a name to the face in her fantasies. *Tanner.* What a great name, too. She nearly skipped down the hall to her apartment door, juggled the takeout container with her attache case as she dug for her keys, and let herself in.

She felt like dancing, she was so giddy. She swung herself around the galley kitchen as she got herself a plate and emptied the contents of the takeout container onto it. How perfect the encounter had been, how natural! She could barely wait to finish her dinner to call Maddy and tell her all about it. She knew she was obligated to call Hannah first. She would keep her news from Hannah for now. She didn't want to flaunt her good luck to Hannah, who was mourning so severely over the abrupt termination of her love life.

Brynn swallowed her cheer and called Hannah to see how she was doing. If Hannah seemed receptive, she would tell her about her encounter with her mystery man; otherwise, she would keep it to herself for the time being. Brynn could tell right away from Hannah's tone that she was not, in fact, receptive to hearing about Brynn's good fortune.

"It was the most humiliating experience of my life," Hannah sobbed. "I went there for closure, and it's just getting worse and worse!"

"What do you mean, Hannah?"

"They think Pauly was murdered, and they think I had something to do with it!"

"What?" Brynn was floored. "What did they say?"

"They said they don't think his fall was an accident. They grilled me from head to toe about our relationship, and made me come up with a timeline of everywhere I've been since Pauly left for his trip. I just can't believe it! They treated me like a criminal. Here I just lost my husband, and they made me sit there for over *six hours* and repeat myself over and over again what I already told them."

"Why would they think it wasn't an accident?" Brynn asked.

"They didn't come right out and say," Hannah was hysterical. "They said there was evidence inconsistent with a fall, and there were drugs found in his system – drugs that he never would have taken for recreational purposes. Not that he would have taken drugs anyway. And certainly not first thing in the morning. I'm beginning to think I didn't know my husband at all. Who would want to harm Pauly?"

"I don't know …" Brynn stammered.

"Lots of people, when you think about it!" Hannah answered her own question. "He was a cruel person. He was cut-throat at work; nobody liked him. They admired his skills, and tried to stay on his good side, but none of those creeps actually liked him. They all stood to gain if Pauly wasn't in the picture. Hell, I stand to gain two-million dollars in life insurance. No wonder they think I had something to do with it!"

"Simply because you have something to gain doesn't mean you would commit murder. Plus, they released you. If they truly thought you were involved, they would have charged you."

"They said I'm a *person of interest*," Hannah said with a snarl. "What does that even mean?"

"It means they think you can help them with the investigation," Brynn explained calmly. "You are the person who knew Pauly the best. It doesn't necessarily mean you're a suspect."

"It sure feels like I'm a suspect!"

"Hannah, do you have a lawyer?"

"No. The only lawyer I know is the one who handled our closing on the house."

"You're going to want a lawyer who knows how to handle this type of situation. Let me do a little research. Is your brother still there?"

"He's here now, but he's leaving in a little while. They wouldn't let him come in the room with me. They made him sit in another room and wait. And they asked him questions, too. He doesn't even know Pauly. He doesn't think I'm a suspect, but he wasn't in that room with me for *six hours*! I can't believe this is happening. I honestly can't believe it!"

"I can't believe it, either," Brynn agreed.

"The truth is, I'm glad he's gone!" Hannah continued with barely a breath. She laughed a little at the irony. "He was a cruel, abusive, selfish man. He treated me terribly, and I'm glad he's gone. And do you want to know the truth? I'm glad he's dead! If he wasn't, he'd still be sucking the life out of me. Even if I would have filed for divorce, he would have made my life a worse hell than it already was. Look at you and Michael. Getting a divorce is nearly just as bad as staying married."

Brynn didn't know what to say. No matter how bad things were with Michael, she would never wish him *dead*. She was beginning to worry about Hannah's sanity.

"I'm glad he's dead," Hannah went on, "but I didn't kill him. I didn't even have the balls to divorce him, how could I have killed him?"

"Hannah, I know you're upset. The loss of your husband is devastating, especially under these circumstances. I think you need to go see the doctor and get something to calm your nerves." Suddenly Brynn had a startling thought. "Hannah, Leo can't hear you talking, can he?"

"God, no! He's still at the police station, as if he can be of any help. He hasn't seen his brother in nearly two years. What the hell does he know?"

Brynn sighed with relief. At least Hannah wasn't incriminating herself in front of her brother-in-law. Her own brother knew her well enough to understand she was merely venting; Leo would assume the worst.

"Hannah, I want you to take my advice and make yourself a doctor's appointment. If you don't go today, at least lie down and take a nap. In the meantime, I'll do what I can to find you a lawyer, just for peace of mind if nothing else."

"All right," Hannah agreed. "I don't know if I can sleep, but as soon as Jeff leaves, I'll lie down."

"Good." Brynn was surprised Hannah was being so cooperative. She had never seen her this upset! Of course, none of her friends had ever experienced something this traumatic. "I'll check in with you later."

"Thanks, Brynn," Hannah told her. "I'll make a doctor's appointment, too. I just needed to get it off my chest."

"I understand," Brynn assured her. She hung up and pulled out her laptop to research decent criminal lawyers in the area. She forgot all about calling Maddy, her encounter with Tanner miles behind her. It wasn't until she went to bed that she allowed herself to relive the scene in the elevator over and over in her head.

Her dreams started out pleasant that night, having fallen asleep thinking about Tanner. The romantic notions were soon replaced with visions of Pauly falling to his death, his head hitting the rocks on the way down. Then, it wasn't Pauly falling anymore, but herself, sailing past the jagged cliffs speckled with blood. She could see Hannah at the top of the mountain, looking down at her and laughing. When she was about to hit the ground, she made herself wake up.

Several seconds passed before she realized it was the ringing of her cell phone that had awoken her. She groped for it on the nightstand, noticing the time was 5:06AM as she swiped to answer.

"Mrs. Kehmen?" the voice said. "This is Verna Teall, calling from Northside General Hospital. We have your husband here. He was brought into the emergency room by ambulance. He has you listed as emergency contact?"

"M-my husband?" Brynn stammered.

"Michael Kehmen."

"Is he alive?" she blurted.

"He is alive, Mrs. Kehmen. He's apparently been in a car accident. I can't give much information over the phone due to HIPA restrictions, but you are listed here as next of kin in his records. I thought you would want to be here."

"Of course," Brynn said breathlessly. She couldn't even remember the rest of the conversation. She jumped out of bed, dressed and drove to the hospital in such a flurry, she was lucky not to have had an accident herself.

Brynn parked by the emergency room entrance and ran in. They took her in right away, explaining that Michael was stable but unconscious, and needed to have surgery. They asked her to sign the consent forms so they could operate right away. When the doctor finally came out of surgery to talk to her, he explained Michael's leg had been broken in three places. He would possibly need additional surgery, but that remained to be seen. One of his lung had collapsed, and he was going to be moved to the intensive care unit once he was out of recovery. They would follow-up with an x-ray in a few hours. They would watch his progress, but expected he would fully recover.

Brynn thanked the doctor. She was allowed in to see Michael for a few minutes once he was moved to intensive care. He was awake but too groggy to know she was even there. She supposed she had better call his parents and let them know, although she had very few details herself of what had happened.

The police pulled her aside for a few minutes and told her what they could. Evidently, he was crossing the street at the airport from the parking garage to the main terminal, when he was struck by a car. The car had hit-and-run, she was informed, and the police were reviewing airport security video in an attempt to identify the car. The officers asked her a few questions, but Brynn explained she and Michael had been separated for some time, and she hadn't even been aware he was going on a trip. They took her information and advised they would be in touch.

Brynn's mind raced until her head ached. She was surprised the hospital had called her, but they had no way of knowing she and Michael were going through a divorce. In all the divorce discussions, she had never once thought about their living wills and the fact that she was still Michael's healthcare proxy, as he was hers. When all was said and done, she needed to change that! It didn't appear any life-affecting decisions would need to be made, thank God. Michael should recover fully, although his badly broken leg would take some time. *He could have died,* she kept thinking. *He could have died.*

Michael's parents arrived a few hours later and hugged Brynn in spite of their current differences. Brynn held nothing against them, other than the fact that Michael was a product of their upbringing. Still, they were not to blame for their son's deteriorating marriage and eventual split. Brynn told them what she knew and then left Michael in their able hands. There was no point in her sitting around the hospital any longer. She was probably the last person Michael would want to see when he regained consciousness.

Brynn felt like she was in a fog, as she drove home. She realized she had forgotten to call work. She pulled over and sent her secretary a text message, *family emergency, taking the day off, will see you Monday.*

She nearly pulled out in front of a car when she merged back into traffic. She shook her head to clear the foggy feeling. All she wanted to do was get home and take a nap. She was exhausted, but the more she thought about falling asleep, the more she feared the bad dreams would return.

How could the dreams be worse than everything that's happened? She made herself a salad and took a shower. She couldn't believe how quickly life could change. Michael could have died. She was almost a widow instead of a divorcee. She had a new appreciation for what Hannah was going through. She was genuinely grateful she wasn't widowed. She couldn't imagine having to go through with planning a funeral, picking out a casket, a headstone. She would have had to do all those tasks, even though she and Michael were getting divorced. They were still married on paper, and she was financially and legally bound to care for her husband's burial. No matter how vicious Michael was being over splitting their assets, she would have given him a decent burial. She expected he would do the same for her. Fortunately, she would never know.

Brynn sat on the couch with her legs tucked up under her and stared around the living room as she thought. The silence was occasionally interrupted by a door closing in the outer corridor or a horn blaring in the street below. It had been a crazy day – a crazy week! Her friend's husband had died. *Paolo was murdered,* she reminded herself. Her soon-to-be ex-husband had been hit by a car. *Hit-and-run. Had it been intentional?*

Brynn shook the thought from her head as quickly as it had come. *Who would want to kill Michael?* She laughed out loud. The stress was starting to get to her. Michael had been the victim of a random act of negligence. She rose and poured herself a glass of wine. She was going to need a few glasses to help her sleep tonight.

She knew she had promised Hannah she would call her, but she couldn't bring herself to do it right now. She wanted to talk to Maddy, tell her everything that happened today, but she wasn't up to repeating the story just yet. She needed to sort things out in her own head before she spoke with anyone else. Brynn sipped at her wine and resumed her position on the couch, listening to the random sounds of the apartment above her and the traffic below.

One thing was certain. Michael's brush with death had not changed her mind about divorcing him. She hoped he didn't wake up in the hospital and have any contradictory revelations of his own. She laughed again, and poured herself another glass of wine. Maybe his near-death experience would soften his resolve to take her for everything she had. She doubted it, but miracles did happen.

Chapter Twelve

Brynn did not remember dreaming that night, but she felt as though she hadn't rested, nevertheless. She hadn't called Hannah or Maddy yesterday, as she'd intended. She dreaded calling them at this point – she didn't feel like talking about what had happened yesterday to Michael. She called the hospital first, to make sure his status was stable. They promptly provided her the information, he was stable and he was in room 1218. That was more than she needed to know. She certainly wasn't planning to visit him.

Brynn spent the weekend in her pajamas. She didn't feel like talking to anyone, let alone leaving the apartment. Monday morning, she would have to return to work, whether or not she was ready to emerge. She followed her typical Sunday evening routine, applying a facial mask and soaking in the bathtub for twenty minutes. She polished her toe nails and finger nails after ironing her outfit for work. She lounged on the couch with a glass of wine until her nails dried, then set her alarm and went to bed.

Another restless night passed, the dreams merging from one bad scene to another for what seemed like the entire night. First there was Michael crossing the street to the airport, and she was driving the car. She maliciously slammed her foot to the floor and ran him down. He was definitely dead this time. The next dream was the funeral, and she was dressed all in black with a lace veil over her face. She graciously accepted the condolences of the hundreds of people who lined up behind the coffin, the queue meandering through the headstones of the cemetery all the way to the black iron gates marking the entrance, and then some. Her friends were there, Sydney was with Hannah and Amanda was with Paolo, who was very much alive. They shook her hand in turn, Sydney and Hannah leaving arm in arm, and Amanda lingering behind to explain how Paolo had faked his death so they could be together. Hannah didn't care – she didn't want him anymore. She merely wanted the insurance money.

Vision after eerie vision streamed through her head until her alarm sounded before dawn on Monday morning. Brynn wanted to hit snooze in the worst way, but she dragged herself out of bed and climbed into the shower. She couldn't afford to take another day off from work. She had the time coming to her, but she had absolutely too much to do at the office. She forced herself to go through the motions and try to accomplish at least a little. She received a voice mail from Michael's mother thanking her for everything she did and letting her know that Michael was home and recovering. She promised Michael would call when he was up to it. Brynn did not bother to return the call. She also didn't plan on holding her breath waiting for Michael to call her. The likelihood was improbable.

Even knowing Michael was no longer at risk of losing his life, Brynn couldn't stop the nightmares from returning Monday night, flowing from one to the next relentlessly. *The nightmares have to stop eventually*, she told herself.

She dragged through the day again on Tuesday. She was exhausted by the time she returned home that night, but she wanted to check in with her friends and make sure they still wanted to get together tomorrow. She was too tired to call them all, so she sent a group text, which was completely out of character and riddled her with guilt for behaving so impersonally. Eventually they all responded "yes" and she sent a reminder it was "German night." She decided to make something in the crockpot for dinner, which she could throw together in the morning before work. She went to bed early, in hopes of catching a full-night's sleep.

Much to her dismay, the nightmares returned. This time she was being stalked by a serial killer. Amanda and Maddy had already endured their fate, and she was next. She ran all night through her dreams, hiding and looking over her shoulder, staying one step ahead of the killer. Finally, he caught her, only it wasn't a "he." It was Hannah, bending over her with a knife, already dripping with blood, she knew not from whom, perhaps herself and the adrenaline was too fierce to feel the pain. She forced herself awake and opened her eyes, fully expecting to see Hannah looming over her. She had killed once; she could kill again.

It was nearly 4:30AM, but not near time to get ready for work. Brynn couldn't risk falling back asleep to be haunted by nightmares, so she got up, showered and started cutting vegetables to throw in the crockpot. She added some sausage, broth and a bag of lentils to create a stew-like dish her parents used to call *eintopf*. She had always called any soup or stew *eintopf* when growing up, but eventually learned it didn't mean soup or stew, but rather *one pot*. Her friends wouldn't care what it was called, as long as they had something to eat with their wine.

Brynn was in better spirits after preparing the meal she would share with her friends. Cooking was relaxing, and she didn't do it as often as she should. It was hard to cook for one. She was glad to have this opportunity to make a big pot of stew. When she unlocked her apartment door and swung it open after work, the aroma met her nose immediately and reminded her of her childhood.

Her friends timed their arrival, and she only had to buzz them in once. She propped her door open against the deadlock and went back to the kitchen to stir the soup and add a package of fresh kale.

The girls came in with a roar, praising the smell that hit them as soon as they got off the elevator. Brynn pushed the kale down into the crockpot and popped the lid back on, before wiping her hands on her apron and turning to greet the girls. She gave them each a heartfelt hug.

"I feel like I haven't seen you all in ages!" she cried. "It's been such a long, stressful week."

"I know, haven't heard from you," Maddy said.

"I'm sorry I haven't called," Brynn told Hannah as she hugged her.

"Are you overworking yourself again?" Sydney scolded.

"The more you make, the more Michael is going to try to take from you," Amanda reminded her.

"Actually, Michael had a little accident last week. Come in, pour some wine and I'll tell you all about it."

"I brought pinot noir, but the guy at the liquor store said this one was German," explained Maddy.

"Spatburgunder," Brynn perused the label. "Yes, that is German."

"I brought this, but I can't pronounce it," Sydney produced a bottle of white wine.

"Gewurztraminer," Brynn said. "Excellent choice."

"I went with Riesling," Hannah shrugged.

"Blue Nun," Amanda held up her bottle.

"Liebfraumilch," Brynn nodded. "I drank a lot of that growing up."

"Blue Nun is much easier to remember," Amanda insisted.

"I have two choices," Brynn showed them, holding up each bottle in turn. "This is the Jacob Heims Riesling Kabinett, and this one is a Spatlese late harvest Riesling, which is much sweeter and would probably pair better with dessert, had I made any ..."

The others laughed.

"We don't need no stinking dessert!" Maddy jested.

"Good thing," Amanda added. "Let's start with the Blue Nun."

Brynn obliged and opened the bottle Amanda had brought. She divided the bottle into five glasses led the ladies into the living room. Amanda was already drinking, when Sydney raised her glass to propose her toast. She hesitated, as though contemplating spitting it back into the glass, but swallowed it down with a flash of guilt that was quickly replaced with a smile.

"My friends," Sydney began. "We have been through many trials and tribulations together, but none as difficult as we have seen of late. These times are the true test of friendship, and I pray that our friendship withstands the test and flourishes. A toast to friendship, through good and bad."

"To friendship," Amanda repeated and drank, before Sydney could continue. The others followed suit.

They made quick work of the Blue Nun and moved onto the Jacob Heims Reisling Kabinett on Brynn's recommendation.

"How are you doing, Hannah?" Brynn asked kindly once they were all seated in the living room with fresh glasses.

"I have good days and bad," Hannah sighed. "Or should I say I have good and bad times every day? That would be more accurate."

"You've had quite a shock," Brynn comforted.

"You don't know the half of it," Hannah told her. "The police bother me every day, as though I'm going to remember some tidbit I forgot to tell them, that will miraculously lead them to the answer they're seeking. They are convinced Pauly's fall was not an accident and was not a result of his own incompetence, for lack of a better word. Leo encourages them every chance he gets. I can't stand living with that man, but I can't afford to let him out of my sight, either. I've caught him going through Pauly's desk twice now. I don't know what he's looking for, but it's none of his business."

Brynn felt a sudden rush of guilt, realizing she had never finished researching a lawyer for Hannah.

"Can you lock the office?" Maddy asked.

"Yes, I have it locked now, but it's a regular straight lock. You can easily pick it with a penny. It doesn't matter. What is he going to find in Pauly's desk? If someone felt the necessity to kill Pauly, and I'm not saying I believe that's true, and Leo finds evidence in Pauly's desk, all the more power to him. My concern is that he's searching through Pauly's personal papers looking for evidence to point to *me*. I know I had nothing to do with it, but I stand to gain the most by his death, so I'm the obvious choice."

"You have nothing to worry about, Hannah," Sydney assured her. "We all know you had nothing to do with it."

"You know that, and I know that, but they can pin it on me if they want to. I have no alibi. I have a motive."

No one said anything for a moment.

"Tell us what happened to Michael," Hannah turned to Brynn.

"It was the oddest thing," Brynn began, "but first I have to tell you about my mystery man!"

The girls squealed with delight.

"Did you finally talk to him?" Maddy prodded.

"I finally met him!" Brynn smiled with a flush. "Thursday after work I stopped at Tresor for takeout and when I got home, we ran into each other in the elevator. He commented about the food smelling so good, and I told him where I got it and introduced myself. His name is Tanner Evans."

"Nice name!" Amanda approved.

"Isn't it? I was so proud of myself for talking to him, and I saw his hand definitely had no ring."

The girls squealed again.

"Now you know his name. What is your next step?" Maddy asked.

"I don't know!" Brynn laughed. "Wait until I run into him again, I guess."

"It's a start," Sydney said supportively, and held up her glass to toast to Brynn's success. The girls tapped glasses and drank.

"It was a great start," Brynn agreed. "I went to bed dreaming of Tanner, and I was rudely awoken by a phone call from the hospital the next morning at some ungodly hour, telling me my husband had been in an accident."

"That must have freaked you out!" Amanda commented.

"It did! I haven't referred to Michael as my husband in ages. To me, he has been my ex since the day I moved out of the house. I thought I was dreaming at first."

"How did they happen to call you?" Sydney asked.

"I was still listed on his records as next of kin from when he had his gallbladder out three or four years ago. They told me he was stable, but they couldn't really tell me much more over the phone. I didn't even shower. I drove down there as fast as I could, and eventually the doctor came and talked to me. Michael's leg was broken in three places. They had to do surgery, and I guess his lung collapsed, so they had to keep him in intensive care for a while to keep an eye on it. Then the police came and told me that Michael was at the airport crossing the street from the parking garage, and a car hit him and drove off. Now that I think about it, I'm not sure if the lung collapsed because of the surgery or the impact of the car. I was in such a daze the whole time."

"Oh my God!" Maddy cried. "Is he OK?"

"He's home now," Brynn informed them. "I haven't spoken to him, but his mother called to let me know he was recuperating at home and he would call me when he felt up to it. I'm not expecting any calls, nor do I care to get any, unless he wants to tell me that his life-threatening experience changed his mind about stealing all my assets in the divorce."

Brynn laughed, and the others joined in.

"You never know," Amanda said. "He might have a 'come to God' moment and reconsider. Weirder things have happened."

"I can only hope," Brynn agreed. "It would certainly help me to get some sleep at night. I swear, I haven't slept since that phone call from the hospital. Maybe subconsciously I'm afraid of being awoken with bad news again. Who knows. All I know is I am completely burned out!"

"Have some more wine," Hannah offered with a sheepish grin. "I find it helps."

"Let's have something to eat first," Brynn suggested. "I have a German-themed treat for us in the crock pot."

"I've been wondering what that smell was!" Sydney gushed.

"What you are smelling is a stew like the ones my parents used to fix when I was a kid. I always called it *eintopf* growing up, but I learned years later that's not really the German word for stew."

"So, we can say stew," Maddy surmised.
"Sure."

"Good, that's much easier." Maddy brushed her forehead with the back of her hand in jest. "Now let's open that bottle of wine I can't pronounce."

"Which one?" Sydney laughed.

"The red one!" Maddy pointed.

"Spatburgunder," Brynn said. "It will pair perfectly with dinner."

Brynn handed Maddy the corkscrew and started to ladle stew into large bowls. Maddy worked the cork off the bottle, filled her glass and offered some to the others.

Amanda, Hannah and Sydney opted to stick with white wine but Brynn accepted a glass. They took their bowls and wine glasses and filled in around the table. Brynn had seating for four, so she pulled an office chair from her desk in the living room.

"The stew is really good," Sydney complimented.

"How can you tell? It's so hot!" Amanda laughed.

"I'll grab some crackers and bread," Brynn offered and hurried back to the kitchen.

"We can play my game while we wait," Sydney suggested.

"Do we have to?" Amanda whined. "I mean, it didn't end up very good last time, if you remember."

"You stood us up last time," Maddy reminded her. "We had a great time choosing which country we would live in, if we could live anywhere in the world."

"Yes," Brynn added. "That's where I got the idea of having a German theme this week."

"It worked out really well," Sydney agreed, and pushed directly to her question of the week to prevent Amanda from elaborating on her comment. Sydney wasn't sure if Amanda was referring to the "how would you murder your husband" question or the "who would you sleep with" question, but either one might spar bad memories. "I was thinking about my grandmother's birthday coming up next week, and what I would have gotten her if she were alive. I thought, what a great question for our Wednesday Wine Club! If you could choose the most special birthday gift for yourself, what would it be?"

"I always wanted a pony," Maddy laughed.

"You would," Amanda snorted. "I could see you riding it around your back yard."

"The kids would love it," Maddy argued.

"Then it isn't really a gift for you," Sydney pointed out. "What would you want for yourself, more than anything in the world?"

"I would still take a horse," Maddy insisted. "It wouldn't have to be a pony. It could be a full-grown horse, with a stable and a ranch and everything. I could go and ride it anytime I wanted."

"That's better ..." Sydney said, and Amanda rolled her eyes.

"Does it have to be material?" Brynn asked.

"That's what I intended when I thought of the question, but I guess not."

"You can break the rules, Brynn," Amanda told her. "You pretty much already have everything you want."

"You all know what I want. It's no secret, I want this divorce to be over, but I don't want to have to live in the ghetto when it's all said and done."

"That would be a great birthday present," Sydney agreed, "but it wasn't exactly what I meant. I couldn't very well get you that for your birthday."

"You've got a year to figure it out," Amanda joked. "I'll tell you what you can buy me for my birthday, Syd. I would like a new car – something little and sporty, maybe a Porsche – and make sure it's a convertible."

"What color?" Sydney asked without flinching.

"Red, of course," Amanda replied. "All blondes should drive red sports cars."

"This blonde rides a horse!" Maddy laughed.

The others joined in the laughter.

"How about you, Hannah?" Sydney asked.

"I have never been one to get hung up on material things," Hannah said thoughtfully. "I always wanted a dog, but Pauly would never let me have one. I guess I would buy myself one of those tennis bracelets that have every other stone diamond and sapphire."

"That's a good answer," Maddy said. "I wish I had thought about mine a little harder."

"Hannah's getting a bracelet, and you're getting a whole ranch," Amanda told Maddy. "I think you got the better deal."

Maddy shrugged and went back to her bowl of stew.

"The first answer that pops into your head is supposed to be your true feeling," Sydney told them matter-of-factly. "The first thing I thought of was a baby. If I woke up on my birthday, and I was pregnant, it would be the most blessed day in my life!"

"That's sort of like Brynn's answer." Amanda was playfully argumentative. "In order to get pregnant, you need a man, and that's not really a gift you can buy someone."

"She could buy herself *in-vitro* fertilization," Brynn suggested.

"There!" Sydney cried, pointing at Brynn. "See? It's something I could get for my birthday!"

"It's your game," Amanda resolved.

"Yes, it is, and I always win," Sydney bragged.

The others laughed.

"Do you mind if I open this one?" Hannah asked, holding up the bottle of Gewurztraminer Sydney had brought.

"Go for it," Brynn nodded.

"You gonna need a ride home?" Amanda asked.

"No. I took an Uber," Hannah informed her. "I use Uber all the time now."

"You do?" Amanda questioned.

"Absolutely. I don't drive anywhere anymore."

"Isn't that expensive?" Sydney wanted to know.

"It doesn't matter what it costs. It's a convenience." Hannah pulled at the corkscrew, but it wouldn't budge. Sydney held her hand out for the bottle, and Hannah handed it to her wordlessly. Sydney pulled the cork out and handed the bottle back to Hannah.

"Thank you," she said and poured herself a large glassful.

"If you can afford it ..." Amanda shrugged.

"I can't, really," Hannah continued. "I haven't worked in two weeks, and I don't have any more vacation time. But, the police want to know where I am every second of the day, and I already sat through a six-hour interrogation session trying to document *my whereabouts on the dates of April 28, 29 and 30*. Do you know how hard it is to remember where you were every second of the day? It's hard enough to remember what you did that day, let alone what time you did it. I'm not going through that again. They can track my Uber records."

"You're making it easy for them?" Amanda was dumbfounded.

"I'm making it easy for *myself*," Hannah insisted. "Besides, I have nothing to hide."

"I'd still watch my back," Amanda warned her.

"Why is that?" Hannah asked pointedly, her voice unusually bitter.

"Hey, don't get mad at me," Amanda defended herself. "You're the one who said you would want him to die in a mysterious rock climbing accident."

"And I was just as serious as you were when you said you'd snip off Nate's balls stuff them in his mouth until he suffocated."

"I was exaggerating, and you know it," Amanda defended herself.

"It was a game," Maddy attempted to referee. "None of us were serious."

"Maybe not, but it still happened exactly like Hannah wished," Amanda pointed out.

"How do you know how it happened?" Hannah demanded.

"Come on, Hannah," Amanda retorted. "You know what I mean."

"I know exactly what you mean," Hannah raised her voice. "You think I had something to do with it, just like the police. I suppose you think Brynn had something to do with Michael's accident, too. Well, Brynn? Who did you hire to run over your husband?"

"That's not funny," Maddy interrupted.

"Enough," Brynn stood adamantly. "First of all, it never occurred to me that Michael was run over intentionally. It was an accident. It was very early in the morning. It was still dark out. Secondly, for all I know the police may have already caught the person who did it. There's surveillance videos all over the airport."

"Calm down, everyone," Sydney stood as well. "We are best friends. We have to stick together, no matter what."

They all exchanged glances, some eyes still fiery, others softening to their norm.

Chapter Thirteen

Hannah took her Uber home and opened herself a bottle of wine. Leo was presumably asleep in the guest room. She poured herself a glass and kicked off her shoes, leaving them in the middle of the kitchen where she never would have dared leave them when Pauly was alive.

This is my house now. I'll leave my shoes wherever I damn please.

She wandered into the living room and made herself comfortable in the side chair, with her feet propped up on the ottoman. She usually enjoyed her night out with her friends, but tonight had been more stressful than pleasant. It was her turn to host next week, but they had left it undecided, since they were barely speaking by the time they broke it up. She saw Amanda speed off in her car as she waited by the curb for her Uber. *Amanda was full of it tonight!* She had a lot of nerve to insinuate that Hannah and Brynn had anything to do with their husbands' misfortunes, especially when Amanda had told the most gruesome tale of all! Her description of her husband's demise was downright disturbing.

Hannah shook her head and took a sip of wine. She couldn't stop thinking about Brynn's surprise at Amanda's accusation. She found it hard to believe it had not crossed Brynn's mind that an attempt may have been made on Michael's life. It had crossed her mind immediately. She didn't think Brynn had anything to do with it, but she had to admit it was a horrible coincidence that Michael was a victim of a hit and run, which could certainly be within the realm of capability of a paid assassin. When Brynn had originally said *paid assassin* during the game, Hannah had imagined a skilled sniper, but getting run over by a car was more likely that getting shot, when she really thought about it. They didn't live in that big a city where assassins were readily available for hire, but anyone could be paid to drive a car over your soon-to-be ex-husband. Hit and run seemed pretty easy to get away with – much easier than staging a rock climbing accident. Hannah laughed to herself.

She sipped at her wine and relaxed back into the chair. It had been a long, stressful, two weeks. She had gotten a lot done, but she had more to do yet. She was going to have to go back to work sooner or later. The bills would be piling up before she knew it, and she wasn't getting the life insurance money until the police signed off that Pauly's death wasn't a suicide – or murder. She still had trouble believing anyone would kill Pauly. He certainly wasn't well liked, but he was respected in his circle. She couldn't imagine anyone would go through the risk of murdering him.

And that led the trail straight back to herself. She had the most to gain. No wonder the police suspected she had something to do with it. Her friends should know better, though. Amanda was flat-out accusatory, when she had no right to be. She had to know Hannah wasn't capable of killing anyone!

Hannah didn't have an explanation for Pauly's death. The fact that it coincided with her rendition of having him killed was one of two things. Either it was complete chance, a self-fulfilling prophecy, or it was staged to frame her to look guilty. It had to be chance, because her friends were the only ones who knew what she'd said about a rock climbing accident, and none of them would have a motive to kill her husband. Unless ... Amanda was having an affair with Pauly and they'd had a fight. Maybe Amanda wanted him to ask for a divorce, and he'd refused her. It was the only logical explanation.

Hannah finished her wine and set the empty glass on a side table. She contemplated getting another, but she had a nice buzz already, and wanted to think clearly for a few more minutes.

How many other explanations were there? It had supposedly happened early Sunday morning. Maddy was home with her husband, and Sydney had spent the night on Maddy's couch. Brynn apparently had no alibi, but she had no motive either. Amanda was the only one left. It certainly could have been one of Pauly's coworkers, or even some disgruntled client who'd lost out on a great real estate deal, but Pauly didn't make it a habit of leaving his clients less than one-hundred-percent satisfied. The police said something about drugs in his system – it could be related to something she didn't even know Pauly was involved in, like a drug deal gone bad or an overdose.

Either way, it wasn't her, and she needed to get the police's focus somewhere else. She was never going to be able to get on with her life until her name was cleared. She dozed off in the chair while playing scenarios over and over in her mind.

She was awoken early the next morning by Leo dragging his suitcases down the stairs.

"I am leaving," he announced.

Hannah sat up straight and blinked questioningly.

"My father is very ill, and although my desire is to see this through to the end, my brother's killer must come second to my father's health. I do not know how long he has left to live."

"I see," Hannah said drowsily, trying to appear alert. "Would you like a ride to the airport?"

"I called a taxi," Leo informed her curtly. "Do not think I have given up. On my brother's behalf, I will take whatever steps necessary to bring his killer to justice."

"As will I," Hannah's response was equally as blunt.

"Thank you for your hospitality," Leo said, and turned toward the front door.

"Leo, wait!" Hannah pushed herself up from the chair, as Leo turned back with raised eyebrows. Hannah stood and approached him. She stopped very close to her brother-in-law and stared him in the eye. He had those same olive-green eyes Pauly had, inquisitive and piercing, like he could see her thoughts in her brain right through her skull.

"Please give your father a message," she began, and paused while she figured out how to word herself. "I wish him good health. I swear on the life of my own brother I had nothing to do with Pauly's death. He was my husband, and I loved him. When my name is cleared, I will travel to Italy to tell your father in person, and I will bring him a token from his son."

She looked down at Pauly's wedding ring she was still wearing around her thumb. She quickly looked back to Leo and met his gaze. His eyes narrowed slightly, and then relaxed.

"Very well," he said dryly. "I will bring the message. It may be too late to deliver it."

"I understand," Hannah nodded. "Thank you."

Leo left. Hannah breathed a sigh of relief. Her house was finally empty! Had Pauly been alive, she would have immediately cleaned up the guest room. Instead, she went up to her room to take a nap without even picking up her dirty wine glass from the living room table. She slept longer than she had in weeks. It was well after noon when she got up and showered. She had some errands to run and wanted to make good on her promise to Leo. The first matter of business was to apply for a passport, so that when her name *was* cleared, she would be able to travel abroad. Hopefully she would have her insurance money by then, and she could take a nice, long vacation.

She fetched her birth certificate from the safe, where she had seen it last week while going through the insurance papers. She gathered all her dry cleaning and put it in a grocery sack. She ordered an Uber to take her to the dry cleaner, and then she would walk across the street to the post office to apply for a passport.

It didn't take nearly as long as she had figured to get her passport picture taken and fill out the application. It would take a month or two to come, but she was in no hurry. She checked her phone as she exited the post office, intending to access the Uber app to summon her ride, when the fading red of a neon sign across the street caught her eye. Next to the dry cleaner was a tattoo parlor. She had noticed it before, but had never considered going in there. Pauly would have killed her! He had expressly forbidden her to get a tattoo.

I'm free of Pauly.

Hannah smiled to herself and crossed the street, knowing exactly what she wanted. In no time at all she was on her way out of the tattoo shop and climbing into the Uber with a beautiful little hummingbird on her forearm to replace the bruise Pauly had left there.

By the time she got home, she was feeling refreshed. She cleaned the guest room and cooked herself some dinner – egg noodles doused in butter with a sprinkle of parmesan cheese. Pauly would have been appalled if she'd tried to feed this to him. Hannah laughed out loud at the thought and poured herself a glass of wine.

She made the decision to go back to work. She had to get herself into some type of routine, and the bills weren't going to pay themselves. She called her boss, and he told her she could come in on Saturday for a few hours to ease back into things. Friday, she spent the day trying to sort through her finances, and Saturday she took the plunge back to work. It felt good to be around people, but it was also difficult to face the sorrowful faces of her coworkers. She knew they meant well, but she wished they would simply act normal towards her. They were being so kind and so gentle, it made her feel uncomfortable. She wondered how long it would take for things to go back to the way they were. Would things ever be the same again?

Nothing would ever be the same, she knew, but she believed things would get better once her name was cleared. She realized how far she was from that happening when the police pulled her in again on Monday for more questions.

She felt more confident this time, as she sat across from Detective Harris and Detective Rowley in a cold interrogation room with bland, gray walls. She still hadn't hired an attorney, but she had gone to the doctor, who prescribed her an anti-anxiety medication. The pills, paired with her careful planning of every move she made outside the house, had calmed her nerves considerably. She had nothing to hide. She clasped her hands together in front of her and waited for the firing squad to commence.

"Thank you for your cooperation," Detective Harris began.

Hannah smiled, trying not to show her disdain at the detective's presumption.

"We have made very little progress since we last spoke," Detective Harris continued. "In spite of the immense amount of information we've taken in from your husband's colleagues and major clients, we are no closer to determining who may have been responsible for his death."

"But you are convinced it wasn't an accident," Hannah concluded.

"The evidence gathered at the crime scene, combined with the coroner's findings suggest that your husband did not, in fact, die as a result of injuries sustained in a fall. Rather, he was already deceased, and his body was placed in such a way to appear as though he had fallen. Without divulging details that could prove vital in identifying his killer, we can tell you his death was unmistakably deliberate."

"So, you're telling me someone killed my husband and dumped his body at the bottom of a cliff, or whatever, but you're not going to tell me how you've come to that speculation," Hannah surmised.

"Basically, yes," Detective Harris confirmed. "There are details around your husband's manner of death that only the killer would know, and we intend to use that information to locate our perpetrator."

Hannah forced her breathing to remain steady and looked from one officer to the other. Their expressions were not particularly empathetic, but not accusatory either. She tried to let this new bit of information settle before responding. Her mind was racing.

Pauly was murdered. Someone purposely killed him and attempted to make it look like an accident.

"How is it that I may be of assistance?" she asked cautiously.

"You knew him best," Detective Harris explained, pointing the tip of his pen in Hannah's direction. "Who would want your husband dead?"

"Apparently, I didn't know him best," Hannah retorted. "I have spent many sleepless nights thinking and thinking who could have done this, and I have no answer. Pauly knew a lot of people, and attended a lot of events without me. He didn't have a close circle of friends; he had an immense circle of acquaintances and contacts, some of which aren't even in this country. I never realized it while he was alive, but Pauly had many, many people in his life that I didn't know. Maybe I did realize it, but I had no reason to question it. His business transactions didn't involve me."

"We have interviewed a number of his colleagues, and have obtained copies of his recently completed sales, as well as transactions in progress. Did he discuss his work with you? Were there any particular clients he spent an excessive amount of time with? Anything you can tell us is helpful," Detective Harris insisted.

"He did not discuss work with me," Hannah told them. "He would tell me he was working on a big deal, or we would celebrate a big sale, but he was very private with his clients. He rarely involved me in any of his transactions. If he was meeting a client for dinner or cocktails, he preferred to go alone."

"How often was that?"

"He met with clients all the time."

"How many hours a week would you generally say your husband worked, whether at the office or meeting clients?"

"He worked more often than not," Hannah said. "We had dinner together a few nights a week. Otherwise, he was working."

"Did he have friends outside of work that he socialized with? Anyone at the gym or anyone he went rock climbing with?"

"No, he had a trainer from time to time, but they didn't socialize outside of the gym."

"Any mutual friends or couples you did things with?"

"No. I have my small circle of friends, and Pauly had his vast array of contacts and clients. He knew people wherever we went, but I wouldn't call any of them his friends. Pauly wasn't one for socializing without a purpose. He was all about his career."

Detective Harris was quiet for a moment.

"What would be a typical day for your husband?" Detective Harris took a different direction.

Hannah had trouble piecing together a "typical" day for her and Pauly. They didn't have a routine, because they both worked most evenings. She described their lifestyle as best she could, including their many trips to the gym each week, whether together or separately. He would come home for dinner some nights, and not others. She left out the part that he always expected her to have dinner ready and waiting, even if he wasn't coming home. Many nights he would go back out to an appointment after dinner.

The detectives took it all in, jotting notes in their steno pads. Hannah looked from one to the other, but their expressions seldom changed. They were two pan-faced professionals going through the motions.

"How would you describe your relationship with your husband?" Detective Harris asked next.

"We had a good relationship. We've only been married a little more than two years."

"And no children?"

"No. We weren't ready for children. We both were happy with our jobs, and our routines. Things worked between us, if you know what I mean."

"It sounds like a co-existence," Detective Harris commented. "Did you have any hobbies or activities you did together?"

"Other than go to the gym, where we worked out separately, no. We didn't have many common interests."

"And your relationship was good?" he asked doubtfully.

"Of course."

"No domestic disputes of any type?"

"You would already know if there had been," Hannah reminded him.

"If the police were involved..." Detective Harris's blue eyes studied her icily. "Did you have any disagreements about anything recently?"

"We had normal, everyday disagreements, like all married couples. You know, the house is a mess, or you didn't call when you said you would, that type of thing. Nothing major." Hannah pulled up her sleeves and crossed her arms in front of her.

"Nice tattoo," Detective Harris commented.

Hannah stared at him icily.

"New hairdo, new tattoo. I guess people all mourn differently," Detective Harris quipped.

"People all mourn the same, they simply express themselves differently," Hannah retorted.

"Do you have any reason to believe your husband may have been having an affair?" the detective asked bluntly.

Hannah paused, considering how to respond.

"Our relationship was largely sexual," Hannah explained. "He was insatiable, to say the least, but I never denied him carnal pleasures whenever he desired. I find it hard to imagine he was not getting enough sex to the extent that he would resort to having an affair, but anything is possible."

Detective Harris raised his eyebrows.

"Men do stranger things," Detective Rowley shrugged.

"The more you get the more you want," Detective Harris added with a laugh to his partner.

Hannah looked from one to the other disapprovingly. The smiles were short-lived.

"Pauly never gave me any reason to believe he was having an affair," Hannah said, but her voice trailed off as though she hadn't finished her thought.

"But…"

"But nothing!" Hannah stared him down with a straight face.

"You can see where we are running into brick walls," Detective Harris said bluntly. "You and your husband had a wonderful marriage. He had no family in the area and no friends. He had many, many acquaintances, but none who would want him dead. He wasn't interested in anything other than real estate, rock climbing and sex."

Hannah hesitated. She had to give them something, or they would continue pursuing her. The wife was always the number one suspect. If they couldn't find anyone else to pin it on, they would use the evidence they had against her. She knew full well she could be convicted whether than had any evidence or not. She saw it happen on TV all the time. She could just imagine sitting in a jail cell the rest of her life, pining over her innocence to anyone who would listen. She had to redirect their interest one way or another. A lover scorned sounded like a reasonable suspect.

"It was nothing Pauly did to make me doubt his fidelity," she said slowly. "When he came home late from his last trip, he made a remark like, 'what if I ran off with a blonde and didn't come home.' He was teasing me. He didn't usually say things like that, but I didn't think much about it at the time. It seems totally unrelated, but recently, I caught my friend, who is a blonde, in a couple of lies. She told her husband she was with me and my friends one night, but she wasn't. I started thinking about a conversation we had, and some of the comments she made about Pauly to me. The timing was when Pauly was out of town. It made me wonder if something was going on between the two of them."

The detectives exchanged glances.

"I'm sure it's nothing. My imagination."

"It's worth looking into," Detective Harris was serious again. "It's very important, Mrs. Gianni, that we don't discount anything without investigating. Tell us about your friend."

Chapter Fourteen

Hannah felt like a load had been lifted from her when she left the police station. She had an entirely new outlook on her life – *her life*. She felt like she had control again for the first time in years. She had given the police enough information about Amanda to keep them off her back for a while. Now she had to play the mourning widow. She was the victim in this, after all. She sent a group text to the Wednesday Wine Club to confirm they were on for this week.

"Wednesday night at my house. The theme is Italian in honor of my late husband."

She spent the next day cleaning the patio for the event. There was no rain in the forecast, although the temperature may be slightly cool. No matter, they could huddle around the grill, which she pulled out of the garage and cleaned. She was excited to try cooking on it. Pauly had never let her touch the grill, other than to clean it. While she was in the garage, confronted by reminders of Pauly everywhere, from rock climbing equipment to lawn tools, she came across a hummingbird feeder her brother had given her as a housewarming gift. Pauly didn't like birds, so the dainty, red, bulbous decoration had been stored in the garage unused. Hannah lovingly retrieved it, dusted it clean and hung it from a shepherd's hook on the back patio. She filled it will a homemade solution of sugar and water, looking forward to the first visit from a tiny, feathered friend.

Keeping with her newly adopted prospect of living her life her way, on Wednesday, she ditched the Uber and drove herself to the grocery store. She would have her receipt to prove what time she had been shopping. This was *her life* now. If the police wanted to follow her around and harass her, that was their business. She decided she wasn't going to help them out any longer.

Besides, the Uber rides were getting expensive, and she had no income at the moment.

She bought Italian sausage and freshly-baked rolls, bell peppers and onions for the main dish. She chose beefsteak tomatoes, a bunch of fragrant, sweet basil sprigs, a hunk of mozzarella cheese, prosciutto, salami and provolone to make a Caprese salad and charcuterie board for sides. Satisfied with the menu, she stopped at the liquor store and selected a bottle of Chianti and a bottle of Asti to accompany the meal.

She opened the Chianti when she got home and poured herself a glass while she prepped the vegetables. She whistled as she worked. She was looking forward to spending a pleasant evening with her friends and enjoying the spring weather. It was her official fresh start to her new life.

Her friends arrived one-at-a-time, Amanda showing up nearly an hour after the others.

"Traffic," she said. "There was an accident on the Thruway."

They all wondered why she was on the Thruway, but no one asked. They all seemed to be avoiding confrontation with Amanda, knowing she was racking up lie after lie, but not certain they wanted to know the truth behind the lies. Sometimes ignorance was easier.

Hannah led them to the patio, where she had the table set for five. It looked exquisite. She had covered the iron, scrollwork table with a thick red table cloth, and placed settings with matching red napkins folded neatly atop the plates. For her centerpiece, she cut several stems off her bleeding heart, arranging them in a crystal vase so the delicate blossoms trailed over the edges in neat rows. The pink heart-shaped flowers with the white "bleeding" droplets did not exactly meet the requirement of her color palette, but they did serve as a reflection of her dedication of the evening to Pauly, her own heart bleeding at the loss of her husband.

She had set out water glasses and a large pitcher of water with lemons and ice. The grilling tools were clean and lined up neatly, ready for their first use of the season. She had layered several strings of white, twinkle lights through the bushes that surrounded the patio to add extra light and contribute to the ambiance. The hummingbird feeder hung off to the side, the twinkle lights reflecting off the red, bulb-shaped section that held the nectar.

Her friends took in the beauty of the setting and seated themselves around the table. Hannah started the grill to let it heat up. She had to follow the instructions carefully, as she had never lit a grill before, but it was an easy enough task to accomplish. While the grill heated, she retrieved the sides she had prepared. The platter of Caprese salad looked delectable, the layers of sliced tomato, mozzarella and basil precisely aligned and drizzled with balsamic vinegar. The charcuterie board was equally appetizing, chunks of meat and cheeses whimsically arranged and dotted with olives to make flower shapes.

"It looks too pretty to eat!" Sydney complimented.

"Please, help yourselves," Hannah motioned to the tray of meat she had retrieved from the kitchen. "These sausages are going to take some time to cook."

"Sausage sounds delicious!" Brynn chimed in. "I love the smell of the grill. It feels like summer."

"It'll be here before you know it," Maddy laughed. "Once the kids get out of school, all hell breaks loose."

The others laughed.

"You love it," Amanda said.

"I do love it, most of the time," Maddy admitted. "I just wish Jim had more time off to do things with us. The kids are growing up so fast!"

"Enjoy it while they're little," Sydney added wistfully. "That reminds me, I haven't given my toast!"

Amanda groaned.

Maddy lifted her nearly-empty glass.

"That won't do," Sydney took the open bottle of Chianti and refilled Maddy's glass.

"Thank you."

"This is a very special toast," Sydney resumed in her sing-song manner. "I want to dedicate this toast to tonight, which is the beginning of all our futures. My dearest friends in the world, you all deserve the very best in your future. I wish every day for that, and I hope this toast brings with it the good fortune you all deserve."

Sydney's eyes were still closed, but she lifted her glass, so the others followed suit.

"Salud," Hannah responded from the grill.

"Cheers," Maddy added.

"Why do you subject us to this every week?" Amanda's question was more of a demand, stated as though she were kidding, but they all knew she was serious.

Sydney crossed her arms and pouted, her brown curls bouncing with the jerk of her head.

"It was a very nice toast, Sydney," Brynn affirmed, tapping Sydney's knee for assurance.

"Thank you, Brynn."

"You're lucky we love ya, Syd," Amanda told her.

"I love you guys, too!" Sydney gushed. "That's why I want you all to be happy. We are going through a bit of a rough time right now, especially our Hannah, but I honestly feel deep down in my heart, things are going to get better."

"I hope so," Hannah agreed, rolling up her sleeves to start transferring the sausages to the hot grill.

"Is that a tattoo?" Maddy shouted.

Hannah's face flushed in acknowledgement.

"It's gorgeous!" Brynn jumped to her feet to take a closer look. "Is that a hummingbird?"

Hannah nodded and held up her arm for her friends to see her beautiful, new, body art.

"I love it!" Maddy cried.

"When did you get it?" Sydney asked.

"Saturday. It was on a whim. I had run some errands, and when I came out of the post office, I saw that little tattoo parlor in the plaza across the street. I have always wanted a tattoo, but Pauly wouldn't let me get one. I figured, what better time than the present?"

"He wouldn't *let you* get a tattoo?" Amanda asked incredulously.

"He wouldn't let me do a lot of things," Hannah answered bluntly. "Get a tattoo, cut my hair, put my feet up on the ottoman … so I figured, what the hell? I've always wanted one, and now I have no one forbidding me to get one. I'm mourning the loss of his life, but I'm also celebrating the beginning of my new life, my freedom."

"It's good for you to pamper yourself," Sydney defended her.

"Yes, it is," Maddy chimed in. "I'm glad you decided to have us over, Hannah. I wasn't sure if you'd be up to it, but I always look forward to our weekly get-together."

"I look forward to it too, Maddy," Hannah replied. "Honestly, I dread getting out of bed every day, but I feel like I have to get back to a routine. I went to the doctor last week, and he basically said the same thing. I worked a few hours on Saturday, and I'm going to work a couple shifts this weekend. My boss is being very accommodating with my hours."

"Are you sure you're ready to go back to work?" Sydney asked with a mother's concern.

"I have no choice," Hannah answered. "I have no income, and I have to pay all the funeral expenses on top of the regular bills."

"But, you will get the life insurance payout for the funeral expenses," Brynn pointed out.

"Eventually. The insurance company won't pay out until the police close their investigation, or at least rule me out as having any culpability."

"That's crazy!" Maddy cried.

"You're telling me," Hannah agreed. "I've never felt so low in all my life. Here I just lost my husband, and everyone from the police to Pauly's family, to the insurance company are treating me like a criminal. My coworkers tiptoe around me like I have the plague. I don't even know how they know what's going on, but they do!"

"It's on the news, Hannah," Brynn said gently.

"Oh my God!" Hannah was disgusted with herself for not realizing it. "Has my face been posted all over the story? No wonder people looked at me funny in the grocery store today."

"There was nothing about you, specifically," Brynn informed her. "There was an article in the paper, 'Suspicious Circumstances Around Local Climber's Fall.' I'll search it up on my phone."

"Don't bother," Hannah told her. "I don't want to see it right now. I can look it up later. Let's talk about something else. I just want to have a nice, enjoyable evening."

"I'm sorry," Brynn said, and put her phone away. "Why don't we sample some of the wine I brought?"

"I can't even pronounce it," Maddy laughed.

"Montepulciano d'Abruzzo," Brynn sounded it out slowly for her. "My colleague recommended it. He said it was excellent."

"He?"

"Just a colleague," Brynn explained. She grabbed the cork screw and went to work on the bottle.

"What's going on with your mystery man?" Sydney asked.

"Tanner? I haven't seen him since our encounter in the elevator."

"That's a bummer," Maddy was disappointed.

"I know! I finally got the chance to talk to him, and I haven't seen him since. I was hoping to keep the conversation moving forward."

"It'll happen. Be patient," Sydney said.

"How is Michael?" Hannah asked.

"Michael is recovering slowly. I spoke to him very briefly over the weekend. He said he was taking pain killers to the point he was sleeping more than anything else. He promised to call me when he's more alert."

"Did they catch the person who hit him?" Amanda wanted to know.

"No, they haven't. He said the police were dragging their feet."

Hannah laughed sarcastically. "That's a surprise."

"I don't know what the status is, to be honest with you. Michael was disgusted about the whole thing, but he was also high as a kite on pain killers. He could have been exaggerating."

"Keep us posted," Maddy said. "Hit-and-run is some scary shit."

"Yeah, it is!" Amanda joined in. "Do they think someone hit him on purpose?"

"I don't know," Brynn admitted. "It was very early in the morning, still dark. It was probably a drunk driver."

"Maybe, but it could have been someone who wanted him dead," Amanda said bluntly, glancing at Hannah, who turned around from the grill to face her.

"What are you saying?" Hannah demanded.

"I'm saying the obvious," Amanda answered flippantly. "You said Pauly would die in a mysterious rock climbing accident; Brynn said Michael would be killed by a paid assassin. What's going to happen to Jim, Maddy? I don't remember."

"If I were you, I'd be more concerned about what is going to happen to Nate," Hannah reminded her bitterly.

"That's what I'm saying!" Amanda threw her hands up in the air. "Who's going to be next?"

"I think you're taking this a little too far," Brynn told her.

"I think you aren't taking this serious enough!" Amanda insisted.

"Fine," Hannah said and dropped the tongs on the table. "I wasn't going to go there, but if you're going to claim everything we wished for is coming true, who do you think you are, sleeping with my husband?"

"What?" Amanda cried.

Brynn, Maddy and Sydney's jaws dropped.

"You said you'd sleep with Pauly. Am I to assume you did, since everything we said during the game is coming true?"

"I didn't sleep with Pauly."

"You're obviously up to something!" Hannah accused pointedly. "You're lying to Nate and you've been lying to us. We know you weren't sick that night you blew us off. There's no way you were home on the couch, and Nate just *didn't notice you*. Come on, Amanda. Do you think we're stupid? You've been lying for weeks. What's your deal?"

"I was sick!"

"What about the night I saw Nate out at the Double Play?" Maddy interjected. "He said you were working, but I stopped into the Diamond and you weren't there. And when I asked you about it, you lied to me. You told me you were working."

Amanda didn't respond. Sydney and Brynn stared at her in disbelief.

"Well, where were you that night?" Maddy crossed her arms.

"I don't remember what night that even was!" Amanda answered defensively.

"Were you with Pauly?" Hannah demanded to know.

"No, I wasn't with Pauly!" Amanda claimed.

"Are you lying again?" Hannah asked bluntly.

"What is this, gang up on Amanda night?" Amanda blurted, avoiding answering any of their questions. "I've had enough. You guys have lost it!"

"You're the one who brought it up!" Maddy said in defense.

"You're the one who cheated with my husband!" Hannah added.

Amanda stood up, the legs of her chair making a loud scratching noise against the cement patio.

"*I did not sleep with Pauly!*" she yelled. "I'm out of here."

"Amanda …" Brynn stood to try to stop her, but Amanda brushed past her forcefully.

"Let her go," Hannah ordered.

"I am so sorry, Hannah," Maddy said immediately. "I shouldn't have said anything. I've been so mad at her for weeks for lying to me – to us – and I couldn't hold it in any longer."

"It's not your fault," Hannah told her, wiping back a tear. "My emotions are all out of whack."

"Understandably so," Sydney comforted and stood to rub Hannah's back.

"The doctor prescribed me Prozac, and that seemed to be helping, but I didn't take it today because I knew I was going to be drinking."

"You can drink with Prozac," Sydney told her. "Why don't you go take one, and I'll get these sausages off the grill before they burn."

"I'll do it," Hannah sniffed. "I'm not going to bother taking one now."

"Do you want us to leave?" Brynn asked, unsure.

"No, don't go," Hannah assured her. "Let's just eat and try to salvage the rest of the evening. I'm sorry I lost my temper. My emotions are all over the place lately."

"Amanda did start it," Maddy pointed out. "Besides, it's been boiling up for a while. Eventually, we had to have it out. I'm just sorry it happened tonight."

"You know what?" Hannah changed her mind. "I'm glad it happened tonight. Things *have* been boiling up for a while, now. I'm glad I got what I was feeling out in the open."

"Do you really think she was sleeping with Pauly?" Brynn asked gently.

"I don't know," Hannah sighed, placing the tray of sausages on the table. "I thought it made sense, but she was pretty adamant. On the other hand, she could be lying to us again."

"She was awfully defensive ..." Sydney noted.

The ladies looked from one to the other, all of them wondering the same thing. Either Amanda was lying about Pauly, or she was lying about something else. Whichever the case, she couldn't be trusted.

Chapter Fifteen

Amanda pulled away from the curb in a huff. She didn't know why she'd even bothered to go to Hannah's in the first place. She thought maybe she could get some answers out of them, but obviously they had their own ideas about her – and those ideas were not good! She drove until she was definitely out of sight of Hannah's house, then pulled over and lit a cigarette. She groped in her purse for her phone, texted "MYAH" to the most frequently texted number in her phone, and turned the car in the direction of Dalton's.

They think I slept with Pauly. She was dumbfounded! The thought of sleeping with Pauly had never crossed her mind. She'd only said that as a joke, because Hannah was bragging about Pauly being so good in bed. Truthfully, she was scared shitless of Pauly. That day he'd come into the Diamond was terrifying. Those piercing, green eyes had bored into her as though they could see her very thoughts.

Why do they think I slept with Pauly? Was Pauly having an affair? Amanda puffed at her cigarette as she zipped through traffic. She tried to piece this new information together in her head. If Pauly was having an affair, and Hannah found out, that gave her a motive to kill, although it seemed more likely she would kill the woman he was having an affair with. That explained why Hannah was so upset with her, but she couldn't imagine Hannah letting her imagination run away with an idea like that! Even worse, if Hannah was unstable enough to kill her husband because she found out he was having an affair, what would stop her from killing the woman he was sleeping with? *She thinks I was sleeping with Pauly.*

Amanda glanced in her rear-view mirror to make sure she wasn't being followed. Hannah couldn't possibly have gotten away from the other girls quickly enough to tail her. She had food on the grill and three sane women in her presence. No, Amanda was certain she wasn't being followed – by Hannah. It wasn't the first time she'd felt like she was being followed. To be safe, she took a long route to Dalton's, making several unnecessary turns and driving around the block. She parked two blocks away and walked the rest of the way.

"What took you so long?" Dalton wanted to know when she arrived.

"You don't want to know," Amanda answered.

"It doesn't matter. You're here now," he said, taking her into his arms and kissing her. He lifted her up off the floor and she wrapped her legs around his waist. Neither of them were in any mood for talking. Dalton carried Amanda straight to the bedroom and lowered her onto the bed. Amanda wriggled her clothes off underneath him, while he kissed her neck. He slowly worked his way down to her bare breasts, as she unfastened his pants. Dalton took his lips off her for only a second while he removed his shirt. Amanda made quick work of unfastening his pants, and he kicked them off onto the floor, wasting no time getting inside her.

Amanda moaned as he entered her. Dalton was always hard and ready, so different from Nate who had to be coaxed into having sex half the time. She was so sick of trying to be sexy for her husband, when he clearly wasn't interested any longer. It was no wonder she latched onto Dalton's affection so easily. He wanted her all the time. She didn't have to wear skimpy lingerie around the house and rent porno movies to get him in the mood. She merely had to walk past him, and he couldn't stop himself from grabbing her.

She pulled his body against hers and kissed him harder. She didn't think she had ever been as aroused as she was at that moment and she slammed her hips against his frantically. His passion matched hers as he kissed her back. He pushed himself further inside her and rolled them over on the bed, pulling her on top of him and freeing her to buck wildly until she orgasmed. He unselfishly let her indulge in the moment before flipping her over and taking her from behind to fulfill his own pleasure.

They were both out of breath when he finished and dropped on the bed beside her. She couldn't imagine sex being any better than this with anyone. Hannah could brag about Pauly all she wanted, but she wasn't getting any more multiple orgasms, was she? Amanda smiled to herself. She would never know what tricks Pauly had up his sleeve, but she could live without knowing. Dalton pleasured her like no one else ever had, or ever would. He was all she needed – sexually.

They lay still on the bed still breathing heavily, feeling blissful and satiated. Amanda stretched and rolled over to rub Dalton's chest. He turned and smiled, blue eyes dancing. She couldn't help but wondering where this relationship was going, but she kept quiet so as not to ruin the moment. The future was ugly and black, as far as she was concerned. The thought of confessing to Nate and asking for a divorce was gut-wrenching. There was no reason for it. She didn't plan on running off to elope with Dalton, or anything so permanent for that matter. It was the best sex she'd ever had, and taking their relationship any further would jeopardize what they had. It was hard not to dream about having more with Dalton, but it was for the best. Dalton knew it too. He didn't pest her to end it with her husband. He took what he could get, and he took it oh, so good.

Amanda smiled back, relishing the moment.

"What happened with your girl's night?" Dalton asked, brushing his hand through his thick, black hair.

"Hannah and I got in an argument, so I left," Amanda sighed.

"I thought you two were tight," he said.

"I thought so, too. I'm beginning to wonder if I ever knew Hannah at all. I know this is a horrible thing to say, but I think she may have killed her husband."

"What?" Dalton was startled.

"Maybe not personally killed him, but she had something to do with it." Amanda rolled over onto her back and stared at the ceiling. "That's not the worst part."

"It gets worse?" Dalton said with a laugh.

"It gets way worse. She's losing her mind. I don't know if she was crazy before he died, or if it happened after he died, but she is definitely crazy. I guess she had to be crazy to marry that son-of-a-bitch in the first place. But she was at least reasonable. Now she's all over the place, bat-shit crazy."

Amanda paused, trying to piece together everything that had taken place over the last few weeks. Hannah was not the same person. She looked different; she acted different.

"I'm kind of afraid," Amanda confessed to her lover. "She's a ticking time-bomb ready to explode. She exploded at me today! That's why I'm here, for God's sake. She accused me of having an affair with Pauly! Can you believe that?"

Dalton was quiet for a moment.

"It's not that hard to believe," he said. "Maybe you haven't been as discreet as you think you have. They might have figured out you're having an affair and just assumed it was with him."

"That's ridiculous. I can't stand that man – couldn't stand him, that is. I get the chills just thinking about him." She shivered. "I don't even blame her for wanting him dead. He was an evil person. This is what I'm talking about. She's losing her mind if she thinks I would sleep with Pauly. She literally accused me of having an affair with him – all because of that stupid game we played. Me and my big mouth. *I'll sleep with Pauly*. Why did I ever say that? Shit, if I knew that was going to come back to haunt me, I never would have said it. It was a joke! I say stupid shit. That's who I am. She should be used to it."

"I'm not trying to defend her or anything, but she probably is a little crazy. I mean, her husband died. He didn't *just die, he was murdered.* That's enough to make someone crazy."

"Which is exactly why I think she had something to do with it! She's crazy! Maybe she found out he was having an affair and she killed him. She's definitely not acting like a mourning widow. She's more like a woman scorned. Do you know she cut all her hair off? She had gorgeous, long hair and as soon as he was dead, she chopped it all off. She said she only kept it long because that's how he liked it. And today, she pulls up her sleeve and there's a big, new tattoo on her forearm. Apparently, he wouldn't let her have one when he was alive. Now that he's gone, boom! Tattoo. That's not normal. I could see if she went and got a tattoo to commemorate her husband, but this is a dragonfly or something, to represent her freedom. Wait, it's a hummingbird. Whatever it is, someone whose husband just died doesn't go out and get a tattoo to celebrate their freedom!"

Dalton generally listened to Amanda's rants without indulging her. He acted no differently today. He had already said more than he usually did. Amanda was opinionated, and some of her ideas were far-fetched, but Dalton wasn't with Amanda for her intellect. He leaned over and rubbed her bare breasts. He was nearly ready to go again.

Amanda's nipples tightened at his touch, but her mind was back at Hannah's. She kept playing the conversation over and over in her head. If Hannah truly thought she had an affair with Pauly, and she killed Pauly, what was she going to do to her? Was she going to murder her, too? And she couldn't get the idea out of her head that someone ran over Michael with their car. That piece of the puzzle didn't quite fit in, but it could easily have been Hannah. Maybe she felt so great after getting rid of her husband, she wanted to do the same for her friend. It was a good thing Hannah was mad at her, then; she wouldn't bother trying to murder Nate.

If I were you, I'd be more concerned about what is going to happen to Nate. Hannah's words rang through Amanda's head. She sat up suddenly.

"Oh, my God."

"What's wrong?" Dalton asked, trying to regain his grasp on her breast.

"I have to go," Amanda pushed his hand away and jumped out of bed. She pulled her clothes on quicker than she had shed them.

"Come on, babe," Dalton said. "You're going to leave me hanging?"

Amanda didn't answer. She was already across the bedroom floor and out the door. She had to get home to Nate before something happened.

How could I have been so stupid? She asked herself the question over and over on her way home. Of course, she still loved Nate. She didn't want anything to happen to him. Dalton was merely a phase. The sex was great, but the relationship had no future. Dalton simply wasn't the kind of guy to settle down, and Amanda didn't want him to be that kind of guy. She wanted him exactly the way he was — free and sexy and forbidden. That's what made him exciting.

Nate was far from exciting, but he was still her husband. She cared about him. She couldn't let anything happen to him, and she couldn't let him find out about Dalton.

She drove home in record time. She checked her hair and makeup in the rear-view mirror before going inside. She couldn't let Nate see her flushed and upset. She had to maintain her composure and act like herself. She needn't have worried about it. Nate was already in bed. She breathed a sigh of relief. She went back downstairs and double-checked that all the doors were locked, before getting ready for bed. After she was assured they were safe for the night, she crawled into bed next to her husband, and for the first time in months wrapped her arm around him as he slept.

Nate had gone to work by the time Amanda woke up the next day. She had to work as well, and wasn't looking forward to it. She felt like she had a hangover, even though she had barely had any wine all last night. It was the stress. She got herself out of bed, showered and hit the road for work. She hoped Dalton didn't show up at the diner today. She wasn't ready to see him yet. She knew she had to break things off with him, but the diner was not the place to do it. She would have to drive over to his place after her shift.

Her shift went relatively quickly until mid-afternoon, when the cops showed up to talk to her.

"Here?" Amanda looked around helplessly, hoping her boss would save her from having to meet with them. She had no such luck.

"Unless you'd rather come down to the station," the officer stated blandly.

Her boss nodded and pointed to an empty booth in the corner.

Amanda huffed disgustedly and led the officers out of the main fairway. She sat with her back to the room, so her coworkers couldn't see her face. She was absolutely mortified to have this conversation at work.

"Mrs. Colling, we are here in reference to the investigation of Paolo Gianni's death. My name is Detective Harris, and this is Detective Rowley. We'd like to ask you a few questions."

Amanda nodded, then looked down at her hands, clasped in front of her on the table.

"When is the last time you saw Paolo Gianni?"

Amanda remembered very clearly the last time she had seen Pauly. She thought back to try to figure out the date.

"It was a Thursday," she recalled. "Late April."

Detective Rowley pulled out a pocket planner and pushed the calendar page across the table for her review.

"It must have been April 19. I was working, and he came in for a cup of coffee."

"Did you speak to him?"

"We said hello to each other. He thanked me for giving his wife a ride home the night before."

"Did he say anything else?"

"No. He got his coffee and left."

"And that was the last time you saw him?"

"Yes."

The detectives were silent for a moment.

"Mrs. Colling, what was the relationship between you and Mr. Gianni?"

"Relationship? He was my friend's husband."

"Did you have extramarital relations with him?"

"No!" Amanda was adamant. "I barely knew him."

"Do you have any idea who Mr. Gianni might have been having an affair with? Was he with anyone when you saw him?"

"He was alone. Like I said, I barely knew him. I was surprised to see him in the diner that day. He wasn't a regular."

"So, he may have stopped here specifically to see you," Detective Harris surmised.

"He stopped here specifically for coffee. Pauly was a real estate agent. He was probably in the neighborhood."

They all knew Paulo Gianni didn't sell any real estate in this part of the city, but he certainly could have been meeting a client. Detective Harris moved on.

"What can you tell us about the relationship between Mr. and Mrs. Gianni?" he asked.

Amanda wasn't one to think before she spoke, but she made herself think about this response.

"They've been married a little over two years," she began. "They weren't really ones to socialize together, like do things with other couples. I've been getting together with Hannah once a week for dinner for years, and our husbands never wanted to come, so it's been a girls' night. I never really saw a lot of Pauly, but any time I did see him with Hannah, it was tense. You could cut that tension with a knife."

"Tense because they were arguing, or…" Detective Harris prompted.

"I think it was because she was scared shitless of him. She was always worried about pissing him off, like she always made sure she didn't stay out too late, and the house had to look perfect. *She* had to look perfect, that kind of thing. And if things weren't perfect, she paid the consequences."

"How so?"

"Physically, I would say. We all saw the bruises on her."

"Who is 'we all?'"

"The Wednesday Wine Club girls. We have dinner every Wednesday, drink wine, catch up. There's five of us: me, Hannah, Maddy – Madeline – Helmsford, Brynn Kehmen and Sydney Mitchell."

The officers exchanged glances at the mention of Ms. Mitchell, with whom they were already familiar.

"And all of you have witnessed bruises on Mrs. Gianni that were allegedly caused by Mr. Gianni?"

"Yes, from what Hannah told us. I mean, she said some of them were from rough sex, not like he beat her up on purpose, but we had our doubts."

"There is no record of domestic violence at the Gianni residence. Why do you suppose Mrs. Gianni didn't report anything?"

"Like I said, she was scared shitless of Pauly. She always defended him, said it was her own fault, that kind of thing. She would tell us the sex got rough, he slammed her into the table one time, and she had a big bruise on her arm. Right where she got the tattoo!" Amanda realized suddenly. "That must be what she meant by a symbol of her freedom."

The officers, having seen the tattoo, understood Amanda's insinuations. They were both writing notes in their steno pads.

"I have to tell you something," Amanda blurted.

The detectives stopped writing simultaneously and looked at her expectantly.

"I told you we get together every week for dinner, the five of us. Well, Sydney always makes us play this game where she asks a hypothetical question, and we all have to answer honestly. It could be anything, what would you do with a million dollars, or who would you be if you could be a movie star. One week a couple of us were complaining about our husbands, normal stuff, nothing major, and Sydney asked us if we could kill our husband and get away with it, how would we do it." Amanda didn't look up to see the officers exchanging glances again.

"Hypothetical, of course," she continued. "Hannah said that Pauly would be killed in a mysterious rock climbing accident. Well, a week later, we find out Pauly is dead, and it was some coincidence how he died." Amanda paused for effect and looked up to see their reactions. She knew she'd opened up a can of worms, but she had to tell them. She could tell from their expressions that Hannah had not divulged that information to them previously.

"So, your theory about Pauly having an affair may be head on, but it wasn't with me. Hannah seems to think there was something between me and Pauly. I know that's why she sent you after me, but this is a dead end. I barely knew the guy."

"What would make her think you two were an item?" Detective Harris asked.

"I don't know. You'd have to ask her that question," Amanda answered tritely. She wasn't giving them any more information than she had to about herself.

"Mrs. Colling, where were you on Saturday, April 28 and Sunday, April 29?" Detective Harris asked.

Amanda was startled at the change in his line of questioning.

"I usually work during the day on Saturday. I'd have to check the schedule, but I'd say I was here. Saturday night, I was probably home. Sunday, too. I really don't remember going anywhere."

"Is there anyone who can corroborate your whereabouts?"

"My husband," she replied.

"Your husband stated he was working out of town that weekend," Detective Harris smugly checked his notes.

"When did you talk to my husband?" she exclaimed. "*Why* did you talk to my husband?"

"It would appear you don't have an alibi at the time of Mr. Gianni's death, Mrs. Colling."

"I don't need an alibi," she retorted. *Oh, my God. I was with Dalton. I'm not telling them anything about Dalton.*

"Seems you do need an alibi," Detective Rowling added.

"What was Hannah's alibi?" Amanda demanded. "It seems to me you should be looking into that, not bothering me. If you don't have any more questions, I need to get back to work."

The detectives looked at each other, then stared coldly back at Amanda, who met their stares, then pushed herself out of the booth.

"One more thing," she said, turning back. "I don't know if you two are the ones investigating a hit-and-run accident that happened a couple weeks back, but you might want to check into it. Michael Keymen was hit by a car up at the airport. It just so happened that his soon-to-be-ex-wife, Brynn said she would hire a paid assassin to kill him. Hit-and-run pretty much fits the bill, wouldn't you say? I would bet my life the two incidents are related. Maybe Hannah has gone crazy enough to start carrying out her friend's fantasies, too. She told me flat out I'd better be worried about my own husband."

She turned to leave.

"Mrs. Colling?" Detective Harris called her back.

Amanda spun back to face him defiantly.

"Curious. How is it you said you would kill your husband?"

"I'm done here," she snipped and walked away.

Chapter Sixteen

Maddy heard her phone vibrate from across the bathroom, but she had Trinity in the bathtub, so she ignored it. It was a text, she could tell by the sound her phone had emitted. It could wait.

After she got Trinity bathed and dried off, she checked her phone. It turned out to be a group text to the Wednesday Wine Club ladies from Amanda, "Canceling Wednesday night at my house. Sorry for the late notice."

Maddy deleted it and tossed the phone back on the counter by the sink. It slid and knocked over the toothbrush holder. She picked up the toothbrush holder, noticing it was filthy inside and needed to be cleaned anyway. She set the toothbrushes neatly on the edge of the sink with their heads balancing over the basin, and took the holder to the kitchen to clean it. She could hear her phone vibrating again.

She ran back to retrieve the phone, and it was Brynn calling.

"I am so irritated!" Maddy vented to Brynn. "What the hell? I get out once a week, and now she's canceling at the last minute."

"It doesn't surprise me," Brynn replied. "I didn't think Amanda would have us over after last week's blow-up. Honestly, I wasn't sure I wanted to go."

"I know what you mean, but it was a risk I was willing to take. I need my Wednesday nights out!"

"We can still go," Brynn offered. "We'll go to a restaurant, like we used to."

"You don't have to ask me twice. I'm game. Do you want me to call Sydney and Hannah?"

"Would it be terrible of us not to invite them?" Brynn asked tentatively. "I'm sorry, but I'm not up to any drama tonight."

"It's fine with me," Maddy agreed eagerly. "You pick the restaurant."

They met at a steakhouse around six and settled into a quiet booth. They ordered a bottle of Pinot Noir to share, since it was Maddy's favorite.

"I feel a little guilty not inviting the others," Brynn admitted, "but I've had a hell of a week, and I needed to talk about it with a neutral party."

"What's going on?" Maddy was concerned.

"Michael called me and told me the police got a good look at the car that hit him, from the video surveillance. They can tell the make and model, but not the color, because the video was dark. They couldn't get the license plate because it was either removed or covered up, which tells us it was either unregistered or purposely concealed."

"Do you mean someone ran him down intentionally?"

"I'm not sure," Brynn replied anxiously. "It could be the car wasn't registered or insured, so the person got out of there as quickly as they could. Or, it could be someone covered the plate, tracked Michael down and maliciously sailed through the crosswalk at the precise moment he was crossing. I tend to think it was an irresponsible kid who didn't bother to license his car."

"What kind of car was it?" Maddy asked.

"It was an older Buick LaCrosse, around ten years old. They said it was hard to tell exactly what year it was, because the video is grainy, but they thought maybe a 2008."

"It could have belonged to a young kid, then. Maybe their first car. What did Michael think?"

"Michael thinks it was random. He was in the wrong place at the wrong time."

Maddy nodded, taking in the information.

"I'm glad they're making progress," Brynn continued. "It seemed to take a long time to go through those surveillance videos."

"You would think the airport would have better security equipment," Maddy commented.

"Oh, the airport does," Brynn told her. "Had he been closer to the building itself, they probably would have caught the person by now. The problem is, he was coming out of the parking garage, so the only video that picked it up was from the rental lot."

"Plus, it was dark," Maddy remembered. "I don't suppose they could see the person's face at all?"

"No, it was a dark blur. I actually saw a snapshot of it. After Michael called me and gave me the news, the police called and asked if I would stop down at the station and review the pictures they compiled from the video to see if I recognized the car."

"You had to go down there?" Maddy asked with astonishment.

"Wait until you hear this!" Brynn drank some wine to prepare herself for the story. "I went down there, and they put me in an interrogation room and showed me the pictures of the car. I honestly didn't recognize anything. I couldn't have told you what kind of car it was, but they knew somehow. I figured that was all. I wasn't much help, but I'd done my civic duty. Then, they tell me they got a tip that it may not have been accidental."

"A tip?" Maddy gaped. "From who?"

"I couldn't tell you," Brynn shook her head. "They said they were investigating another case, and a person of interest in that case suggested that the two cases may be related."

"What other case?" Maddy asked slowly.

"The case of Paolo Gianni's murder," Brynn said with a tip of her head. She raised her wine glass and took a long, calming sip.

Maddy's jaw dropped again, and her eyes became two huge, round marbles.

"Holy shit."

"I was flabbergasted!" Brynn admitted. "They started asking me questions about our Wednesday Wine Club, and if I recalled anything about Hannah saying her husband would die in a mysterious rock climbing accident."

"What did you tell them?" Maddy leaned closer across the table.

"I told them what I remembered, and I told them I took that conversation in jest. I guess I'm used to Sydney and her silly games. They, however, took it quite seriously."

"But, who would have told them about that?" Maddy questioned. "Hannah certainly wouldn't have brought it up, under the circumstances. It points the finger directly at her! Who else would they have spoken to?"

"They spoke to Sydney, but I don't see her bringing it up. It was her game. She probably thought nothing of it."

"It's hard to tell with Sydney," Maddy pointed out. "She's an odd bird."

Brynn nodded and sipped at her wine.

"I know I didn't speak to the police, and they already knew when you spoke with them. If Hannah and Sydney didn't tell them, that only leaves Amanda," Maddy deduced.

Brynn nodded again slowly, mulling the possibilities in her head. Her thoughts were momentarily interrupted by the waiter, coming for their order. Brynn ordered a New York strip steak, medium rare, with smashed garlic potatoes and the vegetable du jour. Maddy ordered the same, only well done.

"When in Rome…" Maddy shrugged.

"That's what I figured. I haven't eaten all week, I've been so sick over this whole thing. I've barely gotten any sleep, either. Do you know what it's like to go to the police station?" Brynn whispered across the table.

"No," Maddy admitted, "and I don't want to."

"You definitely don't want to, but I have a bad feeling you're going to find out."

"I hope not!" Maddy cried. "Do you think they talked to Amanda?"

"I think they did, and I'll tell you why. They asked me if I had any information about Paolo Gianni, and if he may have been having an affair. I don't know much about Pauly, and I don't have any reason to think he was having an affair – aside from Hannah's accusations the other night. My theory is Hannah told them she suspected he and Amanda were having an affair, so they pulled Amanda into the investigation. I highly doubt Amanda and Pauly had anything going on, so Amanda probably told them about Hannah's little 'prediction' to spite her. She was pretty mad when she left last week."

Maddy was nodding now. It made sense.

"Do you think Hannah is capable of … you know, murder?" Maddy asked.

"I wouldn't have thought so a month ago, but now I'm not so sure," Brynn answered without hesitating.

"I get that Hannah could have been so abused that she might have snapped and killed Pauly. Ten to one it was self-defense, if it even happened that way. I don't understand how that could possibly be related to Michael getting hit by a car."

"I don't entirely get it either, but I'm glad I have an alibi," Brynn replied.

"You do?"

"They know I wasn't driving the car that hit Michael. I keyed into the parking garage in my building and stayed there all night. They can check all the video surveillance in my building and see that I didn't leave my apartment until after the accident, when they called me from the hospital. I never would have imagined in a million years that I would need an alibi, but after all that's happened, I am glad I have proof of where I was at the time of the accident *and* at the time they believe Pauly was killed. Thank God for my building's security system!"

"The police asked you where you the day Pauly died?" Maddy was appalled.

"They sure did. It made me feel like such a scumbag. I sincerely hope they don't drag you down there for questioning, Maddy. It was embarrassing, to say the least."

"I can imagine! I guess I better figure out if I have an alibi. What day did Pauly die, anyway?"

"April 29. It was a Sunday morning, although they asked me where I was on Saturday as well. They believe he was with the killer for some time leading up to the time of death."

"I can't believe they asked you. Let me think where I was that day. I was home, with my family, where I always am. Where else would I possibly be?" Maddy said sarcastically. "Actually, that was the weekend Sydney watched the kids. Jim and I had a date night Saturday night. We were together the entire time."

"So, Sydney has an alibi too, then," Brynn surmised.

"For Saturday night, but she was gone when I got up in the morning. I don't know what time she left my house."

"She can account for most of the time," Brynn reasoned.

"That was the night I ran into Nate," Maddy remembered, forgetting all about Sydney. "It was also the night Amanda lied to me – and Nate. She said she was working. We know she wasn't."

"Her work records can vouch for that. You don't suppose she really was having an affair with Pauly, do you?" Brynn asked.

"I find it hard to believe, but I'm starting to question everything."

"Me too!" Brynn agreed. "If you would have asked me a month ago if Hannah would murder her husband, I would have said, 'no, way.' If you would have asked me a month ago if Amanda would have an affair with Hannah's husband, I would have said, 'no, way.' Now I'm having trouble *not* believing it. I can't think of any other explanation."

"It would make sense, if Pauly was having an affair and Hannah found out, that she would be angry. I still don't think she would kill him," Maddy said, lowering her voice at the word 'kill.'

Hannah's words ran clearly through Brynn's mind: *I'm glad he's dead, but I didn't kill him. I didn't even have the balls to divorce him, how could I have killed him?*

"She flat out told me she didn't kill him, whatever difference that makes," Brynn told Maddy.

"I still don't understand why they think the two cases are related. Do they think the same person who killed Pauly tried to run down Michael? Who would know both of them *and want them dead*?" Maddy pondered aloud.

"I don't entirely understand either. If they suspect the same person is responsible, there would have to be a motive for both. If Hannah killed Pauly, which she definitely had a motive to do, what could she possibly gain from trying to kill Michael? It makes no sense."

"I'm sure any number of people had a motive to kill Pauly. He wasn't the most likeable person. Who would benefit from killing Michael?" Maddy wanted to know.

"Michael doesn't have any enemies, that I know of. I'm the only one that would benefit, monetarily that is, and we both know I didn't have anything to do with it. It does freak me out that Pauly died rock climbing, the way Hannah said she would have him killed. It's a sick coincidence that she said that."

"Do you think someone is setting her up to look guilty?" Maddy asked.

"Nobody knows she said that besides us," Brynn pointed out.

"Maybe he was in the mafia," Maddy suggested. "He could have been involved in anything, knowing that man. Maybe he pissed somebody off and they took care of him, and they set it up to look like an accident."

"At this point, nothing would surprise me," Brynn agreed.

Their food came, and they redirected their focus to the beautiful cuts of steak before them.

"I am so hungry," Brynn took a deep whiff of her plate. The steak smelled delectable, and she cut into it to find it cooked perfectly to her liking.

"Me too," Maddy said, diving into her potatoes.

"I do have some good news," Brynn said.

Maddy raised her eyebrows.

"Remember that hot guy in my building, Tanner? We ran into each other in the elevator again the other day. It was funny, because I had just come from Tresor with takeout. I guess stopping at Tresor after work is my good luck charm, because that's where I had been last time I ran into him in the elevator. He noticed I had food, and guessed where I had gotten it. We talked about the restaurant for a minute, and then he suggested we go out to dinner sometime!"

"He did?" Maddy asked, too thrilled to care that she had just shoved a mound of potatoes into her mouth.

"He did!" Brynn smiled radiantly. "We are going to Tresor on Friday!"

This time Maddy swallowed before responding.

"I'm so excited for you!" she squealed.

"Thank you. I'm excited too, but nervous. Do you know how long it's been since I've been on a date?"

Maddy thought about it. She and Jim had been together so long, she couldn't imagine going on a date with another man, especially a *first date*.

"You must be terrified," she said.

"Well, not *terrified*," Brynn laughed at Maddy's dramatics. "I feel a little guilty, truth be told."

"Why would you feel guilty?" Maddy blurted.

"I don't know… Michael is stuck home with a broken leg, and I'm out with another man. I know I shouldn't feel guilty at all, but it's ingrained in me. I'm still his wife. For better and for worse, for richer and poorer, in sickness and in health…"

"'Til death do us part," Maddy finished.

They looked at each other in silence from across the table for a moment. Brynn sighed and took a sip of her wine.

"Sometimes I wonder if I'm doing the right thing," she admitted. "Michael is not a bad person. We simply have different aspirations in life. It's like we started off on the same path, but forked off in two different directions. Splitting up seems to be the best option – the only option."

"You're only questioning your decision because of the accident," Maddy pointed out. "It's the Florence Nightingale effect."

Brynn laughed whole-heartedly.

"I'm not cut out to be a nurse," she shook her head. "Thank you for putting it in perspective for me."

"You're welcome," Maddy said, although she was a little confused why Brynn was thanking her. It was human nature to care about someone you'd devoted years of your life to, even if your lives had recently gone in different directions. She would think it odd if Brynn *didn't* care what happened to Michael. She was sickened at the thought of going through a divorce. She was lucky to have Jim in spite of his faults, leaving the toilet seat up, tracking mud through the house, forgetting garbage day. He was there for her and the kids, and most importantly, they were on the same path in life. Maddy didn't verbalize as much to Brynn, as she didn't want to make her feel any worse about her own situation than she already did. Maddy thanked her lucky stars for her seemingly mundane life. She may not have the career Brynn had, or the sexual passion Hannah and Pauly had experienced, but she had something they didn't. She had roots. Nothing could take that away from her. *Or could it?*

"Brynn," she said abruptly. "I just had a crazy thought."

Brynn had been deep in thought herself, but met Maddy's gaze. Maddy looked suddenly pale.

"You don't think someone is playing out our game for real? It sounds nuts, but how else could the two accidents be related? Pauly and Michael didn't even know each other. Why would the police think they are related somehow? The only way they are linked is through us, and we were the only ones who knew about that conversation. I know I didn't tell anyone about it."

"Why would anyone do that?" Brynn asked, analyzing Maddy's theory in her usual practical manner.

"I don't know, but Pauly is dead. That is a hard, true fact. Michael could have been dead too, but he got lucky. Remember what Hannah said to Amanda last week? Do I need to worry about Jim?"

Brynn remembered exactly what Hannah had said to Amanda last week. *If I were you, I'd be more concerned about what is going to happen to Nate.* She wanted to assure Maddy she was letting her imagination run wild, but a small part of her had been wondering the same thing.

Chapter Seventeen

Maddy kissed Jim goodbye the next morning and told him to drive carefully. She didn't want to believe that someone evil was plotting to kill all their husbands in the matter they had predicted, but she also didn't see any harm in being cautious.

Brynn's prediction that the police would want to speak with her came true. The police paid a visit to her house on Friday. It was an odd experience, but passed quickly enough. Ryan was down for a nap, but Trinity had resisted. She screamed the entire time that the police were there, which probably facilitated the abruptness of their departure.

They had asked her if she knew Hannah and Paolo Gianni, what kind of relationship they had and if she had ever witnessed any violence between them. They asked if she had known either of them to be unfaithful. Most memorably, the asked her if she recalled Hannah stating she would kill her husband and make it look like a rock-climbing accident. Maddy stumbled over her description of that conversation. Her intent was to protect her friend, explain that the comment was taken out of context, but the more she talked, the less convincing she sounded to herself. Trinity was whining and pulling on her arm the entire time, which was distracting. Detective Harris left her with his card, if she should think of anything else.

Like what? She wanted to ask, but she kept quiet. The less said the better. The second they left, she put Trinity down for a nap and called Brynn.

"I don't even remember what I told them," Maddy admitted after describing the brief visit.

"At least they didn't drag you down to the police station," Brynn consoled her.

"That's for sure! I would have had to bring the kids with me, and Trinity was acting awful. I just put her down for a nap."

"Did they ask you anything about Michael and the hit-and-run?" Brynn asked.

"No, nothing."

"They must not think it's related," Brynn concluded. "I don't know who gave them the idea the two cases were related. Maybe it was a ploy to distract them from the real killer. It sounds to me like they think Hannah had something to do with it."

"That's how I felt," Maddy confessed. "I feel so guilty that I didn't stand up for her. I mean, this is Hannah we're talking about, our friend. I should have said more about her character, and told them she didn't have it in her to kill anyone, let alone her husband. I don't even know what I told them. It's a blur."

"I'm sure you did fine," Brynn assured her. "We don't know anything. They undoubtedly need to interview anyone who knew the Gianni's, but that doesn't mean they're going to get any information from those interviews. It's standard procedure."

"I know, they're just doing their jobs. I still feel bad."

"I understand. Listen, Maddy. If Hannah did kill him, we don't know anything about it. We have nothing to feel guilty about. Okay?"

"Oh, I know, but I feel guilty for even *thinking* Hannah might have killed him. I'm sorry to bother you at work with all this."

"Actually, I'm in the car on my way home," Brynn told her. "I took the afternoon off to get ready for my big date!"

"That's right! It's today! Is he picking you up at your apartment?"

"We're meeting in the lobby," Brynn replied. "It's awkward, in a way, that we live in the same building, but it's convenient too."

"It sure is convenient!" Maddy agreed. "I hope you have a great time."

"Me too! Wish me luck!"

"Good luck!" Maddy hung up with a sigh. A first date was so romantic. She and Jim hardly ever got out any more. She hated to ask Sydney to watch the kids again, and Jim's mother was getting a too old to handle all three little ones at the same time. Maybe things would be easier when the kids were a few years older. Maddy went to the kitchen to start dinner. She couldn't stop thinking about her visit from the police. She played back the conversation over and over in her head, trying to piece together everything they'd asked her and how she'd responded, and what it all meant.

Brynn was right, it sounded as though they thought Hannah had something to do with Pauly's death. It seemed unlikely Hannah could have done it on her own, especially if Pauly didn't fall to his death, but was planted at the bottom of the cliff. Hannah couldn't have moved Pauly's lifeless body by herself. Maddy knew how hard it was to carry a sleeping eight-year-old up a flight of stairs to bed, let alone a grown man across rocky terrain, who knows how far. Hannah worked out, but she wasn't a body builder or anything; she was more into cardiovascular workouts and toning exercises.

Maddy was sick of worrying about it. She shook her head and went about her day. The police had gotten her statement, so she no longer had that hanging over her head. And Brynn was right – she didn't know anything. She needn't bother trying to figure out who was responsible, because she simply didn't have enough information. She completely put the matter out of her mind, and went about her life, at least for the day.

Brynn called her Saturday to relay the details of her date. It felt good to talk about something less controversial.

"We met in the lobby, and walked down to the parking garage together. Tanner drove," Brynn told her. "He has a really nice car, an Audi. I was impressed. It was not only a nice car, it was clean!"

"I would hope so!" Maddy commented. "If you drive a nice car, you probably want to keep it clean."

"I think so," Brynn agreed, "but Michael's car was always a mess! Michael was a slob all around, though. He dressed nice, because I made sure his clothes were always dry cleaned and pressed, but his car was always filthy."

"What man isn't a slob?" Maddy wondered rhetorically. Jim would never win a housekeeping award.

"Let's just say I haven't encountered Tanner's housekeeping skills yet," Brynn said.

"And has he encountered yours?" Maddy teased.

"No," Brynn confessed. "We had a great time at dinner, though. We talked about everything you can imagine. We even stayed for coffee and dessert. Then, he drove me home and walked me to my door. He kissed me goodnight, but we both agreed we kind of want to take things slowly. He is also divorced, although he has been a divorcee a lot longer than I have. Technically I'm not a divorcee yet!" Brynn laughed.

"Sounds like it went well," Maddy surmised.

"It went very well. It couldn't have gone better, I don't think. I mean, I would have loved to have invited him in, but I know I'm not ready for that yet. I'm not looking for a one-night stand, and I don't think he is either."

"Are you going to see him again?" Maddy asked.

"I am! We are going out again next Friday. He's taking me to his favorite restaurant. Since we went to mine, he found it only fitting that we go to his, too."

"That's great!" Maddy was glad things were working out for Brynn. She deserved it. She'd worked hard for everything she had, and the divorce was taking a lot of those things away from her. Maybe having a love interest would help Brynn get through the process, or at least have a positive outlook that she had someone in her future.

Maddy couldn't help but compare her friend's life to her own. Brynn's divorce was a financial turmoil, but only because she had actual assets. At least now, she finally had a budding love life to serve as a distraction. Maddy and Jim lived paycheck-to-paycheck, had no assets they didn't owe money on, but they had each other. And they had three beautiful children. Her life was boring, routine, predictable. *It was everything she'd ever wanted.* She realized more and more every day how lucky she was.

Maddy planned a fun weekend for the family. It was hard not to get stuck in a rut when her days were filled with nothing more exciting than cleaning house, fixing meals and caring for children. She wanted to get out of the house and do something fun this weekend. Jim had to work Saturday morning, but when he got home, she and the kids had lunch ready and waiting. They had already cleaned their rooms and put away all the laundry. After lunch, they took a trip to a children's museum, about an hour's drive. The kids spent the afternoon learning, running and laughing, and she and Jim got to spend some much-needed time together as well. The kids fell asleep in the car on the ride home. They ordered pizza for dinner and settled in for a night of movies and popcorn. Sunday, they relaxed!

Maddy enjoyed every minute of their family weekend together. She knew all too well not to take life for granted. She felt satisfied knowing she made some great memories for the kids, too.

Monday came all too quickly. Jim went back to work, Little Jay went back to school, and Maddy was left with two rambunctious toddlers and a messy house. It was her life. She looked around, wondering where to begin. She let out a sigh, realizing it didn't matter where she began, and started picking up the dishes that were scattered around the living room. She welcomed the interruption when Amanda called a little while later.

Maddy hesitated for a moment whether she should answer the call, but she was not the type of person to run from controversy. She wanted to hear what Amanda had to say.

"What's up?" she asked her old friend.

"I just got out of work," Amanda replied. "I'm sitting here at the picnic table, because I'm not quite ready to go home yet. Remember when we used to sit out here on our break?"

"I do remember," Maddy told her. They had had some great conversations around that picnic table outside the diner. Life seemed simpler then, but perhaps it was a matter of perspective. Maddy wondered what had Amanda feeling so nostalgic.

An awkward silence told her Amanda was struggling with something.

"I kinda wanted to talk to you about what's been going on with me," she started hesitantly.

"Sure," Maddy said. *I'm all ears*, said the sarcastic voice in her head, but she told herself to keep quiet and hear what Amanda had to say.

"All right, so, I never had an affair with Pauly. Let me get that out on the table first. I can understand why Hannah might have thought that, since I realize I've been sneaking around, but it wasn't with Pauly. I would never do that to a friend, and honestly, Pauly always scared the crap out of me." Amanda gave a small, embarrassed laugh.

It was no joke. Maddy remembered all too well how intimidating Pauly had been. Sometimes she wondered what Hannah ever saw in him. Probably she could never shake him after their first date. She still shouldn't have married him, but maybe he gave her no choice. Maybe she thought she could change him – a lot of women enter into marriage with that illusion. At any rate, it didn't surprise her to hear Amanda didn't sleep with Pauly. She had been having trouble digesting that idea from the beginning.

"I know Hannah doesn't believe me, and I don't blame her. Maybe Pauly was having an affair with someone, but it wasn't me. You don't have to believe me, if you don't want to."

"I want to believe you, Amanda," Maddy explained, "but you've obviously been lying about something. What exactly has been going on with you?"

She could hear Amanda inhaling and exhaling through the phone, evidently smoking a cigarette.

"I have been having an affair, but not with Pauly, alright? I met this guy at work a few months ago, and there was an instant attraction. Let's just say I couldn't resist. Nate and I have been in a rut, and I guess I liked the attention this other guy was giving me. It was a physical attraction, like I've never had before, but that was all it was. I never planned on falling in love with him or anything. This guy, Dalton, didn't expect me to leave Nate, and I didn't expect any commitment from him. It was just sex."

"Are you still seeing him?" Maddy wanted to know.

"No. It's over now. I realized, with everything that's been going on, it isn't worth it to fuck up my marriage. I mean, Nate isn't that bad of a catch. We have a lot going for us. We're used to each other. I don't want to start all over with somebody else. I went over to Dalton's place this morning before work and told him it was over."

"How did that go?" Maddy asked.

"It went as well as expected. I think he knew it was coming. I mean, he knew we weren't in it for the long haul. We both agreed it was nothing more than a fling, for as long as we were both enjoying it – not that I wasn't enjoying it any more. That's not the case at all. It was pretty hard for me to break it off with him. I still don't even know if I did the right thing ending it, but I was starting to freak out. Hannah warned me more than once to watch out for Nate, and I guess it hit me the other day. Maddy, I'm scared. I don't want to lose Nate."

"I get it," Maddy told her friend. "I would be devastated if I lost Jim."

"Yeah, right? It's starting to hit home – too close to home. I never imagined Hannah had it in her, but Pauly must have pushed her too far."

"Wait, so you think Hannah killed Pauly?" Maddy wasn't convinced.

"Of course, she did!" Amanda exclaimed. "Who else would have done it? And who would have done it in the exact way that Hannah said she would do it? There's no other explanation."

"There's lots of other explanations," Maddy argued. She wasn't sure why she was sticking up for Hannah, but a small part of her was having trouble believing one of her closest friends could commit murder.

"Name one," Amanda challenged her.

"Maybe one of his coworkers did it. I don't know, maybe he was in the Mafia."

"That's a little far-fetched," Amanda responded doubtfully.

"You met his brother. It's not *that* far-fetched," Maddy pointed out.

"I don't buy it, and I'll tell you why. Hannah was an abused woman. He beat her up more than once; he probably raped her more than once. We all knew it, and we did nothing."

"We tried," Maddy interjected sheepishly.

"We didn't try hard enough. Hell, I'm not even sure we *could* have done anything. We could have gotten her out of there, but he probably would have come after her. And in all truthfulness, I don't know if she would have left him. She seemed to like being abused," Amanda said flatly with a snort. "She admitted she got off on their kinky, rough sex. She didn't want to give that up, but sometimes he just went too far. She walked around with bruises all over, for Christ's sake."

"I think we did what we could," Maddy insisted. "We opened the door for her to talk about it many times, and she shut us out."

"Exactly. She kept it all in. Well, you know what happens when you keep everything bottled up inside of you. One day, you explode."

"And you think she killed him?" Maddy concluded.

"I don't think it was premeditated, or anything like that, but I think she snapped. I think she'd had enough. Maybe that night when we talked about it, she got an idea in her head. Who knows?" Amanda exhaled loudly again.

"I don't know," Maddy admitted. "I don't want to believe she could do anything that drastic. I honestly don't know what to believe. You know, the police were here the other day, asking me questions."

"Oh, yeah?" Amanda perked up. "What did you tell them?"

"I didn't tell them anything, really," Maddy told her. "I don't know anything!"

"Did you tell them what Hannah said? About the mysterious rock climbing accident?" Amanda prodded.

"They asked me about that," Maddy replied.

"Yeah, they asked me about that, too," Amanda confessed. "They showed up at the diner last week asking all kinds of questions. What did you tell them?"

"I told them what I heard Hannah say, but I didn't think she was serious."

"Hell, I didn't think she was serious at the time either, but look what happened. I always treated Sydney's goofy questions as a joke, but apparently Hannah took them seriously. She actually thought I would sleep with Pauly! What else did the cops ask you?"

"Not much," Maddy was non-committal. "Trinity was whining and carrying on the whole time. I wasn't really focused on what they were saying, and it's all a blur now."

"Lucky you," Amanda said with her usual touch of sarcasm. "They walked right into the diner and started asking me questions in front of everybody. I wanted to crawl under the table. Did they ask you where you were the night Pauly died?"

"Yeah, I was here," Maddy answered.

"They asked me, too," Amanda told her, without acknowledging she'd heard Maddy's reply. "The thing is, I was out with Dalton all night. I don't know why I didn't just tell them the truth, but it was before I broke things off with him, and I didn't want them going and talking to him. And I sure as hell don't want Nate to find out. I just want things to go back to the way they were, you know?"

"You haven't told Nate yet?"

"God, no! I'm not telling Nate, either! What good would that do besides hurting his feelings?"

"What if he finds out anyway? Won't that make things worse?"

"I'll take my chances," Amanda insisted.

"What about Hannah? Are you going to tell her the truth?" Maddy asked.

"I probably should," Amanda admitted. "She'll be mad at me forever if I don't. I'm the one who should be mad. She has to be crazy to believe I would sleep with Pauly."

"I think we're all acting a little bit crazy," Maddy told her. "I definitely think you should talk to her and clear the air."

"I don't think she'll talk to me one-on-one."

"Talk to her Wednesday night," Maddy suggested. "Sydney's hosting Wednesday Wine Club."

"I guess. How about I pick you up? You can give me a pep talk on the way there and drink all you want."

"I can live with that," Maddy laughed.

"Thanks, kid. You're a life saver."

Chapter Eighteen

Amanda picked up Maddy as planned on Wednesday night and headed north to Sydney's place. Amanda chattered with anxious energy the entire trip. She couldn't wait to tell Hannah the truth and get it off her chest. Maddy didn't get much opportunity to speak, but when she finally did, she said what she felt was most important.

"You're not going to tell Hannah you believe she killed Pauly, are you?" Maddy said pleadingly.

"Hell, no!" Amanda answered without hesitation. "That's like the number one rule on true crime TV. You never tell the killer you know they did it!"

"We don't know she did it," Maddy reminded her.

"You can stay in denial for as long as you want," Amanda told her. "It's probably a safe place to be. You don't have to worry about slipping up and accusing anyone of murder. Believe me, I'm not going there with Hannah. I'm simply going to clear the air about the whole sleeping with Pauly thing. If she knows the truth about Dalton, she's got to believe I never had anything to do with Pauly. So, if she killed him because he had an affair, at least she'll know for sure it wasn't with me!"

Maddy sighed, but couldn't respond. Amanda kept rambling.

"I'm sick of living in fear," she was saying. "First, I had to worry about Nate finding out the truth. Then, I had to worry about Pauly telling Nate the truth. Then, I had to worry about Hannah retaliating against me for something I didn't do."

"Wait. What?" Maddy interrupted.

"Oh, yeah. Pauly knew I lied to Nate the night I drove Hannah home. I told Nate I was spending the night with Hannah, to make sure she was OK, but I went over to Dalton's. When Pauly took Hannah to pick up her car at my house the next day, he must have talked to Nate and found out that I lied. Let me tell you, I was scared shitless. Pauly showed up at the diner that day and *thanked* me for getting Hannah home safely. One look from him and those creepy, green eyes and I knew I was in trouble. I'm not sure how much he knew, but he definitely knew I didn't go home that night, and he sure as hell knew I wasn't at his house. Maybe he said something to Hannah. Maybe that's why she thinks there was something going on between me and Pauly."

"So, he came into the diner and thanked you for driving Hannah home? How did he know where you were all night?"

"He didn't know *exactly* where I was all night, unless that crazy son-of-a-bitch followed me or something. I wouldn't put it past him. I just knew from the way he was looking at me that he knew I lied to Nate. He looked at me as though he could see straight through me. I still get shivers thinking about it – especially now that he's dead."

"Pauly knew you were cheating on Nate," Maddy summed up what Amanda was saying. She was trying to wrap her head around it. It seemed like there was more to it than Amanda was telling her. Maybe encouraging her to come tonight was a bad decision.

Maddy started questioning everything Amanda had told her. It simply didn't add up. Maybe she was lying about everything.

"Oh, he knew all right. You know that look your parents give you when they know you're lying, and they have this half-smile like they already know what your punishment is, even though they haven't confronted you yet that they know you're lying. *You* know that look. You probably use it on your own kids," Amanda babbled, as she changed lanes.

"You're sure he didn't say anything to Nate?" Maddy asked, ignoring Amanda's presumption.

"Nate never mentioned anything about talking to Pauly. I'm pretty sure he would have confronted me, if he knew I was out all night and I *wasn't* with Hannah. Don't you think?"

"I would think so," Maddy admitted. "I don't know how you think you're going to go along with Nate like nothing happened. You're going to keep that secret inside the rest of your life?"

"Damn straight going to try! Mind if I smoke?"

"It's your car," Maddy wrinkled her nose, knowing her answer had no influence over Amanda whatsoever. She lit her cigarette before Maddy even had the words out of her mouth.

"I'll quit next week," Amanda nodded at the cigarette, wisps of toxins filling the car with her every movement.

"Famous last words," Maddy said dryly, cracking her window.

They were the last to arrive at Sydney's house. Maddy was relieved, because the others were already deep in conversation about Brynn's date with her mystery man. Sydney ushered them in and poured them wine.

"I can't believe he asked me out in the first place!" Brynn was saying. "Do you know how long I've been lusting after him in the elevator?"

"Yes, we know!" Amanda chimed in.

"It felt wonderful to be out on a date with someone other than Michael, but it also felt weird. I had a speck of guilt hanging over my head all night."

"You shouldn't feel guilty," Sydney told her.

"No, I know," Brynn agreed, "but it's hard when you're coming out of a failed marriage. The feelings of guilt aren't even that I feel like I'm 'cheating' on Michael, but more because I feel bad I couldn't make my marriage work. When I got married, I never in a million years imagined I would be getting a divorce a few years later. I had my whole life planned out. I had my degree out of the way, and my career was taking off beautifully. I had the husband, and the house, and the travelling. I hoped someday to have children. Now I have this huge feeling of failure and inadequacy. I know I shouldn't feel like that, but I can't stop myself. It's hard starting all over."

"I know how you feel," Hannah agreed, "but you're not starting over completely, just like I'm not starting over completely. You still have your career and your friends, and most importantly yourself. You have enough pieces of your life intact to move forward. I'm not saying it's easy to do, but you have what you need."

"Thank you, Hannah," Brynn said sincerely. "I can't tell you how much I needed to hear that."

"I've given it a lot of thought," Hannah laughed a little.

"You know, you're right," Brynn continued. "Things are going to get better. My date was fabulous! Tanner and I are going out again on Friday."

"See? That's wonderful!" Sydney gushed.

"That's not all," Brynn said with a smug smile. "Michael called me yesterday. Evidently his brush with death made him realize life is too short to squabble about possessions. He decided to compromise with me on everything. He really, really wants the house, so he's buying out my half of it *and* the time share."

"I can't believe neither of you wanted the time share," Maddy interjected.

"It's not that I didn't want it," Brynn explained. "Michael wanted to take the house and give me the time share, and that was not an equitable split. Now he says will take it, if I give him a break on price, since he's buying both. It's fine with me. We've been at a standstill for so long, I'm glad to have things moving toward a resolution – an amicable resolution at that!"

"That's fantastic!" Sydney cried.

"I'm glad things are going well for you, Brynn," Hannah said sincerely.

"Things will get better for you, too," Sydney assured her.

"I know, eventually." Hannah took a sip of her wine and stared idly at the oversize spoon and fork set hanging on the wall of Sydney's kitchen, exactly as Grandmother hung them fifty years ago.

Sydney went to the refrigerator to pull out a tray of assorted vegetables that she had cut up, and set it on the table for the girls to snack. To ensure her appetizers weren't too healthy, she also set out the bacon-ranch dip and horseradish cheeseball she had made, along with some crisp, wheat crackers. Amanda dug in first, shoving vegetables in her mouth like she hadn't eaten for days. Maddy attributed her sudden appetite to her purposeful delay of the conversation she'd come here to have with Hannah. If her mouth was full, she couldn't very well confess her affair.

"You are so good to us, Sydney," Brynn complimented her. "What is in that pot on the stove? It smells incredible!"

"That is Jambalaya," Sydney informed her with a proud smile. "What you are smelling is andouille sausage, shrimp and cod in a meticulously-seasoned tomato sauce. We're just waiting for the rice to finish cooking, and I'll fold some fresh parsley into it to make it perfect!"

"It smells perfect already," Maddy admired.

"Thank you, but I can't take full credit. It's Grandmother's recipe."

"It's sure to be delicious. Grandmother was a wonderful cook," Brynn commented in her politically-correct manner that paid homage to Sydney's matriarch while imparting that Grandmother was, in fact, dead. Sydney spoke of her as though she would walk into the kitchen at any moment.

"This cheese ball is excellent!" Maddy declared.

"Also Grandmother's recipe," Sydney confirmed.

"Of course," Amanda added between bites. "Let me try some of that."

Maddy pushed the porcelain onion-shaped dish that held the cheeseball across the table to Amanda.

"That dish is adorable," Brynn said, then added, "you can't buy things like that anymore," before Sydney could inform them it was Grandmother's dish.

"I didn't use it for the longest time," Sydney admitted, "because I didn't want to risk it breaking. After Grandmother was gone a few years, I thought to myself, *this is silly.* I pulled out all the china and the crystal and the silver. Now I use it all the time. If it breaks, it breaks. It could break just as easily with a routine dusting. I might as well use it and let it serve its purpose."

"You only live once," Maddy said in concurrence.

Hannah sighed audibly.

"I'm sorry, Hannah," Maddy said quickly. "I didn't mean anything by that."

"No, I know," Hannah replied. "It's just hard for me not to think about Pauly sometimes. All the time really. He lived his life the way he wanted to live it. He did what he wanted, and I don't think he missed out on anything, but he should have lived so much longer. It's not fair."

"It's not fair for anyone to die that young," Brynn said consolingly.

"I'm sorry. I need to try to be more sensitive," Maddy apologized.

"It's not your fault," Hannah told her. "I need to stop being so sensitive!"

"No, you don't," Sydney said firmly. "You've been through a horrible ordeal, and it's going to take time for you to come to terms with it. Don't feel like you have to put up a front for us. We're your family. Oh, my goodness! I didn't give my toast!"

Amanda groaned.

"No, no! Let me give it now. It's the perfect time," Sydney lifted her half-consumed glass of wine. "To family, because that is what we are. No matter how our lives digress, no matter how high or how low we are feeling, no matter if we are near or far from each other, we are family. Whatever the future holds, we will tackle it united."

Sydney's eyes were open for once, and she held her glass out towards the center of the table, so the others could tap theirs together accordingly. The ladies followed suit, except Hannah, who set her glass down in front of her defiantly. She pushed her palms against her thighs and drew a deep breath.

"I'm sorry, Sydney. I don't mean to ruin your party, but we need to address the elephant in the room," Hannah said.

Sydney's expression was one of dejection and puzzlement.

"We didn't part on good terms the last time we were together," Hannah went on, directing her gaze on Amanda, who was mid-gulp. "We can't pretend everything is normal."

"We could..." Maddy muttered under her breath and finished off her glass of wine.

Brynn and Sydney were staring at Amanda expectantly.

"It's alright," Amanda insisted. "I came here tonight to set things straight. We might as well get everything out in the open now."

Hannah crossed her arms in front of her chest and waited for Amanda to continue. All of their eyes were on Amanda, except Maddy, who was intentionally avoiding eye contact with all of them. She pulled the dainty plate with the cheeseball back across the table and turned her concentration to it.

"I want you all to know the truth," Amanda said, placing her hands on the table in front of her for support. She stared at her excessively manicured fingernails as she spoke. "I did not have an affair with Pauly. You obviously know I've been keeping something from you, but I swear I had absolutely nothing to do with Pauly. His name is Dalton. I've been seeing him for months. Well, I'm not seeing him anymore."

She raised her eyes tentatively to see how the others would react. Brynn and Sydney looked sad, but Hannah's expression didn't change. Maddy continued to avoid eye contact and got up to fill her wine glass.

"I broke it off with him recently, because I realized I still love Nate, and I'd be stupid to throw away my marriage. That's why I canceled last week. I wasn't ready to talk about it. I've been keeping a low profile, staying home at night and trying to make things up to Nate."

Amanda's gaze dropped back to her fingernails, as she waited for affirmation. Brynn and Sydney were looking at Hannah, who rolled her eyes and took to staring at the giant fork and spoon on the wall again. Brynn and Sydney looked back at each other, both trying to figure out whether to interject or remain silent.

"What did Nate say?" Brynn asked after a brutally long silence.

"Nate doesn't know," Amanda sounded confused.

Brynn was taken aback, her expression atypically shocked. Hannah finally stopped looking at the knickknacks and stared at Amanda disgustedly. Sydney turned away to stir the Jambalaya, and Maddy downed half her freshly-poured glass of wine.

"When are you planning to tell him?" Hannah demanded.

"I'm not!" Amanda spoke up. "If he found out, I would have dealt with it, but he didn't find out. I'm just going to get on with my life and try to make things right with him."

"You don't think he knew something was wrong?" Brynn prodded gently. "*We* knew something was wrong…"

"It doesn't matter, at this point," Amanda insisted. "It's over with Dalton. I'm going to concentrate on being a better wife, and things with Nate are going to be better than ever. If he did suspect anything was wrong, he won't anymore."

"He could still find out," Hannah remarked, seemingly nonchalant with a hint of a threat.

"He *won't* find out," Amanda replied forcefully. "The only one who would have told him is gone. Never mind. It's not important. What's important is that I realized I made a mistake and I'm going to make my marriage work. We're going to get back to the way we were. We're going to start planning a family again."

"You know how I feel about children, but having a baby isn't going to save your marriage," Sydney said, setting down her spoon.

"We're not rushing into anything," Amanda back-peddled with a nervous laugh. "I'm not quite ready to be a mom."

"Pauly knew, didn't he?" Hannah demanded suddenly. "The only one who *would have* told him is gone? I *knew* something was up between you and Pauly. He came in one day and told me he'd run into you. He made some remark about how you were promiscuous and I should pay closer attention to who I hang around with. I didn't dwell on it at the time, because Pauly was always criticizing my friends, but the more you snuck around telling us lies, the more I started to believe you were seducing Pauly all that time. Now you're saying the guy's name was Dalton. If you're telling the truth, and you weren't sleeping with Pauly, why would he call you promiscuous? *He knew.* He knew you were having an affair. What did you do to keep him quiet, Amanda? Murder him?"

"I didn't murder Pauly," Amanda retorted. "That's ridiculous. He was twice my size. Besides, I can prove it. I have an alibi. I was with Dalton all night. One phone call can clear my name any time I want."

"Why don't you?" Hannah challenged her.

"I will if I have to. The police aren't worried about my whereabouts, are they, Hannah? They're more worried about yours. I'm not the only one who's glad Pauly's gone."

"How can you say that?" Hannah lashed out.

"It's true!" Amanda stuck to her guns. "You're glad he's gone. Look at you, with your sassy new haircut and your sexy little tattoo. You've never been happier! Now you're jealous because I actually have a chance of working things out with my husband. Don't you dare mess things up for me, just because your marriage is over."

"My marriage is over because my husband is dead!" Hannah yelled.

"He's dead, alright," Amanda kept pushing. "Michael was almost dead, too. If you know what's good for you, you better stay away from Nate."

Amanda started for the door.

"Come on, Maddy. I'm done here. If you want a ride, the bus is leaving."

Maddy hurried to down the rest of her drink and scurried after Amanda, mouthing, "I'm sorry" to the other girls on her way out of the kitchen. Amanda had already slammed the front door shut behind her, and Maddy had to open it back up to let herself out. She shut it more gently, but hurriedly enough to make a noise. Hannah broke down crying after the second closing of the front door.

"I didn't kill Pauly," she sobbed. "She's right, though. I am glad he's dead. I wanted him to die. I wished for it every time he went rock climbing. One little slip would be all it took. Even Pauly could slip."

Brynn fought for comforting words, but nothing came to mind.

"Amanda was out of line," Sydney filled the silence. "She had no right to come here and act like that. She has a guilty conscience, because she cheated on Nate.

Guess what? She's going to have a guilty conscience until she confesses to her husband; confessing to us probably sounded like it would solve her problem, but it doesn't."

"Sydney's right," Brynn added. "Amanda was trying to ease her own conscience by dragging you down."

"You two don't think I killed Pauly, do you?"

"Of course, not," Sydney cooed.

"Brynn?"

"I don't believe it for a minute, Hannah," Brynn confirmed.

"I didn't do it, but I'm probably going to get arrested for it anyway. The police are so convinced I did it, they aren't even looking for another suspect. I pointed them in Amanda's direction, but that didn't do any good. They showed up at the jewelry shop the other day and pulled me from behind the counter to ask me more questions. I was with a customer when they came in. I have never been more embarrassed in my life! After they talked to me, they asked my boss and coworkers a bunch of questions, too. My boss had been so supportive up until that point. They must have said something to change his mind, because he asked me to take a personal leave until my name is cleared. He said the police showing up was the straw – some of the customers had recognized me from the news. He's afraid of losing customers, because I'm a murder suspect."

"Hannah, I am so sorry," Brynn said.

"I have to figure out who is responsible before it's too late. Do you think Amanda's telling the truth? She supposedly has an alibi with her lover. Or maybe she convinced this Dalton to say he was with her. I have to figure out how Amanda is involved in all this. I still think she had something going on with Pauly. If that's true, he literally took it to his grave. I'm beginning to think I'll never know the truth."

"The truth will come out," Brynn assured her. "People don't go around killing for no reason, especially not someone like Pauly."

"I hate seeing you upset," Sydney bit her lip. "Let's have something to eat, before it gets cold. I made this huge pot of Jambalaya. I'd hate to see it go to waste."

Brynn and Hannah didn't bother to argue with Sydney. Neither was particularly hungry, but they obliged, since Sydney had gone through all the trouble of cooking such an extraordinary meal. They ate quietly, each thinking about the evening's disturbing outburst.

"The more I think about it, the madder I get," Hannah said after a short time. "I can't believe Amanda had the nerve to show up here tonight. You would think she would be ashamed."

"Maddy said she was trying to make amends," Brynn offered weakly.

"Make amends! What a joke!" Hannah cried. "She's been cheating on her husband for months and keeping it from us. Suddenly she wants to come clean, but she's told so many lies, she probably doesn't know how to tell the truth anymore."

"Lies will eat you up," Brynn agreed. "Like I said, the truth will come out, one way or another."

Chapter Nineteen

Sydney was unusually morose through dinner. Brynn surmised a combination of things contributed to her sullen demeanor. Sydney was not appreciative when her hosted events broke up early because of an argument. She hated when her friends fought, and she hated to be left with huge quantities of food. She sulked as she ate, and refilled her wine glass at atypically regular intervals. The fact that Brynn and Hannah barely ate only added to her dismay.

They helped Sydney pack away the leftovers and clean up the kitchen. Brynn suggested they sit outside, since it seemed to be a lovely, June evening. They all agreed they could use some fresh air and transitioned to the back patio. Sydney grabbed some lawn chairs from the nearby barn. She refused any assistance, as the chairs were more awkward than heavy, and attempted to drag all three over in one trip. She dropped one with a clatter half-way back to the patio. The wind flipped the chair over before they could get there to help her, and Hannah chased it across the lawn.

"Take these," Sydney instructed, handing the other two chairs over to Brynn. Sydney returned to the barn and emerged with three cushions, which she positioned into the chairs that Brynn and Hannah had set up. "There. That will be more comfortable. I haven't had the occasion to take the patio furniture out of the barn. What a lovely evening!"

Hannah shivered. She wore a sweatshirt, but her thin, cotton pants were cropped above the ankle, and she had sandals on her feet.

"It's windier than I thought out here," Brynn commented. "We can go back in, if you're cold."

"I'm fine," Hannah leaned back in her seat and took a long swig of her wine. "This wine will warm me up."

Sydney topped off their glasses and excused herself to grab another bottle from inside the house.

"Red or white?" she called over her shoulder.

Brynn shrugged.

"Red, please," Hannah answered for them both. "Red wine will take the chill out of this cool breeze. It is a beautiful night, though. I'm glad you suggested we get outside. It always makes me feel better."

"Fresh air always does it," Brynn answered. "I sometimes regret having an apartment in a high rise. I would have liked to have had a patio, but I feel safer up off the ground floor."

"A balcony would be nice," Hannah offered.

"True. A balcony would be perfect," Brynn agreed. "I wouldn't feel nervous about being outside by myself up on the eighth floor. How are you doing in the house by yourself, Hannah?"

"It's odd. It feels unusual being alone, but I don't feel scared. I'm not sure how to describe it. I guess I felt like a prisoner in my own house, and now I feel … relieved," Hannah struggled with what word to use to describe her newly-found freedom. "I don't want to get used to it, though. All good things come to an end."

"Why? Are you thinking about selling the house?"

"I haven't decided yet," Hannah sighed. "I feel like I'm living in limbo right now. I have no money until I get the insurance payout. The police are going to pin Pauly's murder on someone, and unless they have some leads they aren't telling me about, I'm afraid I might end up their scapegoat."

"They won't get a conviction if you're innocent," Brynn pointed out. "What evidence could they possibly have against you?"

"They don't have any," Hannah admitted, "but I have a motive and I don't have an alibi. They can use those things against me to build a case. It happens on TV all the time."

"Be that as it may, you didn't kill him," Brynn said, with a hint of a question mark at the end of her statement.

"I did not kill him," Hannah confirmed, staring Brynn straight in the eye. "I may spend the rest of my life in jail for a crime I didn't commit, but then I won't have to worry about how I'm going to pay the bills. No, Brynn, I didn't kill him. I may go to my own grave never knowing the truth, but I at least I have a clear conscience."

Hannah took another long swig of her wine and closed her eyes for a moment. She was startled from her thoughts by the sound of a cell phone ringing. Hannah reached into her the deep pocket of her capris, only to realize it was not her phone but Brynn's that was ringing. She slid it back down into her pocket.

"It's Maddy," Brynn advised, looking at the caller ID. "Excuse me."

Brynn answered the phone and stood from her seat on the patio to take a few steps out of earshot. She had no intention of hiding her conversation with Maddy from Hannah, but it was a force of habit for Brynn to hold telephone conversations in privacy.

"I made it home," Maddy was breathless on the other end of the phone. "What a ride that was! Amanda was driving like a maniac, she was so mad. How do I get myself into these things? I thought we could have a nice evening, clear the air and make up, but *no*… We have to go down that same road, you slept with my husband; *well, you killed your husband.* When is it ever going to end?"

Brynn wanted to laugh at Maddy's animosity, but she refrained. The situation was not humorous. It was quite the opposite, and getting worse every day.

"Amanda is convinced that Hannah killed Pauly. She says she did it in a jealous rage. She suspected Pauly of having an affair, and she decided if she couldn't have him, no one could. And Amanda is adamant that she did not sleep with Pauly. She actually drove me past some house claiming it was where Dalton lives. She said she would march me in there and introduce me, but they didn't part on the best of terms. Then she started raving about how Dalton probably won't tell the truth if the police question him about where he was that night, so there goes her alibi. She's losing it, Brynn!"

"Sounds like she's already lost it," Brynn agreed. "Do you think she's telling the truth?"

"I don't think Amanda could tell the truth if it smacked her across the face," Maddy said animatedly.

"But you don't believe Hannah killed Pauly, do you? She has told me straight out several times that she didn't, and I believe her."

"I don't think Hannah would harm a fly, but I can't stop thinking Amanda is involved somehow."

"Do you think she really slept with Pauly?"

"I couldn't say. I think she's lying about something, I just don't know what. I feel like everything she is saying about Hannah is really about herself, like the way she accused Hannah of flying into a jealous rage. Either she has a super-vivid imagination, or she's projecting her own experience onto Hannah to cover up the truth. We've witnessed both of their tempers lately, and Hannah doesn't have a temper like Amanda does."

Brynn wandered over by the barn while Maddy spoke and thought about the implications of what she was suspecting. It was true Hannah only got angry when provoked. Amanda seemed to have a chip on her shoulder at all times, daring anyone she met to try to knock it off.

The wind had blown the side door of the barn back open, and Brynn reached inside to pull it shut. She couldn't help but notice the piles of boxes and furniture and accumulation of items that must have belonged to Sydney's grandmother. In the midst of everything was parked an older-model sedan. It had to have been Grandmother's. It looked like the kind of car an old lady would drive.

"I have to go. Amanda's calling," Maddy said abruptly and clicked over to answer the call.

Brynn didn't have a chance to respond, as she pulled the barn door shut. She turned around to find Sydney standing directly behind her. She jumped, startled.

"What are you doing?" Sydney asked, her face calm, but her eyes enraged.

"The wind blew the door open," Brynn explained, confused at first, but quickly becoming alarmed. She had never seen Sydney react so harshly, although she had always been very protective of her grandmother's belongings.

"Who are you talking to?"

"It was Maddy, but she had to go. She made it home safely," Brynn explained meekly, meeting Sydney's gaze.

Sydney's expression softened slightly. She smiled and gestured back toward the patio. "Shall we?"

"Of course," Brynn replied with a weak smile, walking past Sydney and leading the way back to the patio, where Hannah was enjoying a freshly-poured glass of red wine.

"Is Maddy OK?" Hannah asked, as they approached, seeing what must have been a concerned look on Brynn's face. Brynn smiled quickly and took her seat.

"Maddy is fine," she assured her with a wave. Her mind was racing, but she forced herself to remain calm. She couldn't stop thinking about the car she had seen in the barn. It looked like a Buick. She reminded herself Buicks were a dime-a-dozen. It was no surprise that Grandmother had owned one and Sydney hadn't disposed of it. It was Sydney's uncharacteristically irritated reaction that bothered her. There was something in the barn Sydney didn't want Brynn to see.

She wondered if she should tell the others about Maddy's suspicions of Amanda. It would certainly draw attention away from what was actually on her mind, but she decided against it. She didn't want to get Hannah upset again. Suddenly, she wanted nothing more than to get as far away from Hannah and Sydney as possible, but Sydney was busy pouring her a fresh glass of wine.

"You're not in a hurry, are you Brynn?" Sydney asked, noting Brynn's reaction to the large glass of wine in her hand.

"No, I'm not in any hurry," Brynn lied, smiling. "I don't have any meetings tomorrow morning. I try not to schedule anything on Thursday mornings, if I can help it."

"I don't blame you," Hannah agreed. "When I was working, I always took Thursdays off. I'd rather take days off during the week, when sales aren't as good. You're lucky you don't have to worry about work, Sydney."

Sydney smiled, her expression back to its normal, contented self. Sydney hadn't worked since her grandmother became ill and she moved in with her to take over as sole caregiver. After her grandmother had passed away, she inherited everything along with enough cash to pay off any debt she had at the time. She lived a meager life style and avoided accumulating any new debt, which enabled her to remain voluntarily unemployed.

"I'm going to have a huge garden this year," Sydney said. "I have some more tilling to do for the later crops, but I've already planted spinach, radishes, carrots and snow peas. Groceries is one of my few expenses, so I plan to limit the amount of produce I have to purchase. Don't be fooled, it is hard work, but every single thing I can grow, I grow. Plus, I plan on canning anything I over-produce or selling it at the farmer's market. I guess I do sort of have a job."

"A challenging job," Hannah agreed. "Nothing like getting your hands dirty."

"You're welcome to come over and play in the dirt any time you'd like," Sydney laughed.

"I may take you up on that. I don't know how much longer I can hold out for this insurance money. Losing my job is the worst thing that could have happened right now. There's no point looking for another job, if I'm that much of a threat to business. I suppose I could try to find something outside of the public eye, but I don't know how to do anything technical. I've only ever done customer-facing jobs. I have literally no experience to do anything else. Besides, who would hire me, since I'm apparently a notorious husband-killer."

"Hannah, you haven't lost your job permanently," Brynn assured her.

"I might as well have," Hannah rebutted without pause. "This case could drag on for years, and even if my name is cleared, things will never be the same. If customers recognize me now, they will always recognize me as the woman who was accused of killing her husband. I may never work again. I think I might have to move, but the police told me I can't even leave town."

"What if you disappeared until all this is over?" Sydney interrupted.

Hannah cocked her head and stared at Sydney.

"What are you saying?" Brynn asked, although she was scared to hear Sydney's answer.

"You go underground. You could move in here, hide from the world for a while. You haven't left town," she answered flippantly. "In the meantime, once the police have the real culprit in custody, they'll leave you alone."

"It sounds lovely, but even if I stayed out of the public's view, the police are still focused on me as their number one suspect. I'm beginning to doubt they will ever find the real culprit." Hannah sighed.

"It can't be much longer," Sydney insisted.

"How can you be so sure?" Hannah asked.

"They've been dragging their feet, if you ask me. We all know you're innocent. It's only a matter of time before they catch the real killer," Sydney answered nonchalantly. "I think you should hide yourself away, where you won't be bothered by gawking idiots, and let this whole thing work itself out. After your name is cleared, we should take a trip to Europe – the three of us! We can visit Amsterdam and Ireland, and even Germany, Brynn!"

"I appreciate your optimism, Sydney, but it's not that simple," Hannah replied realistically.

"Do you trust me?" Sydney answered with her own question.

Hannah didn't respond immediately, but tightened her focus on Sydney's face. Brynn looked from one to the other. *Sydney would never tease Hannah like that. What did she know? She seemed so certain the case was close to being solved, but how could she possibly know that?*

"It's not a matter of trust, Sydney. Tell me what you know," Hannah said pointedly, her face portraying a mix of anger and desperation. Sydney was smiling eerily.

Hannah's expression clouded over, but Brynn's jaw dropped. It all came into focus. The car in the barn was a Buick, and she would bet her life it was a 2008 Buick LaCrosse. Michael had been run down by the car in Sydney's barn – Grandmother's old car. Sydney knew it, *and Sydney knew who killed Pauly!*

Brynn opened her mouth to speak.

"I know everything is going to work out," Sydney said with a determined look, raising her hand towards Brynn in a gesture for her to be quiet. "I can't stand to see you suffering, Hannah. Let's finish this and move on with our lives."

"Sydney, no…" Brynn started.

"Stay out of it, Brynn," Sydney snapped.

"I'm in it up to my neck!" Brynn stood and held her hand across her neck figuratively.

Hannah's focus came back to the present. She looked at Brynn sharply, digesting the insinuation.

"What did you do, Sydney?" Hannah cried out. The tears welled up in her eyes and started to stream down one cheek, as she flung herself at Sydney. "*What did you do?*"

Sydney grabbed Hannah's arms in a lightning-fast swoop and pinned them to her sides. Sydney was not a large person, but she was considerably stronger than Hannah. Brynn's memory flooded with photographic snippets, some real – Sydney at the gym, out-lifting them all, Sydney snapping the cork out of the bottle effortlessly after Amanda had struggled with it, Sydney dead-staring her near the shed, and some fantastic – Sydney slamming Pauly over the head with a blunt object, Sydney dragging a dead body on a tarp across rocky terrain, Sydney hitting the accelerator in Grandmother's Buick with a malicious grin.

Hannah was crying hysterically, pieces of the truth materializing in her brain.

"Why?" she cried, trying to shake her arms free, but Sydney held her tight.

"It's all for the best," Sydney said sternly.

"I trusted you!" Hannah screamed, shaking her head from side to side.

"As you should," Sydney said calmly, tightening her grip on Hannah's arms and shaking her.

"Let her go, Sydney," Brynn shouted.

"You stay back, Brynn" Sydney ordered. "I did what I had to do. Pauly would have killed Hannah if someone didn't get to him first."

"No!" Hannah sobbed.

Brynn reached for her cell phone.

"Don't touch it!" Sydney yelled, threatening enough for Brynn to freeze in place. She had never seen

Sydney like this; the look of violence flashed in her eyes like an all-consuming fire.

Brynn held up her palms in defeat, showing Sydney her hands were empty of any weapons or means of communication. Any ideas she had of overpowering Sydney dissipated from her mind. If Sydney had the strength to take down Pauly, she could certainly overcome her and Hannah. Brynn looked around the dark yard, quickly surveying the distance between her and her car. She could make a run for it, as long as Sydney was occupied with Hannah. Sydney would never hurt Hannah, and if she could get to her car quick enough she could call the police.

"You're not going anywhere," Sydney said bluntly, taking in Brynn's movements.

"Calm down, Sydney," Brynn started diplomatically. "Let's not do anything irrational."

"You'll do exactly as I tell you," Sydney informed her. "You owe me, Brynn. Your divorce would never have finalized if I hadn't hurried things along."

"Michael wasn't supposed to live, was he?" Brynn demanded.

"Of course, he wasn't supposed to live," Sydney spat. "Do you think I'm stupid enough to leave a witness alive?"

"What about me, Sydney?" Brynn asked calmly. "I'm a witness now. Are you going to kill me, too?"

Hannah looked up fearfully, trying to control her sobbing.

"Shut up!" Sydney ordered. She pulled Hannah's wrists together and squeezed them securely with one hand, while she pulled a knife out of her pants pocket with the other hand. She jerked her head from side to side, surveying the yard as though they were being watched. "We're all going to go inside and discuss this calmly."

Brynn kept her hands up to reinforce her defenselessness. She took a step toward the house, then stopped to look down at her purse, lying on the ground by the leg of her chair.

"Leave it," Sydney ordered, and waved the knife toward the back door.

Brynn hesitated but obliged, her mind racing frantically, as she stepped slowly to the back door. She racked her brain desperately trying to come up with a way to get her and Hannah out of this. Hannah and Sydney were right behind her, Hannah hiccupping trying to regain control of her sobbing.

Hannah isn't going to be much help, she thought. *I wish Maddy was here…*

Sydney guided Brynn and Hannah to the kitchen, and tied their arms behind them to the backs of the wooden chairs with cooking twine. Hannah stared at her feet. She had stopped crying, but she wouldn't even look at Brynn. Brynn wished she could catch Hannah's gaze to judge her emotional state. She couldn't count on Hannah being in any condition to help her get out of this situation. Hannah appeared to be in shock.

"There," Sydney was saying, satisfied her captives' arms were secured. "It's only temporary. I wouldn't have to tie you up, if you would cooperate nicely. I'm sure you'll see things my way before the night is over, and we can all move forward with our lives.

Sydney has lost it, Brynn thought. *She's always been different, eccentric, but she truly is off the deep end. How could I not have seen this coming? What the hell am I going to do? I've got to talk her down. No, just keep your mouth shut. She's talking. Let her talk. The more she talks, the better. I have to think …*

"You are both going to cooperate, because that's what is best for all of us," Sydney went on. "That's what good girls do. Good girls behave and cooperate, or they get tied to the chair until they promise to be reasonable. Like Mother always said, it's not a punishment; it's an opportunity for you to gain control of your emotions and act appropriately. Mother was not always compassionate in her ways, but her methods were tried-and-true. A few hours of being tied up always made me think twice about misbehaving."

Sydney looked from Hannah to Brynn and back again, her wild curls bouncing side-to-side, her eyes bright as fire. She had taken up possession of the knife again in one hand, and rested her other hand on the back of a wooden kitchen chair for support. She had secured Brynn and Hannah on opposite sides of the table and centered herself between them. Her breathing was deep and deliberate. She exhaled loudly before she continued.

"Hannah has been crying out for help for months. All I did was answer her pleas. We all know she could easily be dead right now, if Pauly were still around. He was a horrible, sinister, monster. You both know that to be true."

She surveyed the expressions of her captives for reassurance. Hannah's head had rolled back slightly and was resting on the back of the chair, her stare now fixated at her lap rather than her feet. Her face bore an expression of exhaustion. Brynn watched Sydney carefully and tried to keep her own expression blank. Sydney didn't sound like she was going to keep them tied up forever, only until they grew compliant. She knew she had to keep a neutral expression and let Sydney think she agreed with her, but she badly wanted to scream and shake some sense into Sydney at the same time. Fighting back wouldn't get her untied. It may even get her killed, if Sydney were so inclined. She wanted to believe Sydney wouldn't kill a friend, but she realized, too late, that Sydney was no friend. She admittedly didn't know Sydney at all.

Her mother used to tie her to a chair? What kind of mother ties her kid to a chair to get them to behave?

"Pauly is never going to hurt you again, Hannah," Sydney assured her in her cooing, motherly tone. "I know how devastated you've been feeling to have lost your husband, but he was no husband. He was a cruel person who did terrible things to you. You're in shock right now, because you're learning that I am the person who took him away from you, but I am also the person who set you free from your living hell. Look at me, Hannah. I want to see your eyes. I understand your natural instinct is to be angry with me, but deep down you know I saved your life. He would have killed you, Hannah. You know that."

Hannah slowly raised her eyes to Sydney. Brynn wished she could tell what Hannah was thinking, because Hannah didn't speak. She merely stared at Sydney. She didn't appear to be angry any more, but she didn't appear to be forgiving either.

"Don't hate me, Hannah," Sydney said. "I couldn't bear that. I did this for you, because I was so scared of losing you. You're my best friend; you always have been. I would do anything for you. I just knew I had to take care of Pauly before he hurt you. It was the only way."

Hannah blinked, but said nothing. Her expression had grown thoughtful, her eyes narrowing slightly as those scrutinizing Sydney's words, trying to gain some insight as to why her self-proclaimed best friend would commit such an unforgiveable act.

"I know you think there had to be another way, but there wasn't," Sydney went on. "I tried to bargain fairly with Pauly, but he wasn't reasonable. I offered to pay him to leave you, but he couldn't be trusted to keep his end of the bargain. Oh, he liked the sound of money, and I offered him a great sum, but he couldn't guarantee me he'd stay out of your life. Do you understand what I'm saying, Hannah? He wanted the money! He was receptive to accepting money from me to leave you, be he wanted to negotiate. He wanted to stay available to you, if you decided of your own free will to reconcile with him. He wanted to take my money and reneg, that's what he wanted to do. You know as well as anyone what a good salesman he was. In the end, he couldn't be trusted. I had to finish what I started. If he left upstate alive, he would have come home and taken his anger out on you. He told me so! He was hell-bent on proving that you belonged to him, and he could do whatever he wanted with you. Don't you see, he left me no choice? It was him or you."

Sydney became more animated as she spoke, her curls bouncing up and down fiercely, her speech quickening with each sentence.

"You're saying you didn't go there with the intention of killing him?" Hannah spoke for the first time.

"No! I mean, I was prepared for all outcomes. I knew it might come to that, but I'd hoped we could come to an agreement."

Oh my God, she is crazy. Brynn's mind was racing, but she kept quiet and listened. Hannah was talking now. That was good. It gave her hope that between the two of them they may be able to talk their way out of this mess.

"So, you did mean to kill him," Hannah surmised.

"No, Hannah. It wasn't like that. I mean, I had to prepare a back-up plan in case he wasn't amenable. I thought if I put a big enough dollar sign out there, he could be persuaded to leave you. Money was obviously a big motivator for Pauly. My mistake was underestimating his thirst for power."

"Dominance fueled him," Hannah agreed demurely, with a nod. "And he was a force to be reckoned with. How did you possibly overpower him?"

"I followed him when he left his motel room and drove closer to the base of the mountain. I brought him coffee, as a sign I was there under peaceful pretenses. I slipped something into his to help him relax. As the conversation progressed, so did the effects of the drug. He became sluggish physically, but his demeanor became more and more volatile. Unfortunately, he couldn't control his temper, so we failed to reach a compromise. However, he couldn't control his motor skills either, which gave me a distinct advantage. I'll spare you the unsavory details."

"I need to know what happened, Sydney," Hannah insisted. "I need to know everything."

Sydney sighed. "I was truly hoping to spare you having to re-experience such a traumatic event."

Hannah stared silently at Sydney, and Brynn realized Hannah had complete control over her. Sydney would unwaveringly do anything Hannah requested of her. Hannah was still bound to the chair with her hands behind her back, but suddenly she was very much in charge.

"I tried to reason with him, Hannah, I did," Sydney blathered. "He was implacable. I have never met anyone more perverse. I had a better chance of convincing the mountain to move than getting Pauly to yield. He was a cocky, obstinate son-of-a-bitch. He actually thought he could take my money and keep you, too. He deserved what happened to him, and the fact that he never saw it coming made it all the more satisfying. He was evil, Hannah. He was a horrible, evil man. I only did what God would have done to put an end to his terrorizing spree. I saw the marks he left on you, and they were nothing compared to what he was going to do to you when he got home from his little mountain-climbing trip. He had big plans for you, Hannah, and they weren't pretty. Somebody had to stop him. I took the work of God into my own hands. However unworthy I may have been to do God's work, I was the only one there to do it. You have to understand, I did what I had to do. There were no other choices left."

"How did you do it, Sydney?" Hannah asked calmly but authoritatively.

"He said he would reflect on my proposal and get back to me with instructions of where to wire the money. I told him it wasn't going to work that way, and he laughed in my face. He said it would work whatever way he wanted it to work. *He* was in charge now. He tried to manipulate me, but he started to become aware of the drug in his system. His speech was starting to slur, and he realized I'd put something in the coffee. He threw it on the ground and tried to attack me, but it was too late. The effects had already diminished his coordination. The struggle was brief. I knocked him to the ground. He tried to crawl away, but I picked up a rock and smashed it into the back of his head. It wasn't a fatal blow, but it knocked him out well enough for me to drag him to the edge of the cliff and dump him there as though he had fallen. I took another rock, a bigger one, and smashed his head again. That one did the trick. I made quick work of setting up his climbing equipment to make it look as though he had fallen. I even climbed up the face of the rock and smeared his blood to make it look like he'd hit his head on the way down. I left no evidence. No finger prints, no foot prints, nothing."

Sydney paused, deep in thought as though reliving the encounter in her mind, and incidentally thoroughly enjoying it. Brynn sat frozen, listening in disbelief. She snuck a glance at Hannah, who was waiting expectantly for Sydney to finish her story. Sydney spoke as though she were talking about someone else, like she was an innocent onlooker rather than a cold-blooded killer.

"It was cold that day. It was April in upstate New York, after all. I was bundled up with hat and gloves. I made certain every lock of my unruly hair was secured firmly under that hat. My hands were protected in my gloves. I left no finger prints. I left no trace of any struggle, and I took no scraps of evidence with me. Every bit of blood I wiped off my jacket and gloves and boots before I got into my car, and I disposed of every article of clothing afterward. There is literally nothing to tie me to the scene of the crime, I swear. The police have nothing to go on – they told you as much. They have no leads."

"They think I did it, Sydney."

"Not for long. In fact, I have it on good authority they'll be making an arrest soon. I've taken care of pointing them in the direction of the killer."

Sydney relaxed her grip on the back of the chair and took a step away from the table. She paced the kitchen a few times, still clutching the knife.

"It wasn't hard to pin it on Amanda," she said, practically bragging. "I took some of Pauly's old camming devices out of your garage, and planted them in Amanda's car. His DNA was undoubtedly already on them, but just to be sure, I plucked a few of his hairs off the clothes in his closet. Your house isn't so impeccable that I couldn't find a couple of stray hairs."

Hannah stole a glance at Brynn, while Sydney's back was turned, catching her eye for a moment. Brynn searched Hannah's face, trying to read her mind. She thought she detected a flicker of a plan in Hannah's expression, which was less filled with desperation than it had been five minutes ago. The color had returned to Hannah's cheeks, and her eyes were focused; she no longer looked like she was about to drop from exhaustion.

"The police already suspected Amanda," Sydney rambled, reveling in the genius of her scheme, as it unfolded. "She shouldn't have been sneaking around, cheating on her husband. Pauly and Amanda both deserved their fate."

"But she wasn't sleeping with Pauly," Brynn pointed out.

"Maybe she was, maybe she wasn't," Sydney snapped. "I knew she was cheating on Nate. I followed her. I also happened to see Pauly stop into the diner one day to talk to her. I saw them together."

"Talking," Brynn refuted.

Sydney shrugged.

"It doesn't matter whether they were having an affair, at this point. Don't defend her. She dug her own grave, so to speak." Sydney laughed at her clever play on words.

Brynn stared, mouth agape. She had no response. Sydney had everything figured out. The only facet that remained to be seen was what she planned to do with her and Hannah. Obviously, she wasn't going to hurt Hannah. All of her actions had been under the pretense of her unwavering devotion to Hannah. *She won't hurt Hannah, but what does she plan to do with me?*

"I think you can untie me now, Sydney," Hannah drew her captor's attention back to the task at hand. "I understand you only tied me still because you needed my full attention. Your mother's method proved effective. Leave Brynn where she is for now. I'm not sure you can trust her yet."

Sydney hesitated.

"Go ahead," Hannah encouraged her. "I'm no match for you."

Sydney moved to the back of Hannah's chair at once and slit the twine with one swift stroke of her knife. Hannah rubbed her wrists where the bindings had been, and ran her hand lovingly over her tattoo, as though soothing the hummingbird. Satisfied it was unharmed, she calmly leaned back in the chair and slid her hands into her pants pockets.

"Why involve Brynn?" Hannah asked. "I understand you did what you thought you had to do to protect me, but why did you try to run down Michael?"

Sydney bit her lip and looked down at Brynn.

"I needed her on my side," Sydney answered slowly, recalling the events at the airport. "Amanda and Maddy would never guess the truth, but Brynn…"

"I only guessed the truth because I saw the car in your barn. If you had left Michael alone, I never would have figured out that you killed Pauly," Brynn pointed out.

"You don't give yourself enough credit," Sydney insisted.

Brynn shrugged and dropped her gaze. *Maybe I would have figured it out; maybe I wouldn't have. The question is, what is she going to do with me now that I know the truth?* She was too frightened of the answer to ask the question. She decided to keep quiet and let Hannah run with the plan she so desperately prayed was developing.

"So, you did mean to kill Michael?" Hannah asked, but it was more of a statement.

"I thought I could buy Brynn's silence, if I resolved her marital issues. We all know Michael wasn't budging. The divorce would have dragged out for years, until there were no assets left to fight over. I thought if I helped speed things along a little, Brynn would owe me. If she ever figured out the role I played in Pauly's death, she wouldn't be able to tell anyone, because I could easily implicate her in Michael's death. Well, his accident. He didn't die, did he?" Sydney made a snorting noise, as if she were making a joke.

"No, Michael didn't die, but the intended outcome was the same," Sydney answered her own question. "The car hasn't been licensed in years, since before Grandmother passed. She couldn't drive after she got sick, but she always believed she would be able to drive again someday. I didn't have the heart to get rid of the car, even after she passed. No one knows it's been sitting there for years. There's virtually no evidence to surface. I can easily dispose of the car, or I can leave it where it is. No one is interested in the contents of my barn."

She's got it all figured out. She's gotten away with so much already, she's starting to think she's invincible. But she did make mistakes. They will come back to haunt her eventually. And now I know the truth.

"Essentially, I am an accomplice," Brynn realized aloud before she could stop herself.

Sydney looked at Brynn with what seemed to be contempt.

"You are my insurance," Sydney answered flatly.

"I'm your insurance, not your friend, that you would do anything for," Brynn noted, hurt that Sydney had used her, yet not surprised. She didn't even know why she said that. It was an inconsequential matter that Sydney killed Pauly out of her deep love for Hannah, while she attempted to kill Michael merely to buy Brynn's silence. The fact remained Sydney was a murderer, and she had to be stopped.

"None of us wanted to see Hannah end up dead at the hands of that vicious monster!" Sydney's voice escalated.

"Tell me, Sydney. What if Maddy learned the truth about you? Would you kill Jim, too?" Brynn demanded.

"Maddy won't find out," Sydney insisted.

"You don't know that. Maddy could stumble across something as easily as I did, and then where would she be? She is a sweet, innocent kitten, and Jim is a decent man. He treats Maddy like a queen. They don't deserve to be tangled up in this sick, twisted plot of yours."

"What does Maddy know?" Sydney's suspicions were aroused.

"She knows nothing," Brynn answered quickly, suddenly regretting challenging Sydney. "She suspects Amanda is involved, but not you." Brynn went on to tell Sydney about her telephone conversation with Maddy, and her opinion that Amanda knew more than she was saying.

"She suspects Amanda," Sydney repeated.

"Yes. She suspects Amanda, not you. You were at her house the night Pauly died. She's your alibi."

"She doesn't know I left her house as soon as she went upstairs," Sydney agreed quietly, speaking more to herself than Brynn.

"She doesn't know," Brynn confirmed. "She got up in the morning, and you were gone. She suspects nothing."

"Leave Maddy out of this," Hannah interrupted impatiently. "Nothing is going to happen to Maddy or Jim. Do you understand, Sydney?"

Sydney nodded meekly. She was slowly losing control to Hannah, her voice becoming softer, her answers more tentative.

"Now, what are you going to do with Brynn?"

Sydney glanced at Brynn hesitantly.

"You have to untie her eventually," Hannah pointed out. "Surely you have a plan for us. We leave this house and never speak of it again? What did you think, you were going to drop this bomb on us and there wouldn't be any aftermath?"

"I … I don't know," Sydney stammered. "I'd hoped you didn't find out."

"You'd have us believe Amanda was guilty and go about your own life without repercussions?" Hannah answered for her.

"I'd hoped no one would have repercussions, but the police won't stop until they pin this on someone. I didn't think they would suspect you …"

"Of course, they suspect me!" Hannah scolded her. "I'm the battered wife. I'm the one who had to live with him and suffer his abuse – physically and mentally. I'm the one who wanted him gone the most! The police don't care that I didn't have the means or the guts to kill him! They only care that I had the motive and the opportunity. Even if they suspected you did the actual deed, they would still think I had put you up to it."

"No, no, Hannah. You didn't put me up to it. I did it all on my own. I couldn't stand seeing you abused day after day. You were turning into a different person; you were deteriorating into a meek, little mouse, running around in your maze, trying not to get zapped at every wrong turn. I couldn't stand by and let him strip away your pride and your vitality!"

"We've established that. You took it upon yourself to kill Pauly and I had nothing to do with it. I understand you felt compelled to kill Pauly to rescue me from my self-inflicted hell. You think your actions were heroic? I think they were disrespectful and callous, but what's done is done. Tell me, Sydney, what are you going to do now?"

Sydney threw herself at Hannah's feet. She buried her face in her hands, the knife still gripped in one hand and resting coolly on her cheek.

"Say you forgive me, Hannah! I did it for you! Tell me what to do, and I'll do it!"

A sudden knock on the door jolted Sydney back to captor-mode. She jumped to her feet, pointing the knife at Hannah. Panic swept over her face, as she swung her head from Brynn to Hannah, then in the general direction of the door, which was not visible from the kitchen.

Chapter Twenty

"Find out who it is," Hannah instructed calmly. "Can you see any cars in the driveway?"

Sydney hesitated, took another glance at Brynn, then backed herself to the doorway without losing sight of her hostages. Hannah sat still, her hands still in her pockets, her eyes glued to Sydney's every movement.

"Stay put," Sydney ordered, tip-toeing across the hall to peek out from behind a curtain, where she could see a car in the driveway. The orange cat slinked into the kitchen, as though taking over in Sydney's absence.

Sydney was gone from the kitchen no more than ten seconds, but long enough for Hannah to pull her phone out of her pocket, text "SOS" to Detective Harris, and shove the phone back into the depths of her pocket. She was sitting innocently still, when Sydney re-emerged.

"I think it's Maddy's car," she whispered frantically. "What could she possibly want?"

"She knows we're in here," Hannah reinforced the obvious.

"I can tell her you've both gone to bed," Sydney suggested.

"What if she insists on coming in?" Hannah asked. "Don't you think you should untie Brynn?"

"She won't come in," Sydney answered adamantly, and moved swiftly across the room to Hannah's chair. "Put your arms behind your back."

Hannah removed her hands from her pockets and did as she was told. Sydney quickly re-secured Hannah's wrists to the spindled back of the kitchen chair with the cooking twine, double-checked the knot was tight, and slid her knife into the back of her pants. She tucked her shirt over the handle of the knife and turned toward the door.

"Silence," she commanded. "If you two care so much about your friend Maddy, you'll be quiet as church mice. I'll get rid of her one way or another."

Brynn stole a glance at Hannah, who nodded reassuringly.

She could hear the front door crack open, and Sydney's voice traveled through the silent hall.

"Maddy, my goodness! What are you doing here at this hour?" Sydney cooed. Brynn felt disgusted at Sydney's ability to change her demeanor so suddenly. She had them all fooled!

"I was worried about Brynn," Maddy let out, as though she'd been holding her breath. "I've been calling her phone for hours, and she doesn't answer. I see her car is still here…"

"She's passed out," Sydney explained. "It's not like Brynn to drink so much, but she was in such a celebratory mood after her good fortune this week! I fixed her up in one of the upstairs bedrooms. Hannah too! It's a regular old slumber party, except the partiers are all partied out."

Brynn rolled her eyes, silently willing Maddy not to believe it. Maddy knew Brynn wasn't one to lose control drinking.

"That's a relief," Maddy was saying. "I was so worried, when she didn't answer her phone. I tried you and Hannah, too. I kept getting voice mail."

"My phone has been off all evening. I always turn my phone off when I have company."

"Grandmother's rule," Maddy recalled. "Yes, I remember. I was just so worried when none of you answered your phones. I drove by Hannah's house, and her car wasn't there, so I thought maybe you were all still here."

"We are all still here, safe and sound. You'll be able to sleep now," Sydney laughed, queueing Maddy to leave.

"That's not all," Maddy rushed on. "Amanda went ballistic on the drive home. Did Brynn tell you? She was driving like a maniac, and ranting the entire time about how Hannah killed Pauly in a jealous rage. I didn't think I was going to make it home, honestly. When she dropped me off, and I ran straight inside and hugged my kids!"

"Yeah, she was angry when she left here. She's got quite a temper, doesn't she? I'm afraid for her. I think she's gotten herself into some kind of trouble. Deep trouble. I think we'd all be wise to steer clear of Amanda for a while."

"You don't know the half of it!" Maddy exclaimed. "I kept thinking how odd she was behaving, and everything she was saying about Hannah seemed to me she was really confessing her own actions. And it turns out it's true! Amanda's been arrested! I have to tell Hannah!"

"Shhh! Hannah is sleeping."

"I think she'd want to be woken up for this news!" Maddy insisted.

"Tell me what happened," Sydney instructed, positioning her body to block Maddy from entering the house subtly but effectively.

"Amanda called me and told me she'd been pulled over. She was all in a panic, because she had been drinking. You know she didn't drink very much, but it was recent enough to show up on a breathalyzer. I tried to calm her down. She wasn't drunk when we left here, just crazed. She hung up when the cop came up to her window, and I never heard back from her. I waited and waited, and I started to get worried, so I called Nate, and he was on his way to the police station! They've arrested Amanda! I don't know what's going on, but they've impounded the car. It's more than a DWI. You weren't kidding, Sydney. She has gotten herself into deep trouble! Why would they impound her car? They must have found drugs, or something worse."

"A murder weapon," Sydney finished Maddy's thought.

"That's what I'm afraid of!" Maddy nodded.

"But, we don't know that for sure," Sydney said slowly.

"No, Nate didn't know what was going on."

"We shouldn't jump to conclusions," Sydney said rationally.

"What are we going to do?" Maddy was frantic.

"We aren't going to do anything, but wait," Sydney said calmly. "There's nothing we can do for Amanda. We need to sit tight, and if the police find something to do with the murder, I'm sure they will notify Hannah. Detective Harris is relentless."

"You don't think we should wake her up?" Maddy reiterated.

"Hannah had a lot to drink, sweetie. I don't think she's in any state to be woken up, especially when we don't know exactly what's going on," Sydney reasoned.

Maddy nodded.

"Trust me. She'll deal better with this in the morning, and maybe by then we'll have more information."

"You're probably right, I just panicked."

"Understandably!" Sydney cooed. "This is a shocking development. I know I won't be able to sleep all night. You'd better get home to your little ones. I'll make sure the girls wake up early. I'll have Hannah call Detective Harris as soon as she gets up, and then we'll call you and let you know what is going on. In the meantime, if you hear back from Nate, you call me. I'll turn my phone back on the second you're gone, in case you need anything. You call me, OK?"

Maddy agreed and said her goodbyes.

"I'm sorry to stop over so late. I'm a little embarrassed." Maddy laughed a little.

"No worries. Drive careful," Sydney said, pushing the door half-way shut.

"Good night," Maddy said.

Sydney shut the door, clicked the dead bolt into place and went to the window to watch the headlights of Maddy's car slowly descend down the driveway and disappear into the night.

Satisfied Maddy wasn't coming back tonight, Sydney scurried back to the kitchen to face her captives.

"Could you hear everything?" she asked, her cheeks flushed.

"It would appear your plan to frame Amanda is well underway," Hannah replied.

"Indeed. Now we just sit tight, and let Amanda seal her own fate. She's such a liar, she won't be able to talk her way out of this one. The evidence is right there for them. She has no alibi. Her goose is cooked. All we need to do is wait."

"We wait, yes," Hannah said, "but we can't stay tied up in your kitchen forever. Eventually, you will have to trust us enough to untie us."

"I need to think," Sydney pulled the knife from its hiding spot and resumed pacing the kitchen floor.

"Sydney, you had to have considered the possibility that we would learn the truth about what you've done," Hannah reasoned. "Either we are going to keep it a secret, or we are going to tell the police. That choice belongs to us, not you. You're not going to keep us quiet if we don't want to be. And there will be no more violence."

Sydney frowned. She looked around the kitchen and surveyed the situation. Brynn hadn't said anything in a while. Brynn appeared to be right that Maddy didn't suspect her. The timing had been ripe to plant the evidence on Amanda. Maddy could easily be convinced that Amanda was guilty – she was already half-way there. If only Brynn hadn't so nosily snooped in the barn. Would

Brynn and Hannah keep her secret? Sydney considered her options.

"What's it going to be, Brynn?" Sydney asked. "If I go down, you go down."

Brynn stared at Sydney, wondering how crazy she truly was. Sydney's actions were becoming more and more careless. The truth would come out eventually, and although Sydney firmly believed Brynn and Hannah would go down with her, there remained uncertainty. However, Sydney could have planted evidence against Brynn already, as she had done to Amanda. Brynn couldn't take the chance to challenge Sydney. She had to allow her to believe she was on her side, for now.

"I defer to Hannah," she answered finally.

"I thought you would," Sydney replied confidently. "You're a smart girl, Brynn."

Sydney looked at Hannah confidently and waited for her to announce her intentions. Her hands were on her hips, the knife still planted firmly in one hand. Her eyes her ablaze with adrenaline.

"We don't know for sure that Amanda is going to be charged with murder, let alone convicted," Hannah pointed out.

"No, but there's more evidence against her than there is against you, and you were certain an hour ago that they could convict you," Sydney reminded her.

"Let me ask you something, Sydney. Do you have any ounce of remorse over what you've done? You do understand what you did is wrong?"

Sydney looked confused. Hannah, realizing she wasn't going to appeal to Sydney's sense of morality, took another angle.

"What's done is done," she said, her patience waning. "My concern at this point, is what you intend to do next. Amanda could very well produce her mystery man, and suddenly she has an alibi."

"At the risk of destroying her marriage? I don't think so. You heard her as well as I did. Besides, people lie. Evidence doesn't."

"The evidence is fictitious. You didn't kill Pauly with a camming device. You hit him with a rock. The autopsy results substantiate that fact. As far as Pauly's hairs you planted in Amanda's car, they are worthless. Anyone who's ever ridden in Amanda's car could have lost a hair or two. There could be more of Pauly's DNA all over that car, if the two of them were truly having an affair. That proves nothing! Just because she slept with him, doesn't mean she killed him. And maybe he gave her the camming devices. If they were sleeping together, maybe he wanted her to go rock climbing with him. Who knows?"

"Like I said, it's more evidence than they have against you," Sydney repeated.

"Your evidence isn't foolproof," Hannah insisted. "It's fake evidence, and Detective Harris will figure it out."

"He hasn't figured anything out yet."

"He will," Hannah assured her. "You've taken the heat off me temporarily, but once Amanda is cleared, the police are going to examine other avenues. Can you honestly live with this lie the rest of your life?"

Sydney didn't answer right away. The distinct sound of a car pulling driveway broke the silence. Sydney's expression darkened. She tucked the knife back into her pants and moved toward the kitchen door.

"Goddamn it, Maddy," she cursed, as she stepped out of the kitchen and into the hall for a better look out the window.

Brynn and Hannah exchanged glances.

"Why would Maddy come back?" Brynn whispered.

"She wouldn't," Hannah shook her head.

"It's not Maddy. It's a police car," Sydney informed them, stomping back into the kitchen, grabbing the back of an empty chair and shoving it across the room.

The adrenaline in her eyes had turned to rage. She surveyed the room maniacally, looking for something else to throw. Her eyes settled on Grandmother's precious onion-shaped dish.

"Stop it, Sydney!" Hannah ordered. "They aren't here for you. They're here for me. Remember?"

Somehow Hannah was able to reason with Sydney, and her expression softened again, with what could be interpreted as realization and relief. The police had no inkling of evidence against her, after all. Amanda had undoubtedly pointed them back in Hannah's direction, and they arrived sooner than she had anticipated.

"Untie me, Sydney. Let me go to the door and talk to them. It's me they want."

"But what will you tell them?" Sydney whined, as she reached for the knife.

"I won't tell them anything, yet. Let me hear what they have to say. Maybe they're here to tell me they've caught my husband's killer."

Sydney nodded and slit the cooking twine from around Hannah's wrists, just as they heard a knock at the door.

"Stay here," Hannah demanded, and Sydney nodded and obeyed like a child who had been scolded.

Hannah took a deep breath and stood, a little unsteadily after having been seated for so long. She gathered her composure and moved toward the door. Much to her expectation, she opened the door to the countenances of Detective Harris and Detective Rowley.

"Good evening, Mrs. Gianni," Detective Harris said.

Hannah caught his eye, shoved her cell phone into his hand and nodded toward the kitchen.

"Are you going to read me my rights?" she asked loudly enough for the others to hear from the kitchen.

"You have the right to remain silent," Detective Harris quoted, nodding at Detective Rowley to investigate the kitchen. "Anything you say may be used against you in a court of law."

Detective Rowley drew his firearm and sidestepped down the hall silently.

"You have the right to consult with an attorney for advice before we ask you any questions and to have an attorney present during questioning now or in the future."

Detective Rowley paused before the doorway to the kitchen, readied himself and then turned the corner to discover Sydney holding the knife at Brynn's neck.

"If you cannot afford an attorney, one will be appointed to you," Detective Harris continued.

"Drop the weapon!" Detective Rowley commanded.

Detective Harris abandoned his ruse, drew his firearm and moved toward the kitchen in a flash. By the time he reached the kitchen door, Detective Rowley had already tackled Sydney and wrestled the knife out of her hand. It slid across the linoleum floor, out of reach. Detective Harris bent to untie Brynn, while Detective Rowley pulled Sydney to her feet and slammed her face-first against the flowered wallpaper. He pulled her arms behind her back and cuffed her.

"Ms. Mitchell, you have the right to remain silent," Detective Rowley began.

"Her full confession is recorded on my phone," Hannah told them. "She's responsible for everything – the murder of Paolo Gianni, the attempted murder of Michael Kehmen… Everything is recorded."

Brynn looked up, surprised. Her wrists freed, she stood and threw her arms around Hannah. The tears she'd been holding back flowed freely in a wave of relief.

"It's over," Hannah told her, soothing Brynn's release of emotions. Brynn wiped the tears from her cheeks and stared at her friend, her incredible, brave, strong friend. Hannah had been perfectly in control the entire time. Brynn wondered how long she had suspected Sydney …

Brynn stole a glance at Sydney, who was being dragged out of the kitchen by Detective Rowley, Detective Harris directly behind them on his cell phone. Sydney's face was flushed. She didn't look at Brynn as she was being dragged past her, but looked longingly at Hannah.

"I did it all for you," she said. "I love you."

"You don't know what love is," Hannah said simply, as they watched Sydney's face change from pleading to pain-stricken, and then she was gone from their sight.

Epilogue

Hannah finished tucking the last item into her suitcase and zipped it shut. Satisfied she could not possibly have forgotten anything, she gave the suitcase a quick pat and lifted it off the bed. She grabbed her keys, passport and bracelet off the dresser. The keys and the passport, she slipped into her carry-on bag. The sapphire-and-diamond tennis bracelet, she slid over her hand where Pauly's ring still rested prominently on her thumb, and positioned it securely around her wrist, where it dangled and danced with her beautiful, little hummingbird.

Hannah studied the ring that had been Pauly's. It was a painful reminder of the physical and emotional duress she had endured. She would soon pass it on to Pauly's father as a token of remembrance to him, and forever free herself of the memories it evoked.

She turned her attention to the dainty tennis bracelet, the diamonds sparkling in the sunlight and casting rainbows across the bedroom wall. The bracelet and the hummingbird flitted without inhibitions, perfectly depicting the freedom she felt, and her gratitude for it. Freedom had come with a price, one she was willing to pay again without hesitation, but one that left her with an emptiness as well. She had lost her husband, and she had had lost cherished friendships, but she pondered if she'd ever truly had those things. Perhaps they were merely illusions in a previous life.

Hannah took every opportunity she could to be thankful for her newly-acquired freedom, no matter what it had cost. She breathed the summer air deeply, felt the warmth of the sun penetrate her skin, took in all the beauty of the world around her with a smile. She took nothing for granted. She had been given a fresh start in life, and she intended to take full advantage of the opportunity that had been presented to her. First, she needed to bring closure to the traumatic events of the past few months.

She had two stops to make before she drove to the airport. She had a two-o'clock flight to New York, where she would spend the night and catch her international flight to Italy in the morning. She had made a promise to Leo, which she was determined to keep. Pauly and Leo's father was miraculously, still alive, although continually ailing. She would make her amends in person, and then go on to tour Europe with a clear conscience.

The first stop was the jail where Sydney was being held without bail while awaiting trial. Hannah had not seen or spoken to Sydney since the night she had been held captive, and she needed to confront her before she could move forward with her new life. She was led to a room with a thick, glass wall between them, where she could speak without fear of repercussions.

"It's good to see you," Sydney greeted her tentatively.

"I came to say goodbye," Hannah informed her.

"Goodbye?" Sydney asked, disappointment clouding her face.

"Yes, Sydney. You won't be seeing me again."

"Please, Hannah. Don't say that. I *do know* what love is." Sydney obviously had given great thought to their last conversation. "Everything I did was for love."

Hannah was unmoved. She watched, as Sydney squirmed uncomfortably on the other side of the glass, like a child who had been caught stealing a piece of chocolate. She felt sorry for that person on the other side of the glass, a person she never truly knew. Poor, misguided, Sydney, obviously abused by her mother, lacking any distinction between wrong and right, hopelessly in love with someone who would never return the affection.

"Maddy went and got your cat," Hannah said. "She couldn't stand the thought of it being abandoned or being turned over to the ASPCA."

Sydney nodded, looking down at her hands.

"Can't you forgive me?" she pleaded abruptly. "Tell me what to do and I'll do it!"

"You can't undo your actions," Hannah said flatly.

"But my actions were justified! Look at all the good that came from my actions," Sydney begged. "Amanda's marriage has been saved. She told Nate all about Dalton, and they are going to try to work it out. Brynn's divorce is finalized, and she got to keep what was rightfully hers. That never would have happened without my interference. Even Maddy got something out of it, a pet for her children. And you, you're alive! That is the greatest gift anyone could ever give."

"I am grateful to be alive," Hannah agreed. "It is true, Pauly undoubtedly would have killed me eventually. At least, he was well on his way to killing me internally. I will never be the same person I was."

"See?" Sydney said meekly. "It's all good."

"The ends justify the means?" Hannah's question was more of a statement.

"Exactly."

"That's the problem, Sydney. The ends don't justify the means. What you did was wrong. I will never forgive you until you accept that as the truth. You committed vile, unforgivable acts, and you have no regret, no inkling of guilt whatsoever. You fully accept responsibility for what you've done, but you don't understand that it was wrong. I can't associate with someone who has no concept of basic, human decency. I made the mistake of marrying Pauly, and I allowed him to treat me badly. I will never do that to myself again. If there's one thing I've learned, it's that all you really have in life is yourself. If you don't love yourself enough to adhere to your own ethical standards, then you can't possibly love anyone else."

"You're wrong if you don't believe I love you," Sydney said.

"I believe you don't love yourself," Hannah replied.

Sydney stared, a single tear creeping down her cheek and settling in the corner of her mouth. She could taste the salt, and it served as a bitter reminder of her loss. It did not bring regret, for Sydney was incapable of reconciling that emotion at present. Hannah could only hope Sydney's time spent alone with herself would enable her to begin the relationship she had been so desperately lacking all her life. With that thought, Hannah stood to leave.

"Goodbye, Sydney."

Hannah turned and didn't look back, essentially closing the door on Sydney for the rest of her life. She felt herself trembling as she walked to her car. Confronting her husband's killer had been more difficult than she had imagined.

She had already said goodbye to Brynn and Maddy in person, but she called them each from the car on her way to her next stop.

Brynn was at work, but answered her cell phone. She wished Hannah well, and told her to call when she returned to the states. Brynn was well on her way to her own new life, finally divorced, dating her mystery man and reveling in her successful career.

Maddy was home sounding frantic as usual, acting as traffic director, while her children chased their new cat around the house. Charlie wasn't used to the activity that enlivened the Helmsford household, but he did take to snuggling next to her on the couch after the children went to bed. Maddy barely heard a word Hannah said on their phone call, she was so distracted by the chaos that was her life. She loved every minute of it.

Amanda was not on Hannah's list of phone calls, as they hadn't spoken much since the truth had erupted. It was true, Amanda had cheated on Nate, but with someone named Dalton, not Paolo. Although Hannah was relieved

Amanda's alleged affair with Pauly was nothing but a stretch of her own imagination, she had no interest in maintaining a friendship with her. After all, if she could so easily believe that Amanda was capable of adultery or even murder, she couldn't justify cultivating a friendship with her.

Hannah was sad to see the end of the Wednesday Wine Club. She had spent many evenings in the comforting presence of her friends, in spite of how badly some of them had turned out. It was hard for her to accept that some relationships, although vitally-interwoven into her very soul, could be so unhealthy. She had slowly been poisoning herself by remaining in an abusive relationship with her husband, and leaking toxins to her closest supporters. She took responsibility for her shortcomings, but also realized that she could only make changes within herself. She would miss the Wednesday Wine Club and the friendships that once existed, even if they were merely an illusion of her imagination.

Hannah pulled into the parking lot of Weston Kennels and found herself giddy with excitement as she parked the car. She was meeting her puppy for the first time today. Hannah had always wanted a dog, but Pauly wouldn't allow it, with his work schedule and travel preferences. Nothing was holding her back now, and she had put a deposit down on a Cocker Spaniel. The puppy would be ready to go home shortly after she returned from her trip to Europe.

There were five puppies in the litter, three males and two females. Hannah picked up each puppy and cuddled closely. They were so sweet, with their big, brown eyes and floppy, oversized ears. They were all so beautiful, it was hard to decide which one she wanted. She settled on the female with the purple ribbon. She seemed to be the smallest of the litter, the most affectionate, and the one who needed her love more than anything. Hannah held her precious, tiny puppy in her arms and dreamed of the future the two of them would have. If nothing else, they would have each other to love.

"You work on growing, and I'll be back in a few weeks," Hannah told her new, little friend.

When it was time to leave, Hannah reluctantly handed the puppy back to the breeder's wife, who plunked her down with her siblings. She stumbled over the bulk of her own paws as she scurried away, but quickly regained her footing and jumped on one of her brothers, who playfully slid her off his back. She rolled over, got back on her feet and was off again in a dash.

Hannah laughed and waved goodbye. She was looking forward to her trip to Europe, but she was even more excited about coming back home to begin her new life.

The End